THE BOOK OF DEBORAH

THE BOOK OF DEBORAH

Maggy Whitehouse

This Large Print book is published by BBC Audiobooks Ltd, Bath, England and by Thorndike Press®, Waterville, Maine, USA.

Published in 2004 in the U.K. by arrangement with the Author.

Published in 2004 in the U.S. by arrangement with Rupert Crew Limited.

U.K. Hardcover ISBN 1–4056–3032–9 (Chivers Large Print)
U.K. Softcover ISBN 1–4056–3033–7 (Camden Large Print)
U.S. Softcover ISBN 0–7862–6826–3 (General)

The text of this Large Print edition is unabridged.
Other aspects of the book may vary from the original edition.

Set in 16 pt. New Times Roman.

Printed in Great Britain on acid-free paper.

British Library Cataloguing in Publication Data available

Library of Congress Control Number: 2004107026

With acknowledgement and thanks to:

Z'ev ben Shimon Halevi

Michael Hattwick MD
Jonathon Clark

Prologue

They say the rebellion is failing. Emissaries from Jerusalem are beginning to arrive here, on the borders of the Dead Sea, carrying religious scrolls and objects of great value to them.

Many Jews know about the caves near Qumran, and how the Essenes—and others—have been preserving and hiding the written teachings against such an emergency as this. Fierce arguments are starting between the factions about whether they may hide their antiquities together. Of course, all sides regard the others as heretic and all think they have the right to own God's teaching—and His land!

They say the Temple in Jerusalem will be destroyed. If so, it is only the physical form of worship, and it has fallen before. This time perhaps the sacrifices really will end, so I, for one, will not mourn.

Maybe it is the end of the Jews. But I do not think so. It will not be the end of the teaching, because the inner teaching is not written, but carried in the hearts and minds of those who have come to understand. The people who hide the Torah in the hills are wise to do so, for it contains much wisdom. The heart of all faith is hidden deep within it for those who

1

have the courage to seek.

Now I will take my own gospels into the hills to hide in case, one day, the Lord should see fit to have them found. The account of the time following Yeshua's death, I will place in one cave; the other, the most precious, my own story of the years spent with my beloved brother and teacher, will lie with my own body elsewhere. It is my time to die and I am more than content to go home.

To you, who has found these scrolls in the many years to come, I send greetings. Read and learn what I learnt, but do not make the mistake of letting the *form* of the teaching rule your life.

You will be living in a different day and a different time and you must adapt this work as appropriate to that time. There will be teachers of the truth around you. Ask, and you will find them.

Deborah Bat Miriam
Written and sealed on the seventeenth day of Tammuz in the year 3830.

1

We were a full day's journey from Jerusalem before anyone noticed that Yeshua was missing.

It was hardly surprising; there were hundreds of us in the long, dusty, straggling trail of people travelling homewards to Galilee: distant relations gossiping and sharing around news of betrothals arranged over the festival; new acquaintances swapping background and lineage; old quarrels added to, or resolved. Everyone assumed that everyone else was somewhere around and you might not see members of your own family for half a day or more.

I was curled up in the back of a half-empty ox-cart owned by my cousin Jonah. On the way down to Jerusalem the old brown ox had hauled sacks of olives and dates, hard cheeses and other Galilean specialities, but now all he had to pull were a few purchases from the big city and the occasional traveller, wearied from the journey. They did not even notice me, tucked away at the back and wrapped from head to toe in an old blanket. The rug cushioned me from the bumps along the way and protected me from the stifling yellow dust that billowed up, all around our path, but mostly it hid me from prying eyes.

Jonah occasionally threw me a word or a question and I would stick my freckled nose out of the blanket in response, but he was a sensible man and did not badger a little girl who preferred to be left alone.

I rested my head on a pile of yellow straw, day-dreaming of my beloved, remembered, silver sea, deaf and blind to the sights and sounds around me and the dozens of shouting and laughing children who ran backwards and forwards with the irrepressible energy of youth.

Through the babble, I still heard Miriam's voice, sharp with worry, calling, 'Yeshua? Yeshua! Where are you?' and sat up, blinking in the clouds of dust, to peer over the side of the cart. We were just pulling up at our lodging house for the night, and it was time for families to regroup.

'Deborah!' She saw me and came hurrying over. 'Is Yeshua with you? Have you seen him today?' Her normally calm face was pinched with worry, her shawl falling back from her long, dust-covered hair.

'No. No, I haven't.' My heart went out to her but before I could do, or say, anything else, she made a gesture of despair and vanished back into the crowd.

Anxious moments passed and I could feel the rumour spreading before I heard the words. As Miriam continued the search, the volume and quality of people's voices changed around her, lifting into a buzz. There was a boy missing! No one knew when he had vanished. Perhaps he was hurt, or even worse, taken by wild animals or robbers on the way. How exciting! Pretty soon, everyone was asking the same question: 'Have you seen Yeshua Ben Joseph? The carpenter's son from Nazara?'

Nobody had, and the buzz rose higher. Its tone changed. People started to say that Yeshua's parents should have noticed earlier that their boy was missing. There were self-righteous comments about those who let their children run free, and the other mothers swept their own broods protectively into the lodging house.

They conveniently forgot that it would have been just as easy to have lost their own child. More than sixty of the travellers were Nazarenes, and Yeshua should have been safe with every one of them. There was constant mixing of adults and children on the route and it was only if something went wrong that people withdrew into their smaller groups and started defending themselves by blaming others for whatever misfortune might have occurred.

It seemed that Salome, my sister, had also been missing for most of the day. James said cuttingly that you only had to look for the moon-struck faces of the silly boys who followed in her footsteps to find her holding court. He did not have much time for his beautiful brown-eyed sister, who turned his friends into gawky idiots who wanted to adore Salome, instead of doing sensible things with him.

Yeshua himself was easy enough to overlook; or perhaps I should say that he made himself easy to overlook. He was a slight, graceful, almost feminine boy of twelve, with a habit of vanishing wherever he was. Even if he had not moved, people sometimes did not see him. In the hubbub made by the dozens of other children weaving in and out of the crowds, he would have found it easy to go his own way—had he even started the journey with us.

Anxious (and embarrassed) enquiries discovered quite swiftly that he had not. No one had any recollection of seeing him after our family group had hurried through breakfast in order to be ready to leave as soon as the morning trumpets signalled the opening of the city gates.

Even Joseph and Miriam's closest relatives laughed at them when they said that Yeshua would not have defied them or stayed behind deliberately. The rule in Nazara was strict discipline and a heavy hand, but our family relied on love, trust and kindness. Even at the age of seven, I could see how people's reactions added to Miriam and Joseph's pain as we gathered together to discuss what was to be done. Everyone obviously thought—and some of them began to say openly—that they deserved what they got for their naïveté.

Seeing their hurt, I lost my temper. 'We are trustworthy!' I shouted. 'If Yeshua is missing it's because he's hurt or lost. He wouldn't disobey.'

'Deborah, don't be rude to your elders,' Miriam's words were gentle, and too late I saw that I had done more harm than good.

I did what I usually did at such times and ran away. I should be honest and say I never actually ran, but did my usual lopsided trot on my stiffened leg. My ears were ringing with what I imagined the women were now saying about me and I tumbled into the lean-to that served as a stable and hid behind the manger, the sound of the ox and the donkeys' steady munching drowning my tears of self-pity.

Joseph came to find me a little later, when he knew the worst of my tantrum would be over. He sat down beside me in the straw and waited until the last hiccuping tears were finished. Then he took my hand.

'We have to go back, Deborah,' he said. 'We're leaving first thing in the morning, just you, your mother and I. James and Salome can go on with Simon, Jonah and Judah and their families, but you are too young. You must come with us.'

'I'm not! I'm not! I'm not too young,' I wailed desperately. 'I can go with them. Please

7

let me go with them.' I began to cry again, but I knew I would have no choice.

Joseph picked me up, holding me in his dear, strong, slightly uncomfortable masculine way, patting just too hard in just the wrong place. Somehow that never mattered with him; he was full of his own rough kindness. I nestled into his jerkin and entwined my hand in his comfortable, long grey beard. If only I could tell him that I was afraid of Jerusalem and the pain I felt there. If only I could tell him that only that day I had vowed never to return, but I did not dare.

Not for the first time, I wished that he were my real father, and Miriam my real mother. Perhaps then I would have the courage to speak. But if I had been their child, perhaps I would never have been so afraid.

*　　*　　*

James, Salome and I were born in Bethsaida, a prosperous little fishing town in northern Judaea, where the Jordan River flows south into the Sea of Galilee. I was not lame then and I spent most of my early years running and playing by the water or watching the fishermen pulling in their catch. We were Jews in name and Father was a pious man in his way, but we did not count ourselves as orthodox and it was only later that I discovered how very lax we were. Mother's ancestors came from Petra, the home of a proud and arrogant race, and that meant more to her than any Jewish heritage. Two or three evenings each week she would shut the door of our house, blocking out the people and the busy streets, and set torches in the walls to create a golden, flickering light. She shook loose her golden-red hair and lifted down a musical instrument that her father had given her: a strange kind of drum with coloured ribbons and loose metal pieces, which made a thrilling, rippling sound when she shook it. She began by beating a slow rhythm, building steadily in speed and passion before beginning to dance around the room, faster and faster until you were giddy from watching her. Just as you thought she must fly up into the air, she would stop, in one sudden but graceful movement, her arms held high in the air and her head thrown back.

Once she had finished that first explosion of movement, Salome and I were allowed to join in with her. She was impatient when we were clumsy, but the magic and wildness of the dance were usually enough to inspire us into being nimble. We spiralled round and round, in Mother's footsteps, our hearts pounding and our faces shining up with delight until we could dance no more and half fell and half sat against the walls, exhausted and panting. If Father were there, he would watch us from the doorway of the other room, never saying a word, but usually we danced alone. Mother did not dance like anyone else I had ever seen and she never danced in public.

Later, after supper, she would tell us stories of the battles, quarrels and triumphs of Petra. The Petrans were the race who spawned Vashti, Queen of Persia, who defied her husband and returned home in disgrace to make way for Esther, the holy woman who saved the Jews. Once a year, at Purim, we celebrated Esther as a saviour and condemned Haman, who had tried to destroy her and the whole Jewish race; but Mother scorned Esther—a milk-sop woman, she called her—preferring Vashti's defiance and pride.

'She was a real Petran,' Mother said. 'She was not afraid even of the King of all Persia. She left behind every gift he had given her, every item of clothing but a plain shift, and rode home on an old, lame donkey.'

'But why would she leave all her jewels and clothes behind?' Salome asked, not understanding.

'Because she wanted nothing of Persia,' said Mother. 'She was a Princess of Petra and she despised a mere warlord with no ancestry. His baubles were nothing to her.'

Salome wriggled uncomfortably. She loved beautiful things and her pride and joy was a pair of carnelian earrings that Father had given her for her ninth birthday, but she would never have dared to contradict. None of us would. Sometimes I wondered what it must have been like for a simple Jewish girl to follow such a fiery beauty onto the throne of Persia, but I kept my mouth shut and sided with Vashti, because Mother told me she hoped I would grow up to be just like her.

Many people in the village were afraid of Mother, and both Salome and I had plenty of practice in ducking to avoid her ever-ready hand. But she did not hold grudges and she would captivate us with stories of strange gods and demons, and heroes and heroines, while we made bread in the morning and before we went to sleep at night. Father adored her, and so did we.

It was because of Mother that Father was estranged from his family, the Nazarenes who lived in the hill country to the south-west. Like them, he was directly descended from the line of Jesse and David, and it was well known that Nazarenes looked down their noses at other less well-connected Jews—as they in turn were looked down on by the Jews in the south. It seemed that all Jews criticised all other Jews either for not being stern enough, well bred enough or for being too rigid in their beliefs.

Arguments would break out even in our little town over what seemed to me to be the strangest things and several families did not talk to each other because they differed over tiny points of law. Father thought the more orthodox enjoyed quarrelling with each other, and one of his favourite jokes was that a Jew

11

finding himself in a strange country would have to build two Synagogues; one he would go to and the other he could criticise and pointedly avoid.

The Nazarenes had gone even further than that; they had founded their own village called Nazara from the Hebrew *netzer,* meaning the shoot of a plant or a tree, so they did not even have to walk the same ground as less well-connected Jews. The Messiah, they said, would come from the branch of Jesse and they had to keep their blood pure.

With an attitude like that, Father's defiance of custom when he refused a suitable Nazarene girl and chose to marry Mother, was simply asking for trouble. He left the little hamlet in disgrace and was often heard to say (at least at home) that if the Messiah was as big a snob as the rest of his race, he would rather He did not come at all.

For all that, Father still went to Synagogue each Shabbat and took James along with him, but I don't think Mother had ever been to a service and I know I had not. I remember Salome asking her why we did not go, and her answer: 'The Jewish religion is for men and brings nothing but servitude to women.' Such things stay in your mind if you hear them very young.

Mother's Petran ancestors had moved away from the rose-red city and come to the fertile Galilee of the Gentiles more than a hundred years before. They and the other unbelievers in the hills and valleys were forcibly converted to Judaism by the Hasmonean conqueror, John Hyrcanus and his successors, who brought the first peace to the warring area for many years. But many of the people converted in name only, without letting go of their old tribal lore, and that had not changed down the generations. 'They can make us behave like Jews, but they can't tame our hearts,' Mother said once, with a flash of her bright blue eyes and a toss of her head.

She still visited the Mikvah, the Jewish ritual bath, once a month, mostly for the pleasure of immersing herself in the cool water and learning the latest gossip. It was wise to go so no one could openly accuse her of being impious. Even though women in our area were not necessarily expected to attend Synagogue, the Mikvah was still thought to be important and most of the women obeyed the laws of purity; keeping apart from their husbands, publicly at least, for two weeks in each month.

Mother was wild but, in those ways, she was careful. 'It is important to take care of yourself,' she said once. 'Fight when you want to, not because you have to.'

James left us when he was thirteen and I was five. I can just remember the quarrels about his leaving but it was only later that I understood how shaming it was for Father that his only son refused to follow in his footsteps.

James wanted to be a carpenter and a Nazarene, not a fisherman. One day he walked out of our house without a scrap of food or fresh clothing. From then on, Father said he had no son.

I missed him very much, but Salome's distress and continual tears were the hardest thing to bear. Both Mother and Father snapped at her as she trailed around miserably for weeks and, though I dared not say anything in front of them, I would hug her tightly in bed at night to try and comfort her.

We got messages regularly, via pedlars and other travellers, that James was happy and apprenticed to his Uncle Joseph in Nazara. He even sent gifts of furniture, but Father never accepted any of them and he sent no message back.

Instead he channelled his love into his work and his two daughters. He was proud of Salome's budding beauty and he would play rough and tumble with me in the evenings, both in and around our two-roomed home, with its yard full of scratching chickens and piles of fishing net. I would end up hiccuping with breathlessness and laughter as he gathered me up in his arms and threw me up into the air.

One cold, windy spring morning when I was six, Mother sent me down to the sea front on my usual errand of fetching Father home for his midday meal. At that time of day Father would be mending his nets with his fellow fishermen and sharing companionable gossip. By the time I arrived, having been diverted by a pedlar, a baby donkey and a handful of figs from the garden of a friend, the weather had made one of its swift turns for the worse. The wind rose, bringing sudden horizontal, slashing rain as the sea welled up to meet it. All over the harbour, men were lashing the boats to the shore and I can still see Father, his black hair plastered to his face, standing on the edge of the pier with the others, hauling on the ropes and shouting.

Father's left foot caught in the nets as they began to slide, out of control, towards the water. He lost his balance, just as another squall hit us with a force that completely knocked me over—but I still saw him fall as the netting, wrapped around his leg, slid over the wooden structure and into the sea. I remember staggering up, my mouth wide with horror. All was noise and confusion and my tiny shout was whipped away in the roaring wind. I raced between the huge men who were trying to catch hold of Father below and my feet too slipped away from me. There was a crack as I hit the side of the boat, as it swung heavily inward on its fatal journey. Then nothing.

*　　　*　　　*

Most of the days that followed I was left to my own thoughts, lying with a strapped leg and bandaged head in the dimness of our whitewashed house. The strong wind that had killed my father whistled around the building and worried at the loose wattle for three days. I have always associated that impatient, heartless wind with the sound of the mourning women sitting, swaying and wailing, on the stools in the middle of the room.

Salome told me later that Father's fishing colleagues came in, one by one, and explained to Mother how they had tried to save him and how they had caught me just before I too vanished beneath the water. She said they each stroked my forehead and called me a poor child, but fever had already taken me and all I could see were strange and frightening gloomy figures and all I could hear were the sounds of inhuman restlessness and all too human grief.

Someone obviously nursed me, but it was not Mother. Salome was there often, bringing me water and bathing my brow. I remember asking her if Father were dead. She said yes, but I did not really know what death was, although I was afraid that I would die too. I tried to ask Salome but she became agitated and told me not to talk of such things.

One night I grew maddened with the wind and the pain and the mourning and I too began to cry out and wail. Mother came then, but instead of offering comfort, she shouted at me to be quiet. I subsided and hid below the covers, afraid that she too was only a ghostly part of this strange new world of pain and fear.

I never saw her again.

By the time I could get up and pull myself painfully around the town, the inhabitants of Bethsaida seemed to have erased her from their memory. She was as dead as my father and my first, halting questions met with such a bustle of avoidance and hostility that I quickly learnt to stop asking and wrapped my misery up in a tight little ball inside me, where no one could see it. Salome asked too but stopped abruptly after one elderly woman slapped her across the face with a stern admonishment to 'Hold your tongue and forget her, lest it happen to you too.' Something twisted in my mind and heart then, as my hip and leg were twisted beneath me.

For a few weeks we were cared for by friends—we had no relatives in Bethsaida or in Kfar-Nahum, the nearest big town. Salome and I were too bewildered to wonder what would become of us, so we bit our lips and struggled on, while holding onto each other tightly and weeping at night. Even though her arms around me were painful to my still-battered body, I think I would have died without that warmth and the certain knowledge that here was something I knew and understood. She took comfort from me too, but we were so afraid that we never spoke, even to each other, about our mother's disappearance or anything to do with it.

Our future arrived one evening in the form of James, grown lanky and bronzed beyond recognition, and with him a big, burly, grey-haired man with warm, hazel eyes, who told us that he had come to take us back with him to Nazara.

Losing our parents was bad enough, but now Salome and I were to be taken from the home we loved with its beautiful seashore, familiar streets and the secret places where we could play and hide. Even if life had been horrific of late, Bethsaida was all we had ever known. While we stayed there, we could still believe that everything would be all right and we might wake one day to find the last weeks had been nothing but a terrible dream. To be told that we had to leave felt like having our hearts torn out. And nothing we had ever heard about the devout Nazarenes and their uncivilised hamlet up in the hills could make the idea attractive—for all Uncle Joseph's seeming kindness.

He had borrowed a donkey and cart to fetch our few possessions and to carry Salome and me. He said it would be best if we started the following morning at dawn and travelled all day and part of the night so we could get there as soon as possible. That way we would not have time to fret and worry about leaving. It was kindly meant and we were too frightened to protest.

I was too lame to go and say goodbye to any of the places I had loved—the little cove to the west where I played in the rock pools, the market place with all its exciting colours, scents and sights, or even the formerly much-loved harbour place, where Father had worked with his friends.

That night I barely slept. I did not know how to pray, or who to pray to, but I remember begging someone, something, anything, to let us stay in Bethsaida and to let Mother come home.

Morning came, a dull, cloudy day, and nothing had changed. There was no alternative but to allow myself to be lifted into the cart and to bury my head in the straw as our home vanished slowly behind us.

All that terrible morning I wept in grief, pain and confusion. Salome tried to comfort me, but even she lost patience when I refused to listen and she left me to my misery.

Uncle Joseph did his best to entertain us and talk of the life we had to come, and James was as matter-of-fact and solid as he always had been. Salome had begun to enjoy the journey by the time we stopped for a lunch of barley bread and olives half-way up the hillside and was chattering away to her heart's content. She blossomed under Uncle Joseph's good humour and interest, but I would not talk to anyone. Instead, I stared inconsolably at the great sea spread out below us, knowing that soon it would be out of sight—perhaps for the rest of my life. I stopped my ears to Uncle Joseph's words of encouragement and could barely eat for sadness.

I slept for most of the afternoon and into the dusk of the evening. The strong beams of a full moon met my eyes as my sister woke me gently.

'We're there!' hissed Salome. 'Look!'

I sat up, wincing with pain and stiffness. The sleep must have cleansed my mind a little because I found I did care, after all, what Nazara was like.

The huge moon threw silver shadows on the village's outline and turned it into a magical, fairyland place, even to our grief-exhausted eyes. Salome held my hand tightly, both of us half-eager, half fearing this first sight of our new home.

We could hear whispers of sound, for it was a warm night and many of the residents were sleeping or talking quietly on the roofs of their whitewashed houses. Animals moved around contentedly in their stalls and the soft, warm scent of living hides sat comfortingly in the still air.

As we came into the main street there was movement; a wisp of a boy ran, light-footed like a deer, to meet us. Joseph swept him up in his great arms with a roar of welcome, which must have woken half the town. When they had finished embracing, we were able to see a slight boy of about eleven with bright eyes, who looked at us with a grave but not unfriendly face, then bowed to us solemnly.

'This is your brother Yeshua,' said Uncle Joseph proudly. For a second, the boy grinned from ear to ear, but before we could take a closer look in the half-light, he had turned and started running home to tell of our approach.

A few sleepy voices called out to Uncle Joseph as the cart rattled over the rough road and he called back, 'Yes, it is I! Say a welcome to my daughters!' And suddenly from, it seemed, a hundred directions came soft voices on the wind: 'Shalom! Shalom, daughters of Joseph, shalom!'

In our exhaustion it seemed like a dream or a greeting from another world. Back home in Bethsaida, Mother's stories often told of spirits and voices on the wind; of silvery elves and of strange foreign places where magic hung in the air. She told us too of princesses with laughter like the sound of tiny bells, and with faces so beautiful the animals would bow down before them. We, so tired, and so dirty, half-delirious with the strain of the last weeks, tumbled down from our cart at the end of our journey, before just such a creature. She was standing motionless in the halo of light from her front door, her pale skin glowing and her eyes smiling a welcome, which caught our battered hearts. As she held her slender hands out to us, both Salome and I fell forward into her arms, dissolving into exhausted tears.

She washed our hands and feet with a touch so light we could barely feel the rippling of the water on our skin, and put us to bed with a drink of warm goat's milk and a honey-sweetened oatcake. Then she sat with us, looking at nothing in particular, but singing a strange, sweet melody in a soft and beautiful voice until Salome and I felt soothed and comfortable enough to curl up together and fall into a deep, if not contented, sleep.

*   *   *

In the weeks and months that were to follow we discovered slowly, but surely, how blessed we were. We had been adopted by a kind and loving family, who took us to their hearts without question and we were never considered to be anything but a part of the whole.

Nazara was quite a pretty little place, and the house where we lived not unlike our old one. But it was all small, parochial and poor compared with Bethsaida and there were only about 120 people living in the village at all.

It was true that everyone was related. We did not have to introduce ourselves and we did not have to tell our story, because everyone already knew it. Joseph had three full-grown sons from his first marriage, Jonah, Judah and

Simon. They had wives and children, and their wives had their own families. Then there were Joseph's late wife's parents and sisters and brothers, and their families. Miriam's parents were dead and she was an only child, but she had cousins who had other cousins and dozens more distant cousins, so before you knew it, two-thirds of Nazara had the right to call me 'sister.'

Everyone was kind, especially to me as I crept painfully around with my suspicious and frightened eyes, missing everything familiar and liable to burst into tears of grief or confusion at any point. I grieved for my parents and the old familiar things; for the sea and the open space along the shoreline, and for the privacy of a home where no one worried where you were or cared about your business.

Here, there were always people to notice you or—as I thought—to poke their nose into your business. You could not walk along the street without six different relatives calling your name, and any quarrel or illness, or good or bad news, was around the village within seconds. I felt stifled, especially during the frequent family meals, for Joseph and his children all held open house for each other.

From the very first, Joseph was a good guardian to us. He was stern but fair, and his manner seemed so similar to our own father's that it was easier than it might have been to adapt. But Miriam was by far the most important person in our new world. She was Joseph's second wife, young and slender and with an inexplicable elf-like appearance, which she shared with her only natural child. Salome and I were at first afraid to love her in case she too should be taken from us, but Miriam's constant gentleness and warmth were such that no child could resist her for long. She acted as if we had been born her own children, telling us that she had always wanted daughters of her own.

I stayed wary and withdrawn for several weeks, but the ever-open offer of two gentle arms to nestle in, her inability to be offended or upset if you did not respond to her, and the sound of her deep and gentle voice in song were irresistible.

Miriam sang to welcome in the morning; to celebrate the rising of the bread; as she walked to the well or as she laid us to bed. Her voice was like water and moonlight, and when anyone asked why she sang so much, she said it was her way of giving thanks for the beauty of the world.

Her son was just like her and they would exchange glances and smiles almost as though they spoke a secret language. Surprisingly, this did not make others feel excluded; instead, in a strange way, you felt almost honoured that they were part of your life at all.

At first I wondered why Yeshua did not

mind this invasion of cousins into his home, but once you got used to who he was, the idea that he might object was simply out of the question. He, too, acted as though we had always been there, and shared everything he had with a smile. Salome tried to provoke him several times, just to see how much he would take, but he never once rose to the bait.

'He's like a girl,' she said scornfully. 'He's soft.' And she would stamp her foot with frustration as, yet again, Yeshua politely removed himself from her taunting and wandered off in his own little dream world.

James used to joke that Yeshua was so removed from things that even mosquitoes would not notice him and would forget to bite.

I thought they were both wrong; I thought Yeshua was more real than anyone I had ever met. It was everyone else who seemed unreal whenever he was around. If anyone were baiting an animal, a bird or a child, Yeshua would be there in an instant, putting himself between the two, his wide grey eyes flashing with a depth of anger unexpected in such a mild boy. He never said much, but the person he was challenging would back off and walk away as though that slight boyish figure were a man twice their size. If they did not, and acted as though they wanted to fight, Yeshua would flash them a look of withering fire, gather up the animal or child and walk away. He never looked back at them and, somehow, they never followed him.

This did not make him popular, but he was not afraid of anything, not even the dislike of the other village boys, who enjoyed taunting animals or stealing milk and fruit. Yeshua did not care that they hurled insults at him for being a goody-goody.

'That's their opinion,' he would say. 'Why should I believe it?' and he would get on with his work. If anyone said something he thought untrue or unkind, he would stare at them as though he saw right into their soul. Grown men sometimes flushed and turned their head away when Yeshua looked into their eyes.

I was too shy to talk much to Yeshua. Sometimes I felt I wanted to be one of the little hurt creatures that would crawl into his arms, but I was afraid he would look into my soul with those great eyes and find nothing there that he could love.

James was happy in Nazara. He loved his work in the carpenter's shop and enjoyed his travels around the area, building stables or helping out in a new house. He looked exactly as you would imagine a son of Joseph should look, strong and sturdy and dark-skinned from the sun. I think he, not Yeshua, was the one who found it difficult to have two stupid sisters around. Having chosen to leave home, he could not appreciate the extent of our mourning or how we missed the old life.

For those first few weeks, Salome was

almost as withdrawn as I was. There had been plans for her to become betrothed to the son of Father's fishing partner, but there was now no chance of that and she felt she had little hope of making a good match here.

Seeing Nazara in the unkind light of day with its narrow streets and basic houses, she pronounced it a dump, but her poor spirits revived steadily when she realised that, after all, there were more than enough young boys in the village to make good her loss—and that none of them smelt of fish! I thought rather sourly that her grief had been less for our parents and more for her own self-esteem.

Salome's prettiness included some of Mother's fire though none of her colouring. Her hair was raven black, her eyes dark and she had dancing and grace written in her bones. She danced the Petran way once, at a family group, twisting and swirling in such a beautiful haze of movement that I felt the easy tears prickle behind my eyes. No one else was impressed and Salome swiftly understood that no woman in Nazara danced in such a way. She accepted the change with her usual good temper and learnt more orthodox steps instead. I could see how important it was for her to be thought lovely and good, and if that meant dancing different steps it was no trouble to her to learn them. I thought the Nazarene dances were nothing in comparison with the Petran ones, but I held my tongue.

Our names were all wrong too. The Nazarenes pronounced them differently, and even when we pointed out that we preferred the Greek versions we were given at birth, many of the villagers would not adapt and it was a source of much irritation, to me especially. I developed a deaf ear to 'Devorah!', which did not endear me to many.

We found that every town and village had different opinions on the appropriateness of Greek, Aramaic or Hebrew and on the different pronunciations of names and places. Father would have said it was the Jews loving to disagree again, but we did not think jokes like that would be well received in Nazara.

Miriam told us we could call her Mother if we felt comfortable with it, or Miriam, if we did not. We called her Mother Miriam, which she liked. But as time went by we dropped the Miriam and both she and Joseph became just Imma and Abba, as though they had always been so.

Often, in that first year, I would dream of Father's death or of Mother shouting at me as I lay ill, and would wake rigid with fear. For Father I could let go and grieve but the pain for Mother had no relief. She had left and I did not know why. If I tried to talk to Salome about it, she would only say, 'This is our life now. There is no point in looking back,' and I would turn away holding my head high to show I did not care. I could only assume that

Mother had no longer wanted us, or that she blamed me for living when Father had died—or that she herself was dead too. Her death, though terrible, was the only solution I could live with, so that was what I taught myself to believe.

Even though Imma was kind, fair and so understanding that it was impossible not to love her, there was so much emphasis on good manners in Nazara that I thought talking about my other parents, who were, effectively, outcasts, would be rude. Salome and James never mentioned them, so neither did I.

There was one other thing I did not tell Imma, or anyone else. My wounded hip and leg refused to heal completely and I was constantly in pain, but I was too proud to act the weakling. I pretended that my crookedness did not hurt and helped to fetch the water, or went on errands, or stood to hold the thread as Imma wove the fine cloth she made on her loom, because I wanted her to love me and to think me useful. My own mother had been loud in her irritation about cripples who wallowed in their suffering, so I lied and pretended but I could not help being bad-tempered and irritable when I wanted so much to be good.

'You are a funny child, Deborah,' Imma would say, stroking my forehead. 'You say so little and look so serious. Why don't you play with the other children?'

I would say I did not want to, when I ached to be able to rough and tumble and race around like the others. In Bethsaida I had not needed other children. Mother, Father, Salome and my beautiful sea had been all the playmates I wanted. Now I wished with all my heart to be a normal child who could run and play but I dared not, in case my weakness showed. I was a very lonely little girl for all the love that was available around me.

* * *

As time slipped by, the old life became almost like a dream, half-remembered and confused. It seemed easier to put it away and forget about it altogether. Salome was still inclined to be quite snobbish about Nazara, but once she realised that her arrival in the little village had caused quite a sensation—she was by far the prettiest girl there—she began to enjoy herself. She gathered around her a little court of both boys and girls, who were as impressed by her big-town ways as they were by her beauty, and she made best friends with three other pretty Nazarene girls. The four of them would run across to Japhia just a short walk away where there were shops and pedlars and merchants and less-observant Jews, who were quite prepared to flirt with pretty girls. Imma had to be quite firm with Salome sometimes. Very soon, preparations were under way to make

30

her safely betrothed to Zachariah, a tall, good-looking Nazarene, who worshipped the ground she walked on.

We settled down and adapted, as though we had always been Nazarenes, apart from knowing how to deal with the one member of our new family who did not make any sense at all: the God of Israel.

Abba, James and Yeshua together with most of the other men from the village went to the Synagogue three times a day. Imma went once or twice during the week and took Salome and me every Shabbat—a completely new idea to us. At home we had paid lip-service only to the Sabbath day but here, in Nazara, all the rules of the Torah were followed in detail.

We carried nothing outside the village limits and did no work on Shabbat. We ate cold food prepared the day before, and we spent hours in the Synagogue praying and worshipping this strange deity, who seemed to demand constant and fervent obedience.

Imma led us, each week, into the women's section of the Synagogue. We sat behind a beautifully carved wooden balustrade with gauze hung across it so that none of the men could see us. Imma would listen with great attention as the men read the Torah and tracts from the Prophets, and Simeon, the Rabbi, translated the meaning of the Hebrew text into Aramaic in his sermon. Salome and I went only because we had to. She fidgeted, sighed and looked bored, and I put my face to the gauze so that I could see the outlines of the men and tried to understand what was going on.

The Lord and His prophets were always talking about duty and sacrifice and vengeance. They did not seem to have anything to do with reality, and most of the Nazarenes seemed perfectly normal away from the Synagogue. I could just have disregarded it, as I thought they did, had it not been for Abba and Imma's insistence that we should involve the Lord in everyday life.

Once Imma realised how poor a religious upbringing we had had, she used to explain things carefully and clearly so that we could understand the rules and regulations. But in that, as well as everything else, she was unusual. Most of the other women, even if they were from the Netzer-shoot of Jesse, were less pious. They gossiped quietly during the Synagogue service and eyed up each other's clothes and jewellery. Many of the men too (from the little I could see through the veil of gauze) seemed bored and restless. After feeling first curiosity, then irritation, at all this senseless fuss, I slipped into boredom, and eventually resignation. I spent most of my hours at the Synagogue in my own little dream world, where I had a tiny multi-coloured boat and could float on my dearly remembered sea. In my mind I put in at unoccupied coves, and looked at beautiful flowers and lush green hillsides and played with imaginary friends. Then I could dance again and I would run, jump and cartwheel on the sand and in the bright summer grass. Imma asked me once what I was thinking of, and when I confessed shamefacedly (though I did not tell her about the dancing), she said that being joyful was as good a way of worshipping the Lord as any. I didn't understand, but I was glad she was not angry.

Abba, Imma, James and Yeshua went to Jerusalem three times a year for the great Jewish holy festivals, but for the first year after Salome and I arrived only the men went.

'You two have had enough disruption in your life for a while,' Imma said when we protested. 'There will be more than enough time to see Jerusalem.'

Salome, who was intrigued by talk of the city's legendary beauty, felt hard done by, and I was curious at what it would be like to go, but glad not to have the strain of a long journey. I could walk comfortably only as far as Japhia, which I loved, and which was much larger than Nazara and more interesting than Bethsaida or even Kfar-Nahum, which I had visited once. It was often full of Herod Antipas's soldiers and merchants from the south and the east (I once saw one with skin that was the palest creamy pink and hair that was almost white) and there was nothing nicer than sitting, watching the hustle and bustle, while Abba or Imma went about their business there.

We women enjoyed the times when the men and the rest of the village were away. Nazara took on a dreamy, restful air and there was extra time for picnics and play. Imma was as good as a sister to me. When she had time, she would play with me in gentle versions of the childhood games I enjoyed so much but was afraid to play with the other children. She never, ever told me I was silly or stupid the way all the other children (except Yeshua) did.

Spring comes to Galilee in a great rush of wind and colour. The buds seem to erupt overnight into daisies and poppies, and the beautiful blue teasels appear from nowhere, making the hillsides as bright as the sky. Imma's songs would change from warming winter carols into bright ripples of sound to welcome the new life. Often, newly fledged baby birds would land right by her hand as she was grinding barley and, instead of shooing them away, she would chirrup to them and offer them a handful of food. If Salome and I were nearby, they would come to us as well, so at first we thought that all the birds in Nazara must be tame. They came to Yeshua too and they seemed cautiously fond of Abba and James, but as soon as anyone else came to our bright little home, they fled.

That second year in Nazara we were all to go to Jerusalem for Pesach, the Festival of the

Passover and the exodus from Egypt. The whole village bustled with preparations for days before every big festival and this time we felt a part of the excitement too, arranging for the animals to be looked after, drying food for the journey and airing our best clothes.

All the Nazarenes who were going started the journey together at dawn, with those to be left behind waving us off. I felt quite confident, as I had grown a little stronger over the year and I had had enough time to plan my strategy carefully. There were plenty of carts to sit in, as the Nazarenes took the opportunity to take wares to sell, other than those for the obligatory Temple tithes. I could perch on sacks of grain or beans, or among cages of chickens and geese, and though that felt sore after a while, it was quite bearable. Some people rode on donkeys and they too would happily offer a lift to a tired little girl who was stiff from the bumps on the road.

If there were no other way, one of my many uncles or step-brothers would let me ride on his shoulders. I was a slight and bony little thing and they would hardly notice my weight. Playing this game let me believe that no one really noticed my crooked hip and ungainly walk.

Salome and I had never been further south than Nazara, so we were sleepless with excitement the night before we left. We expected to see many new and exciting things but, even so, we had no idea how swiftly and how much the countryside would change as we began the journey south. Even though we followed the fertile route of the River Jordan, and it was a bright and abundant spring in Galilee, the land grew steadily more and more barren as we moved towards Jerusalem. Our feet and legs became covered with dust from the road, which slowly crept in through everyone's clothing until we all felt grimy and many began to cough. The bright spring sun burnt into us and the lush spring grass by the side of the path gave way to a harsher kind, already yellowing and dry. The rocks too were different; not dark and spotted as on the hills at home, but pale yellow-white. I thought they must have been bleached by the heat.

We carried food for the journey, but there were plenty of places to stop and eat and rest-houses with long, low dormitories each night. In spite of the heat and the dust we were a cheerful crowd, singing psalms and local songs, and even a reserved little girl like me found that smiles and friendship come easily when you are on the move. Every hour we met up with more people, and by the time we were a day's journey from our destination you could not see any part of the road ahead or behind us that was not filled with the faithful going to the Holy City.

On the morning of the fourth day we saw Jerusalem; a huge, golden, walled city with whole villages, each as big as Nazara, clustered around it, like courtiers bowing to a King. I had never imagined anything so impressive or so frightening.

But worse than the size of the place was the stink.

You can smell festive Jerusalem long before you can see it clearly. The stench of blood and burning flesh from the Temple hovers on the winds and curdles the blood of children like me, who have never considered the reality of religious sacrifice. This great and wondrous place, the centre of all the Jewish faith, was also a charnel house for a fearsome God, who wanted worship through the death of small and beautiful things.

Instead of staring at the wonderful sight in awe, I felt the heavy air turn my stomach and I was sick, violently and ashamedly, by the side of the road.

We entered the city through the Damascus Gate, and the walls stretched so high above us that I was afraid they would topple over and fall. I shrank back in Jonah's cart and tried to make myself invisible among the sacks full of grain, hiding my eyes as we approached the lodging house where our close family group was to stay.

We left our belongings in the long dormitory room, washed and changed and joined the queue of people going to the Temple. It seemed as though everyone coming

37

for Pesach was buying, or carrying animals and birds for the sacrifices, staring in wonder at the fabulous Temple or gazing in fascination at the strange people and the exotic wares for sale along the way. I did look, but I could not bear the sight of all those living things, which so soon were to be slaughtered, and I hid my face in Imma's skirts and wept as Abba bought a beautiful fluffy lamb for our family's Pesach offering. I was sick again when the women added a basketful of gentle white doves to the haul, and though Imma was as kind as she could be, she didn't seem to see what was wrong. I felt betrayed that she, who loved all wild things, could condone killing creatures for the Lord. I was unable to speak to her or explain how I felt because of all the others there. Even worse, I was afraid she would stop loving me because I did not understand.

Jerusalem is beautiful. Its streets are wide and crammed with colours never seen in the parochial north. Spices and fruits add their tang to the busy air and everywhere fabulous peoples from unheard-of cultures haggle and bargain and laugh and shout. To Salome and I, the pale golden rock walls of the Temple, wholly magnificent, seemed higher than a mountain and larger than the whole of Japhia. I should have felt all the wonder and joy that my sister did, but I was tearful and sorry, and resentful and incapable of enjoying myself. I made it worse of course by making a friend of the lamb and stroking him. I bawled when Imma took me away, scolding me for upsetting myself by becoming fond of the animal and forbidding me to go near it again.

So we came, tear-stained and tense, to the Mikvah, the ritual bath everyone took before being allowed into the Temple itself. The men went to their section and we joined the crowd of women queuing for ours. I sulked through the formalities of washing both hands and feet, but Imma wisely said nothing, just held my hand tightly and led me firmly to the water. As we stepped in together she said a prayer, softly, so that only she and I could hear. 'Lord, we, thy servants Miriam and Deborah, come in humility to thy gate. Cleanse our soul and our spirit, O Lord, as the water cleanses our body.' Then she lifted me and together we sank down into the cool, clear water, dipping below the surface so that our hair mingled together as one.

Time stopped. Light became like pearl and sound was soft—muted as though we had entered another world. Comfort, even peace, rose inside my body as though there were a femininity and an understanding greater than the two of us enveloping and loving us. For those moments, the Temple was holy even to me.

And then it was over; hands reached out to help us up the steps and the next women slipped into the water. The world resumed its normal shape and colour and Imma turned to help Salome. We were just another mother and her daughters in the company of a bustle of women.

We met up with the men inside the perimeter walls and began pushing our way through a throng of people all milling around as they met up with acquaintances and exchanged news. Unbelievers, pedlars and travellers keen to see this marvel of architecture were allowed into the outer Temple court and some even called it the Court of the Gentiles. To go further within, towards the holy place itself, meant death if you were not a Jew. On this festival eve, however, it was mostly the faithful who gathered together to worship.

To Salome and the others there was an air of excitement, but all I could hear were the plaintive cries of the animals and birds able to smell the scent of death ahead. Among the flocks of people were dozens of traders offering cages filled with livestock for those who had not had the foresight to buy outside, or who wanted a last-minute extra offering.

We joined the queues through into the Court of the Women, and Imma, Salome and I, with the others of our sex, waited there as the men took the animals through into the Court of Israel. Imma had warned us that we were excluded from the inner courts, although there was a balcony where we could watch on special occasions. This day, none of the women seemed to be watching and I was glad of that.

Who would want to see these strange and inexplicable male rituals anyway, I wondered, and why did Yeshua, who was all that was gentle, want to go in with the other men? It was unanswerable.

Even after the surprise and the pleasure of the Mikvah, I had decided that I hated the Holy One and his Temple and the cruelty that was worshipped in the name of goodness, but that was something else I knew I would have to keep to myself.

Of course I would not eat the sacrificed lamb at the Seder supper, which marked the beginning of Pesach, even though it smelt delicious. Luckily, I was not the youngest child, so I did not have to speak up and take part in the service and most of the time I could hide, dismally, at the back of the room. I could not escape entirely, for all the children at the Seder were expected to drink wine with the adults, to mark each section of the service. I know now that Imma watered my wine, and gave me as little as she could, but even so, the disgusting taste made me choke and the effect of the alcohol only made me feel worse.

I was sulky and withdrawn for the whole week of rituals, services and sacrifices; for the family meals and meetings. I took little notice of the beauty and excitement around us and

41

made no new friends with the other children, who regarded the city as a great adventure. Instead, I spent hours plotting ways of staying behind in Nazara whenever the others came again. Several times Yeshua came to sit next to me at meetings or meal times and he would smile at me invitingly. But he never asked me what was wrong and, though part of me knew that he would have listened, I could not make myself speak. Not even he seemed to think as I did and I would rather have been thought sulky and bad-tempered than mad.

I shook the dust of Jerusalem joyfully from my feet when we finally left and promised myself that, whatever happened, I would never return.

And now, because of Yeshua, I had to go back.

2

Abba, Imma and I rose as the cock crowed and retraced our footsteps. This time there was no one to offer me a ride or to help me on my way and I was already irritable and angry before we began. Abba and Imma were too worried to offer me the game of a lift, and I was too upset and proud to ask.

My anger made me strong and I allowed them to set a pace that was too fast for me.

Before long, I knew I was in trouble but my stubbornness refused to acknowledge it. I walked until my head sang with agony and I could no longer see, until, eventually, I was incapable of speech or even breath. My exhausted body screamed and shook and betrayed me, leaving me to fall down in a shamed and defeated heap by the side of the road.

Abba lifted me up without a word but Imma, normally so patient and kind, was sharp with me. 'Why didn't you tell me how bad your leg is?' she said. 'Deborah, you make it so much more difficult with your pride.'

I wept and they both ignored me. Looking back, I wonder where I found so many tears.

Within a short time we found a small rest-house and, as Abba was carrying our baggage as well as me, he was glad to stop for a drink and something to eat.

We were not the only visitors; a man with his three sons had stopped too and, by then, I was recovered enough to notice the strange flurries of avoidance as our two parties tried not to talk to or sit near each other. The father of the group kept looking at me and I felt confused by the stranger's intent eyes. Abba and Imma appeared not to notice.

During the meal I spotted the men's donkey with its colt, tied at the back of the inn and when I had finished my food, I slipped away, fuelled by the resilience of youth, to stroke the animals and to feel their sweet breath on my face. As I nestled into the warmth of their flesh, the man who owned them suddenly appeared behind me.

He had a kind face and, after a first rush of fear that he would be angry, I was reassured when he told me his name and knelt down to pat the colt. He told me how old the little donkey was and asked whether I thought he was beautiful and his hide soft.

'I think he's wonderful,' I said shyly, looking up at the stranger through my tousled hair.

'Maiden, why do you limp?' he asked suddenly—and, without knowing why, I answered him honestly.

'I hurt my leg last year,' I said. 'It won't get any better. It hurts to walk and we have to go all the way to Jerusalem.'

To my surprise, the man's eyes filled with tears and he turned away swiftly and left me.

When we started off again, Abba, rather shamefacedly, was holding the colt. 'You're to ride on this,' he told me brusquely. 'It's been lent to us. Come on now, hurry up.'

The kind man walked just behind us as we continued our journey, but there was no conversation between us. I thought Abba and Imma were being rude, but I knew I had already caused enough trouble and embarrassment with my sulks. I tried to make up by beaming at the man and waving whenever we turned a corner and I could look back without losing my balance.

Nothing could have made that journey a delight for me, but I sat comfortably on the warm back and found myself crooning to the little creature and watching his ears flicker as he listened to my voice. If I hadn't been so bitterly angry inside, I would have allowed myself to be happy.

Even riding the donkey, I was still tired by the time we approached the city and as the faint but familiar stench crept across the land to greet us, a terrible fear nibbled its way into my stomach. The time for the festival was past, but there were still the daily rituals of atonement, worship and cleansing, all of which required the death of a baby animal and the burning of its entrails on the holy altar. I huddled over the neck of my little mount in horror.

At the edge of the city walls, Abba told me to get down and I did so, but instead of following Imma, I limped back as fast as I could towards the people behind.

'Deborah!' Abba called, but I ignored him. The kind man signed to him that he would bring me back and went down on one knee to hear what I wanted to say.

'What is it, little girl?' he asked with great tenderness.

'You're not going to sacrifice the donkey, are you?' I blurted out. 'Please don't. Please! I couldn't bear it.'

'Deborah!' Both Imma and Abba were outraged at my bad manners, but the kind man smiled.

'No,' he said. 'Of course not. Donkeys are never sacrificed. In any case, our family does not make sacrifices in Jerusalem. He is quite safe.' Then he turned to Abba. 'I have been thinking,' he said. 'The maid has a long journey home again and I should like to give you the colt to carry her back. She reminds me of a daughter I once had, much loved. I lost her when she was seven. It would be like giving a gift to my Ruth.'

I stared at him in disbelief and the easy tears sprang to my eyes. He reached out as if to touch me, but withdrew his hand sharply and looked up at my parents.

Both Abba and Imma began to protest and I could see that they meant to refuse the wonderful, wonderful gift. Something came over me that was more than my usual stubbornness; I simply felt that the gift was right, the donkey was meant to be mine and, without thinking, I said over both Abba's and Imma's voices, 'Yes. Thank you. I should like the colt. Thank you very much. I will love him as your daughter would have done. Thank you. I won't forget you.'

It seemed as though accepting the donkey was like giving a gift to the man. I could not explain it, but the tears in his eyes as he turned away told me I was right.

We found Yeshua in the Temple, of course. I say 'of course' because Yeshua was always worshipping the Lord somewhere or other, so the Temple seemed the obvious place to look.

Imma and I stayed in the Court of the Gentiles while Abba went in. He was gone for only a few minutes and Yeshua came out with him, his head held high.

Imma threw her arms around her son.

'Jesus,' she said, crying a little, saying the Greek word she used as a pet name for him. 'I was so worried.'

Then this strange, beautiful boy, who had caused us so much trouble and anguish, looked at her with his clear grey eyes and said, 'Didn't you know I must be about my Father's business?'

And she accepted it! So did Abba. They were obviously hurt and put out, but they did not say anything else. If I had behaved like that, they would have been very angry, and rightly so. I was so furious that I refused to speak to Yeshua at all.

I sulked all that night, which we spent in the same boarding house as before, and I was still so upset and confused that I hardly appreciated the little donkey, which loyally carried me home. I don't think I spoke at all for four days, apart from making the necessary polite answers. Even Imma gave up asking me what was wrong. I was seething that they could not see.

But even I could not go on sulking once we were back in the lush green countryside of Galilee. Yellow and white daisies, red anemones and deep blue iris were dancing in the dark grasses and Nazara itself was surrounded and filled with a dozen different colours of green as every home's little vegetable patch blossomed with the abundance to come.

Our home too was cool, welcoming and peaceful and Salome and James were glad to see us. Salome had made a herb and bean stew for our coming and James had news of new work for Abba and himself in Kfar-Nahum.

I was happy to see the flowers and vegetables in the garden and interested in Abba's plans for stabling the colt. He and Imma had had a donkey once before, he told me as we tethered the beast at the back of his workshop and he began to look out some spare wood for the structure of a stable. 'It was a gentle beast,' he said. 'Old when we got it. Your mother needed to ride on a long journey as she was carrying Yeshua at the time, but typically she chose a beast that was past its best and sick, out of pity.' He laughed. 'I didn't think it would make it, but I was wrong. It stayed with us for another four years. Yeshua will remember it if you ask him—oh, for

Heaven's sake, child!' as my face contracted from smiles into a frozen mask at Yeshua's name. 'Why are you still so angry with him?'

'She's not,' said Yeshua coming up behind us. 'It's not me she's angry with, it's the Lord.'

As he said the words, something inside me snapped. I ran away, peg-legged as usual, as fast as I could, out of the village and down the hillside.

I don't think I knew what I was doing; my mind was like a cloud of black smoke. Perhaps I was simply past thought, over-tired from the journey and mentally exhausted from the tension. It seemed that no one followed me as I ran, and for that I was grateful. But it made me angry too, because no matter how much Imma and Abba tried to love me, I truly believed I belonged to no one, and with my hip so crooked and weak, I could hardly be any use if I did. I was nothing but a bad-tempered burden to my adopted parents and I had nothing in common even with my own sister. Salome was pretty and willing and helpful; I was sullen and small, and people's faces when they saw me told me that I was plain.

Once I was safely out of sight of the village, I threw myself down in the long grass and sobbed my heart out.

When I finally sat up, Yeshua was sitting a few feet away, chewing a piece of grass and looking up, at nothing, as though it were some sight of great beauty. I stared at him with hatred and he looked back at me with more kindness than anyone could expect in a twelve-year-old boy.

'Tell me about it,' he said.

I did not want to. I wanted to go on sulking, but as he looked at me, some great, ancient roar came from my stomach and, from my mouth, words that I hardly understood myself.

'Your Father's business,' I said spitefully. 'Your Lord. Your cruel, heartless Lord, who demands killing for worship. Wonderful. You were about your Father's business. What about me? I don't have a God. I don't *want* that kind of God. One that's selfish and unkind. I hate that God. All He's ever done for me is hurt me. Why don't women have a God? Why are we shut away behind walls and veils? Your God is for men. Why don't we have a God?'

'You have the same Lord,' said Yeshua simply. 'Everyone does. Look again. You are not seeing.' I snorted rudely and turned my back on him, but I was too tired to run away again, so, eventually, I had to begin to listen.

We sat together, my brother and I, at the foot of the little valley, as the sun began to set behind us, and he spoke to me of things I had never heard before.

'Look for the good in every situation before you say the Lord is absent,' he said. 'There was good for you in my decision to stay behind in the Temple. See if you can find it.'

'Don't be stupid,' I said, but Yeshua was not

50

offended. Instead he rolled me over and tickled me until, despite myself, I was laughing.

'Try again,' he said. 'Where was the good for you?'

Intrigued, I tried to find some good in it, but failed.

'Silly Deborah!' he said. 'You got a donkey and made a friend. Isn't that good?'

Even I had to admit that it was. 'But that only came about because I was in pain.'

'Yes, you were in such pain that you had to admit you could no longer walk,' said Yeshua.

'What's good about that?'

'You overcame your stubbornness and accepted that you needed help.'

'I am ashamed of it. That doesn't feel good.'

'But how can the Lord help you if you won't ask, or you pretend you don't need Him or us? It is you who tries to turn your back on Him, not He on you. If you hadn't been honest about your pain, you would not have been given the colt.'

It was hard to understand and I wept a little more at the thought that everybody now knew how lame I really was. Yeshua patted me gently on the shoulder, just as Abba would have done, and waited until I had finished crying.

Then he made it a game. The donkey and the strange man's kindness were obvious good things that had happened, but soon we were sitting hand in hand as the sun slipped behind the hills and trying to find more and more good from the journey back to Jerusalem.

I had been given aubergine to eat for supper at the boarding house, which was a new experience. Had I been in a better mood, I would have enjoyed it.

I had a bed to myself for once. Usually I slept with Salome.

I had the opportunity to talk alone to Imma and Abba and to see how much they truly loved me. I could have talked to them about how I really felt about myself, and what a burden I felt to them, with no interruption from the others. I could have talked to them about how I hated the sacrifices, without James or Salome to tell me I was a silly baby.

And as I saw—because somehow he made it easy even for a stubborn seven-year-old girl to see—I realised that all those opportunities had been given to me by heaven. It was I who had chosen not to take them. Just for a moment I felt again the strange sensation of light and love that had blessed me in the Temple Mikvah.

Then a flood of guilt and self-hatred overruled this and I was ashamed of myself. So much so that I hid my face in my hands and began to wail like the mourning women after my father's death.

Yeshua took my hands gently, and moved them away from my face. 'Look at the moon,' he said. 'Look how lovely she is and how she

52

lights up the night. Nothing is so bad that it cannot be given light and solved. You don't have to feel bad. You didn't know any better. Now you do. Isn't that wonderful?'

Then he gave me a broad, boyish grin and teased me, until I laughed with him and moved from guilt into delight at the knowledge he had given me. So much so that my head felt filled with the moonlight and I wanted to know more.

'But what about Imma?' I asked. 'What good came for her? And what for Abba? And what for James and Salome?'

'For James and Salome the chance to be independent before they both get married,' said Yeshua. 'Maybe more things, but those may be none of our business!

'For Abba and Imma, well, why not ask them yourself? They'll answer you.' And I knew he was right.

'I know!' I said. 'I know the greatest good of all. It's you. Well, it's us. You and me, Yeshua. Now we are friends and we can talk of these things.'

'Yes,' he agreed. 'That is good. Very good, but not the best. The best is that you are finding your own way to the Lord. Not my way. Not the Rabbi's, not anyone else's, but yours. And it's not you and me, but you and me and the Lord.'

Any other day I would have rejected that, but for once it appeared as though the Lord might be on my side. We walked home together in the gloaming, and it seemed to me that my leg hurt less and my heart felt lighter.

* * *

I wish I could say I was transformed from then on, but of course I was not. But from that day Yeshua and I had a bond that felt like both safety and light in one. I never felt without a friend again, whether he was in the village or not.

We continued the game of finding good in all things, though sometimes it was a sad challenge to a little girl of seven. Yeshua taught me that it was only habit that made us judge all happenings as bad or difficult, when they could be opportunities to live a happier life.

But grazed knees, which taught me to look where I was going, still caused tears of pain and grief. Household chores, which taught me the arts I would need as a woman, were still boring and sometimes painful. Sharp words from our neighbour, Sarah, when I bumped into her while she was carrying her water, brought both tears and resentment, though Yeshua used the situation to teach me that it was often other people's problems that made them so angry.

'It usually has little or nothing to do with the person they take their temper out on,' he explained. 'They hit out at others because they cannot face the pain within themselves.'

Sarah's husband was unkind to her, he told me, but she was too proud to let her unhappiness show except in bad temper.

'Why not take her a bunch of wildflowers to brighten her house?' he suggested. 'If you can return good for evil, you change everything.'

Though it was very hard, and I couldn't face her directly, I picked some blue iris and laid them outside Sarah's door. She never knew who gave them, so she was never any kinder to me. But a week later a pedlar passing through the village gave me a piece of sugar-cake as a gift because he said he thought my hair was pretty.

'That was the Lord,' said Yeshua. 'He was saying thank you for your kindness. He sees all that you do and He will always thank you, even if the person you do good to does not.'

I thought that very strange.

When I remembered to play Yeshua's game, everything did feel brighter. It also made it easier to love and be loved and I needed that lesson. Imma joined in with us (Yeshua said she was a natural at the game anyway) and Abba tried hard to join in, too.

Yeshua told him about the game when he and James were home from their assignment in Kfar-Nahum, and he had a good chuckle and said anything that made people happy had to be a good idea. James and Salome both thought we were silly, but as they were both being very grown-up and betrothed, they did not want to be bothered with little-girl games.

One day I managed to find the courage to ask Imma about the good that came from my leg.

'That is one of the Lord's hidden goods,' she said, stopping work at her loom to give me her full attention. 'We don't know yet, and it may take many years before we find out. Some good has already come—the donkey and your friendship with Yeshua—but there will be more. You have to trust that, Deborah, because as you grow up, it will seem very unfair at times.'

Even at seven, I knew what she meant. Springtime taught young people in our village all they needed to know about the facts of life. James was to be married in a few weeks' time and Salome the following year. A girl with a crooked hip was unlikely to marry and have children—any crippled animals born to the Nazarene flocks were not allowed to live, let alone breed. There were even whispers that the same thing happened to deformed babies, although no one ever spoke openly of these things.

At seven it did not seem to matter very much; all I wanted was to stay with Yeshua and Abba and Imma, but sometimes I would feel resentful of some unrealised longing.

'Promise me there will be good?' I said,

holding on to Imma's skirt for reassurance, and looking up into her kind face.

'I promise,' she said, putting her hand on my head and stroking my curly red hair. 'I promise you, Deborah, that one day you will come to me and say you are glad your hip is crooked. That you could not have had such a wonderful life if you had been the same as the other girls.'

Imma, Yeshua and I even found good in the day that the donkey broke out of his pen and ate all of the new young plants in the garden. That took us quite a few minutes, as our crop of food for the winter ahead had been destroyed, which could have meant considerable hardship.

'At least the good food meant the donkey didn't run away,' said Imma.

'He could have hurt himself, or kicked someone,' I said.

'And we won't be so upset at losing him when he grows old and dies, because we'll get to keep our vegetables at last!' said Yeshua and that made us laugh.

'What in the Lord's name are you so cheerful about?'

An old lady who was passing stopped by the wall, to look at us in amazement. It was quite obvious what had happened and her face was such a picture that we laughed again.

'We are praising the Lord,' said Imma, giggling. 'We're in a pretty pickle, but He will sort it out for us somehow.'

The woman looked at us long and hard. She was one of the few Nazarenes who was no relative of ours and almost a stranger to us. She seemed to be making up her mind about something and it was quite some time before she spoke.

'You and your children are good-hearted,' she said to Imma. 'I've often seen you out and you always look cheerful. You are devout and I've heard good things of you. I'm growing old and I'm on my own now since my husband, may he rest in peace, passed on. My back is stiff and if your children could do a little weeding for me in my garden, you can share all my vegetables and take some seed for next year.'

'That's quick, even for the Lord,' said Yeshua.

I was the one who did the weeding for Rosa and, in the old days, I would have resented that. But I tried hard to see the good in the extra work, and only grumbled a little when I set off for my first day's gardening.

Rosa lived the far side of Nazara and her patch of land was surrounded by a wall easily as tall as I was, so I had no idea what kind of work I would have to do.

She welcomed me kindly and gave me a cup of mint tea and an oatcake while she made all the polite enquiries about my family that manners dictated. I was the model of a quiet, good-mannered little girl and I'm sure she wondered why she had even invited me. But all that changed when she led me through into the garden.

I gasped and exclaimed, and changed in seconds from a stiff and solemn little creature into an excited child with shining eyes. The cascade of colour and beauty, so rare and unexpected, in front of me was overwhelming; it was paradise, filled with every imaginable flower and scent, and humming with the wings of busy insects.

'Yes, it is lovely, isn't it?' she said, her eyes lighting up at my appreciation of her life's work. 'Many of the plants have come from faraway lands and there is a story to every one of them. Maybe I will teach you one day, but today, we will start at the beginning.'

She took my hand and led me round, pointing out her favourite plants. Within minutes we were the best of friends.

Rosa's garden was a place of bees and butterflies and scents. Bougainvillaea, roses, pansies and lilies and many bright flowers I could not begin to name tumbled over the ground in great cascades of coloured light. The vegetables were neatly laid in rows in the middle of this paradise and fruit trees lined the far wall, already heavy with the first crop. In the corner, by a patch of vines, was a beehive, which made me nervous at first.

'The Lord bless you, child, they won't hurt

you!' said Rosa. 'Leave them be and they will leave you alone too. They are here to pollinate all the beautiful plants, and to give us honey to sweeten even the sourest bread.'

She was right. In all the years I worked there I was never stung, and I came to love watching the bees dancing in and out of the flowers and rubbing the bright yellow pollen onto their legs.

What I had thought would be drudgery was a joy from the very first day. As the weeks passed and I looked forward more and more to the days I would spend there, I came to know the names of every plant in the garden and how to tend each one. That patch of land became my garden, my own special place as well as Rosa's.

It was filled with herbs and sweet-scented plants, so just to walk through it lifted a haze of delightful essences from the ground, which could waft you far away from the sometimes scruffy, often smelly, streets of Nazara into some strange, exotic land. I was naturally a dreamer and could imagine myself in a Sultan's garden, or paradise itself, as I worked steadily at the fertile soil.

Rosa had been in charge of the women's Mikvah at the Synagogue in Japhia and was not a Nazarene by birth. 'I'm not orthodox enough for the Synagogue here, my dear,' she said as she brought me a bowl of fresh camomile tea and a herb cake on a golden late-summer afternoon. 'My husband was from Nazara but I always kept my links with Japhia. I used the herbs to help the women's aches and pains and fears and troubles. The Mikvah was often the only place they could come to tell someone their woes—and their joys.

'But now, this land is half wasted. My successor at Japhia doesn't use these balms, so I grow them for old time's sake and for those who still come and see me for a drink and a chat. The Rabbi doesn't approve, nor his wife, but their daughters come here sometimes, and we talk. There's plenty to talk about among the women.'

Rosa was a gruff old soul in her fifties (which seemed ancient to me). It was unusual for anyone in Nazara to live alone, but she did. Her children had gone to Tiberias, which was a scandal in itself as it was a Roman city built on old graveyards, and ritually impure to the orthodox. However, Rosa was not the kind of woman who overwhelmed you with her loneliness.

Plenty of people—I should say plenty of women—came to see her for advice and herbs, but it was not a fact that was generally known. Often a woman would knock tentatively at the door, keeping her face covered in her shawl, and as Rosa made her welcome, I would sometimes see the woman's shoulders shake as she let go tears of anguish. I always kept away and tried not to see or hear what was going on but, of course, I was curious. Luckily I did not understand what snippets I did hear, but somehow I knew that these matters were secret and not to be spoken of, even between Rosa and myself.

She was kept busy; women came from far and wide to avail themselves of whatever skills she had, but she always made time for me, bringing me drinks and a home-made treat as I sat on the soil, pulling up the weeds and enjoying the ever-changing sight of plants growing, flowering and fruiting. We would chat a little about the garden and the season, and I found myself learning steadily which herb would help which simple problem and how to recognise and use it.

Rosa taught me basic first aid: how to treat shock and bruises and burns or grief; how to select the leaves or root of a plant and dry them, and then to pound them into powder with pestle and mortar so that they could be used in potions and salves.

She also taught me how to infuse a precious drop of oil from lavender, rose and other sweet-smelling flowers and to mix it with the golden unguents that she bought on her monthly trips to Japhia. But although she seemed so open and frank with me, there were many plants she never spoke about and many powders and teas that were kept hidden in the solid wooden chest in her bedroom.

Rosa never failed to say 'thank you' for my

efforts and, after each day's work, she made sure I took home two great baskets full of the season's best: peppers, onions, garlic, flowers, beans, oranges and figs.

Even the sourest child will blossom from knowing he or she is valued and appreciated, and there was such pleasure in seeing Imma's smile of welcome and exclamations of delight each time she saw what I had brought back to our little house.

I began to offer my small amount of herbal knowledge as well. When James burnt himself on a heated iron, I made a salve of lavender and goose grease to soothe the pain of his blistered hand, and I would brew teas for stomach pains, tiredness and to help bring sleep. The family drank them bravely but doubtfully, until it became apparent that they worked. Then they praised me in ways that made my heart lift.

I began to sing at my chores as Imma did, and I fleshed out a little, so that I was no longer quite such a skinny, ugly little girl.

Rosa's water was collected by her niece, Joanna, who would come in for a chat and a drink and a handful of figs or olives with Rosa's delicious wheat bread. Most of us in Nazara ate coarse, long-lasting barley bread, but Rosa always had a sack of wheat, which she would grind and bake herself. Sometimes she sent a loaf home with me and we would feast on it for supper, preferring to eat it

63

alone, with perhaps a dribble of olive oil, instead of dipping it in the vegetable or chicken stew or spread with beans.

For all that we did not have wheat, we were richer than many of the other Nazarenes. Abba, as a carpenter, was a village elder, second only to the Rabbi, and his work brought us enough prosperity to have our own chickens and a goat which our cousin Philip drove out to pasture with the other village animals each day. The animals and the donkey's stable took up much of our plot of land, which was why the colt's eating the rest of the garden had been such a problem.

I was a little squeamish about killing the chickens, even though we did not do it ourselves—they went for ritual slaughter, according to the Law. But I still felt sorry for them and found the little bodies pathetic as we sat plucking them, either to eat ourselves or to exchange for other goods with the other Nazarenes.

Sometimes Imma would give me an extra plump bird, trussed and plucked, to take as a gift to Rosa.

'I know the food you bring is your wages,' she said. 'And I know you work hard for what you are paid, but I would like to thank her for all she is teaching you about herbs and flowers and give her something she may not have, even in her wonderful garden.'

As time passed, I began to make friends with many of the people who went by Rosa's garden on their daily errands. The patch of land was on the route to the spring, so all the women passed at least once every day to fetch water. I could not see out of the garden, but they could look in, and though I already knew nearly all of them, it was a warm feeling to hear their voices greeting me and their compliments on the garden.

One of the many who passed was a Pharisee, and some said a holy man, Judah, from Kerith. He was married to one of my many distant cousins, Rivkah, and now lived in Cana, to the south. Every month he would bring the wares from his sandal-making workshop all the way to Nazara and Japhia and he would call out a cheerful 'Shalom!' each time he saw me. I began to look out for him, watching for the familiar gesture when he would push back his floppy black hair from his face and smile broadly at me, showing his white, even teeth. His eyes were a deep, glowing brown and his beard neatly trimmed and oiled. I hardly dared speak to him at first, but as soon as I began to reply to his questions with sensible comments, he began to stop and pass the time of day with me, sitting on the wall, telling me jokes and sharing a handful of sunflower seeds or dates. I thought he was wonderful and I added him to my day-dreams.

Each time we parted Judah saluted me with 'Death to all Romans!', his farewell to everyone (except, I expected, the Romans). It did not fit well with his greeting of peace, but I was too young then to wonder about the ways of grown-ups.

As far as I knew, I had never met a Roman, but no one seemed to like them much. They very rarely came to Nazara, though you could see a few soldiers in Japhia from time to time. I rather admired their uniforms but I kept that to myself. I had long known that it was not the thing to say anything good about the Romans. They were our enemies who had stolen our land and tried to corrupt us with their heathen gods and wicked ways.

One day in the hot summer Rosa brought me out a cool drink made of lemons and honey. 'Let's have a good look at you,' she said, holding me by the shoulders.

'Child, your skin burns so easily, you need some aloe to protect you. And I've got a thought about your leg' (neither Rosa nor Imma ever referred to it as 'your poor leg', as so many people would insist on doing). 'Will you show me where the accident happened?'

Never before had I shown anyone voluntarily, but this time I went into the dimness of her two-roomed house and allowed her to look closely at my crooked hip and feeble limb.

66

'I wonder,' she said. 'It's not all that wrong, is it, Deborah? I mean it's twisted, that's for sure, but I think half the problem is the way the joint has stiffened. I've got some special joint oil here, which came all the way from Babylon. Do you know where Babylon is, child?'

I did not, so as Rosa mixed up the oil with some ginger and herbs, and heated it so that my skin would absorb it better, she told me all she knew about the magical city of Babylon with its famed hanging gardens.

'They must be watered every day by hundreds of slaves,' she said.

I had heard only vaguely about slaves, so as she applied the salve, she told me about slavery and what it meant. It was as bad as sacrifice. A human being bought and sold, treated as his master or mistress wished, and not allowed to be with his or her own people.

'Now don't you fret about them,' said Rosa wryly, seeing my outraged expression. 'There's many a wife worse off than a slave, and there's enough trouble right in front of our faces in Nazara if you want to save the world.' And she laughed and hugged me, and gave me a pot of the precious oil, with specific instructions to rub it on each night and to wrap myself in cloth to make sure it did not rub off on the bedding.

No one ever knew if the oil was the reason why, but my hip and leg eased tremendously that summer. The limp and the crookedness were still there and I did not like to walk too far, but the continual nagging ache was gone in two months.

'It could be your age, or the work in the garden, or it could be the oil,' said Imma. 'It doesn't matter what caused it, all that matters is that you feel better. I think it's because you are growing happier in yourself.'

Rosa was delighted with the result and even more so when we discovered that the improvement was maintained even when the oil ran out.

'We'll give you a top-up every now and again,' she said. 'Just to make sure. But the Lord is looking after you, child.'

I wondered why the Lord did not look after slaves. I thought about them quite frequently, and the next time Judah went past the garden, I steeled myself to ask him a question that had been burning inside me.

'Do the Romans have slaves?'

He looked at me, surprised, for our discussions had never gone further than child-like things. The dark lock of hair on his forehead fell forward over his face and his dark eyes narrowed.

'Of course they do,' he said, pushing the hair back with one strong, brown hand. 'They even have Jews for slaves in Rome.'

'There's nothing good about that,' I thought and from then on I gave back to Judah the salutation that he gave to me: 'Death to all Romans!'

3

James was married that autumn to Rachel, daughter of Imma's cousin Micah. She was a robust, black-haired girl with dark skin and a bright smile and it was obvious that James adored her. She was far too practical a girl to waste time being in love but she seemed satisfied with her parents' choice of husband for her.

The wedding was celebrated at Micah and Dorcas's house, as was the custom, with coloured awnings and plenty of dancing. Simeon the Rabbi was there to give his blessing and spent much of the time grumbling that we Nazarenes were getting less and less devout. Most Jews had no religious aspect to a wedding at all, but most Nazarenes used to be insistent that the Rabbi was there to supervise the proceedings.

'Now stop grumbling, Simeon,' said Abba, putting his arm round the old man's shoulders and offering him a cup of wine. 'This wedding does need you, so don't spoil it by moaning about all the ones that don't. This is a joyful day, not one for recriminations.'

It was a wedding to be remembered for

other reasons as well. We had the usual three days of celebration, but James also had a special gift for his bride, which caused a few raised eyebrows and not a little jealousy.

The husband's present to his wife marks the official moment of betrothal, and is given and received a year before the marriage ceremony takes place. There is much debate beforehand about what might be suitable and James felt that his own gift, a hand-carved wooden bowl, had not been sufficiently costly or appropriate. For the wedding, however, he made it known that as well as the ring, he had an extra wedding gift for Rachel. What it was had been a closely guarded secret and everyone was agog to see the surprise. At the appropriate moment James proudly produced a tiny parcel wrapped in yellow cloth.

Rachel took it with a slight pout, thinking at first it was rather small and insignificant for all the fuss that had been made, but her face changed in shock the moment she realised that inside the wrapping lay a magnificent coin of pure gold.

All the Jewish women wore coins as jewellery at weddings and celebrations and the value of the coins showed the prosperity of the family. Copper was the norm and we thought silver special—but a golden coin was the crown of crowns and one of those could buy enough for a family to eat for a year. To country people like us, it was very rare and much prized. Only rich merchants' wives or the aristocracy wore gold.

Amid cries of amazement and demands that he explain how he came by such a treasure, James told us that he had been given the coin for mending a broken-down cart on the road outside Japhia. A rich foreign merchant had been desperate to get his wares of soft cheeses to Tiberias and James's prompt service had earned him a rich reward.

'He couldn't speak Aramaic but he told me in sign language I could have whatever I wanted if I could mend the spokes before midday,' James said, watching his wife as she danced around with delight, the coin shining on her forehead. 'He spilled out his money into his hand to count it and I saw the golden crown. I asked if I could have it instead of a handful of the others, and he was pleased I wanted so little. I don't think he knew how special it would be to us.'

Special it was, and Rachel's face was as bright as the coin on her forehead as she began the women's dancing. I usually sat out at weddings because I could not dance without losing my balance, but I did not mind. Watching the other women in their colourful clothes with smiles on their faces was quite diverting enough, even if the dances were not Petran. The men's dances, on the other side of the house, grew steadily more lively as the drink flowed and the hand-clapping encouraged them, but I preferred the grace of the women to the vigour of the men.

Yeshua usually danced with the best of them, but this time he did not seem willing. He had helped with all the preparations, but when people greeted him with a cheery 'Your turn next, my boy. Who have you chosen for your bride?' he shrank back and shook his head.

His diffidence disturbed me. Since we had become such friends I was fiercely protective of him. It was a common sight around Nazara to see this slender, graceful boy passing by with a fiery red-haired little girl with a crooked gait trailing after him, behaving for all the world like a devoted little dog. He never minded; in fact he confided in me. He did not have many friends of his own age.

'I don't understand the other boys,' he told me once. 'I don't think the way they do. Even the ones who really care about the Lord don't seem to hear Him or understand Him. At school the Rabbi thought I was a troublemaker because I always asked questions about the teaching, and sometimes I got different answers in my head from the ones he told me. I know it's the Lord talking and making things clearer. I'm sure everyone can hear Him if they just listen, but they all think I'm strange.'

He was strange. Most boys his age only studied what they had to, and treated the Lord as a distant, fearsome being who had to be attended to on Shabbat. But Yeshua talked to

Him in his head all the time. Even so, his faith was not off-putting; he was fun to be with and you could talk to him about anything.

That night he did his disappearing trick while the men's dance gathered pace. After looking all round for him, I followed my instinct and walked the few yards home, finding my way easily in the moonlight into the little stable where Zoresh, the donkey, named for his kind owner, was munching his hay.

I was right. Yeshua was standing there, one arm over the donkey's neck, staring into space.

He started when he heard me, then relaxed. 'Do you want to go up the hillside and look at the moon with me?' I whispered, knowing that for some reason he was feeling sad. He smiled and nodded and, taking my hand, led me out of the stable and up the street, away from the noise and the music and the lights.

'What is it? Why are you unhappy when they ask you who you will marry?' I asked as soon as we were out of sight of all the others.

Yeshua sighed and rumpled my unruly hair with his hand. 'Let's sit down on that outcrop of rock,' he said. 'I'd like to tell someone and I'm not sure even Imma would understand this time.'

We sat for a while in silence, with the echoes of the music behind us. I did not mind waiting for him to speak. It was enough, always, just to be with him. This time though, he said nothing for a long, long time.

'Is the Lord talking to you?' I asked, eventually, for he looked as though he might be listening to someone, or something, far away.

Yeshua looked down at me with love. 'Yes,' he said. 'Yes, He is always talking to me. Deborah, you won't laugh at me like the others, will you?'

'Of course not!' I was outraged. Yeshua was my hero and I would defend him to the end.

'No. No, of course you wouldn't.' He gave another sigh.

I waited, feeling peaceful with his arm around me. I thought I would be happy if the night never ended and Yeshua and I could just sit together, looking at the moon and the stars.

'I have to go away and study,' he said at last. 'I know what the Lord wants me to do with my life and I have to study before I can do it.'

My heart sank. 'I'll miss you,' I said, bravely.

'It won't be yet,' said Yeshua. 'And I'll come back regularly. But I won't be getting married. That's the difficult part to tell people. It wouldn't be fair to get married.'

'Fair to whom?'

'To my wife. I've got a lot of work to do and not a lot of time to do it. She would suffer, and that's not part of the plan.'

I did not really understand him, but I could feel his sadness.

'Couldn't she go with you and learn with you?' I asked. 'You're going to be a Rabbi,

Yeshua, and all Rabbis have to have a wife.'

'Then I won't be a Rabbi,' he said, looking down at me and squeezing me gently. 'I'll be something different. I'm not sure what, but I know I've got something different to give.'

'Is that what the Lord is telling you?' I asked.

'Yes.'

'Then I don't think I want to hear the Lord,' I said. 'I know both you and He would tell me to find the good in your leaving us, and in your being lonely, and I don't want to listen to that.'

'There will be good.'

'Yes, but it hurts.'

'Oh, Deborah,' Yeshua hugged me tightly. 'If you would listen to the Lord yourself, you would understand better.'

I made a face. 'Well, I don't want to,' I said. 'I'd be frightened. He might shout at me or tell me to sacrifice something.'

Yeshua grinned at that and slipped down from the rock onto the grass, where he could lie on his back and stare up into the night sky.

'He does get pretty cross at times,' he said thoughtfully. 'But only when we humans are being stubborn. Most of the time He's all that is loving. People miss that part of Him, because they see things only their way. Honestly, Deborah, He wants what is good for us and to see us happy. His plan for me is the right plan. It's only my stubbornness that sees any regret or difficulty in it. Listen for yourself,

Deborah. I can't prove it to you. You can hear Him any time you want to.'

'Why would He want to talk to me?'

'He is always talking to all of us,' said Yeshua, narrowing his eyes against the brightness of the moonlight. 'He doesn't just talk to the priests or the Rabbis, or to the holy men. He doesn't just talk to me. He talks to us all. We just don't listen, that's all.'

We sat in silence for a while, and I closed my mind off as hard as I could, in case the Lord wanted to talk to me to try to make me understand why He wanted to take Yeshua away.

I knew He was not quite the ogre I had thought him to be when I came to Nazara, but I was still too shy to ask Abba or Imma or Yeshua about many of the things I did not understand. Where, for example, was the good in my parents' death? And if I could not ask those I really loved, I was not about to start asking the Lord. I could see that James, Salome and I were happy, but it seemed very cruel to everyone that it had to happen that way. Why could we not just have been born as Joseph and Miriam's natural children? But then, I told myself, our own parents would not have had any children at all and that would not have been fair, either. My head went round and round until I felt dizzy when I tried to think these things through, and it was easier to put them aside and get on with something I did understand.

I did ask Yeshua about the sacrifices, though, one bright winter morning when we were out collecting firewood.

'There have always been sacrifices,' Yeshua said. 'I don't like them much either, but the idea has always been that the animals are sacrificed instead of us. Sometimes, Deborah, the amount of ignorance and anger in the world has required men—and women—as real live sacrifices to atone for all the evil thoughts and deeds we have done over the centuries. They wouldn't be needed if everyone obeyed the ten commandments and loved each other.'

Then we talked about eating animals, birds and fish and Yeshua said that some of the very holy men in Judaea had decided that it was wrong to do so and would not eat flesh, but only vegetables and fruit.

I thought that was a very good idea (heroically, I tried not to think of chicken soup).

'Yes,' he said thoughtfully. 'Except that we kill plants just as much as we kill animals. They must hurt too.'

I'd never thought of that and I burst out laughing at the thought of plants having feelings. 'Perhaps we should talk to them, and encourage them to grow, so we can have more food!' I said, giggling.

'You mean you don't?' said Yeshua, and I went red, because I did talk to the flowers and

77

the vegetables in Rosa's garden. I did it just as a game, for I'd never thought about it any other way.

'I talk to the plants all the time,' said Yeshua. 'I talk to the things we grow, and the wood in the work-room, to ask it to make the shapes I need. And I talk to the sky and everything.'

I could see that most people would find that stupid, but I thought it was nice.

Yeshua went on, thoughtfully, 'I don't think I could eat anything unless I knew the Lord had given it all to us to eat. It would seem so unkind.

'I used to worry about it, and I read and read the Torah to find the answer. The Lord did give us the animals and the plants to eat so that we could live, so I thought maybe if we take good care of them, and bless them and thank them for their lives, it changes it all and makes it holy.'

He told me then how he always tried to be the one who carried the lamb for the sacrifice at Pesach. 'I talk to him and explain to him, and bless him and thank him for his life, which is given for us, and he always lies peacefully in my arms,' he said. 'I can't always carry him because I can't explain to everyone what I'm doing and often the other men want to do it. But when I can, I do and I think the lamb understands that it is holy. Does that make sense to you?'

'No,' I answered. 'No, but that's because I don't understand. I don't know the Torah and I don't understand the Lord. What you do, I think must be right.'

Some of that was the loyalty between two children who loved each other and who were strangers in their own town. But his sincerity shone through and something of what he said seemed to make a deeper sense than I was ready to understand.

'Have you ever told anyone else this?' I asked.

'Imma knows some of it,' he said. 'Not all. I once said some of it in class, but I was beaten by three of the other boys afterwards. They didn't like what I said.'

I remembered that day. He had come home with a black eye and a bloody nose, but refused to say what had happened. 'Did you give as good as you got?' I asked.

He laughed. 'Oh, Deborah, you should have been a boy! You'd fight anything. No. I defended myself but that's all. I'm not a fighter. Fighting doesn't solve anything. You can't change anyone's mind by hurting them. They may say they agree with you, but they don't inside where it really counts.'

'I still don't like the sacrifices,' I said. 'I don't want to go back to the Temple.'

Yeshua nodded his head. 'I understand,' he replied. 'There must be a better way.

'One day,' he went on, after a long pause, 'a

79

Messiah will make the ultimate sacrifice and choose to die for the errors and angers of man. Then there will be no more animal sacrifices because the Temple will fall.'

I was frightened by his words.

'The Temple will fall? That's terrible.'

'Is it?' He looked at me with his clear, bright eyes. 'The Temple is the place of sacrifice. No more Temple, no more sacrifices. Won't that mean we have thrown away the need for hatred and anger? That we will be spiritually clean, that we do not need ritual cleansing? By then, perhaps, people will realise that we can all talk to the Lord ourselves and all listen to Him inside us, instead of having the scapegoat to say sorry for us.' I managed, heroically, not to be distracted by the thought of the scapegoat, a male kid which was sent into the wilderness from Jerusalem once a year, as an atonement for our sins. Instead I concentrated as hard as I could on what my brother had to say.

'Here.' He pointed to his heart. 'That's where we start—by listening to our own hearts. Only then can we listen to the Lord and make life joyous.'

It was all a bit much for me to take in and we sat in silence for a while as I tried to understand. Yeshua picked a piece of grass and started chewing it thoughtfully.

'You'll have to say sorry to that grass for picking it!' I crowed and he rolled me over,

80

both of us shrieking with laughter. Somehow, my leg never hurt when I was playing with him. After that, we played rolling down the hill until we were dusty and exhausted, and we knew we would be in trouble for getting so dishevelled.

'Don't fret, Deborah,' he said, as we dusted each other down, picked up the wood we had gathered and started the climb back up to the village. 'I'll get myself sacrificed in Jerusalem to save your beloved animals.' He laughed; we both did. It was a beautiful day, and we were young.

*   *   *

I managed to avoid going to Jerusalem for the whole of that year. At Pesach the weather was so hot that no one could travel down the Jordan valley without great discomfort, so pilgrims had to take the higher route through Samaria. Jews and Samaritans were not the best of friends, to say the least, so this would not be an easy journey and Abba suggested that he and the boys went alone.

For the festival of Tabernacles, in the month of Tishri and for Hanukkah in Kislev, Rosa was kind enough to offer me space in her home and for the first time I discovered that my injury could be an asset. It gave me a reasonable excuse for staying behind as, although I was definitely feeling better, my hip and leg still did not stand up well to long journeys. It was quite difficult not to go, because Yeshua was leaving us for the two months between the festivals and going to visit the Essene community near the Dead Sea, even further to the south. He had prevailed on Abba to let him study there for a time and, because Abba had enjoyed meeting and talking with the Essene men who travelled around the country from time to time, preaching and teaching, he saw no harm in it.

I wanted to spend those last few days with my brother, even in Jerusalem, but I knew that letting him go south without me would help harden me for the day when he would leave for good.

Rosa knew well how to distract a pining child. In the summer, she and I spent all our time in the garden together or going for short walks, looking for new plants to add to her collection as she taught me the healing powers of the wild plants as well as the ones we grew. We celebrated each festival together in our own way, which meant excluding the Lord as much as we could, for neither of us believed we could have very much fun by bringing Him into the proceedings. For Tabernacles, we built a beautiful bower of plants and flowers as a sukkah for me to sleep in, so I could pretend I was one of the children of Israel, homeless in the desert. Rosa stayed in her house but she enjoyed seeing the fun I had, making house inside my fragrant, green cave.

Hanukkah was nearly as exciting. We sat inside on the long dark evenings and lit lights in memory of the miracle of the oil two hundred years before, play-acting the story of being under seige without enough oil to keep the sacred flames burning in the Temple in Modin. On the last night, Rosa let me pour the oil and light all eight wicks myself, and it was magical.

As we watched the lights burning we cuddled up together before the hearth, and Rosa told me of far-distant places where women were allowed to worship with men, as equals. It seemed that even the Romans allowed their women far more privileges than the Jews did. But these intriguing stories never seemed to involve places that acknowledged the one Lord. Instead they had many deities, including some that were women, which seemed most peculiar.

One night I asked her why only the men prayed in Synagogue and why we women were kept behind the veil. She snorted. 'Because Judaism is a religion run by men for men,' she said. 'Women, if they are wise, toe the line in public and get on with their lives as best they can. There are women who have a little knowledge who can help the others when there's a problem, but they keep themselves to themselves if they know what's good for them. That's the way it is, child, and there will be no changing it, so don't even try!'

Her answer reflected my own blood-mother's views on Judaism but somehow it did not seem right to me. I could see it did not bother Imma, for she prayed and sang wherever she was and both she and Abba seemed to understand that her prayers for us and for our home were just as important as those said or sung in public. For myself, I did not want to join in the service in the Synagogue, but I grew more and more confused about *why* we were not allowed to do the same as the men.

One day I asked Abba. His reply was as considered and gentle as it always was, but he warned me not to go asking such questions elsewhere.

'It is the Law, Deborah,' he said. 'And maidens—or even grown women—are not supposed to question the Law. But, for myself, I have my own belief about why it was decreed that women should sit apart. Have you noticed that you sit one step higher than we do in the Synagogue?'

I nodded.

'I believe that a woman is naturally closer to the Lord than a man, and she is seated higher to show that,' said Abba. 'She is the bringer of life and the nurturer of all. I don't know about the other men's beliefs, because I have not talked to them about it, but when I pray and read in the Synagogue, I pray to become as near to the Lord as your mother already is.

And I like to think I serve her with my prayers, so that she may listen and enjoy them and talk to the Lord in her own way in her own heart without having to bother with the form of our service.'

'And in the Temple?'

'There I serve your mother—and you and your sister—by taking part in the sacrifice so you do not need to dirty your hands. That's how I see it at least, but then I am blessed with a devout and loving wife and the best of children.'

I pondered his words, seeing everything that was good about him in them, but there was still a niggling doubt at the back of my mind.

*   *   *

Yeshua's game of finding the good in things continued, even when he was not there. Eventually even Salome joined in, but it stayed very much a family game. The more we played it, the more we realised that it made us different from others.

I tried to introduce Rosa to it, but she thought it was silly. She enjoyed expecting the worst so that she would not be disappointed, and she thought I should do the same.

'Most people enjoy moaning,' said Imma, one afternoon, when I asked her why someone as nice and friendly as Rosa should not want to play.

She was weaving cloth for Abba's new tunic. Salome was spinning the flax and I was rolling the coarse wool to hand over to her.

'That doesn't make them wrong,' Imma added hastily. 'But it doesn't make them happy, either. It's a habit most people have, so that others don't think they have got above themselves. If you go around being happy all the time, people will envy you and they might even hate you for having what they don't. So most people won't risk it.'

'But you are happy. You are always singing and laughing,' said Salome.

'Yes, and people think I'm strange,' said Imma with a smile. 'You know they do. We are different from the others and sometimes they find that hard.'

That was never more obvious than in the Synagogue each Shabbat. Salome and I were used to going there now, but it was still noticeable that, apart from the ritual responses, most of the other women spent the majority of the service talking to each other in hushed voices, complaining about the Romans, their bad harvests, their aches and pains and the quarrels they had with other people. But, for all that lack of real interest in their religion, they were hawk-eyed if there was a transgression of the Law to be spotted, and would tear the offending person apart with their tongues, given the chance.

When Rachel, newly married, bright-eyed

and obviously happy, came to the Synagogue on a festival day with the golden coin displayed on her forehead, you could almost feel the excitement in the air at the chance to hand out some well-deserved blame. It was forbidden for anyone to handle money on holy days, which were separate from the working week, and the women enjoyed using the Law as a valid reason to vent their feelings of general discontent, and, in this case, envy. Rachel, cowed by their stern reaction, stammered that she thought the coin was an ornament and not money, as it was one that was not in general circulation. She was soon put in her place. The Law would not allow her to carry the coin in her hand or in a pocket on a festival day either, so poor Rachel had no idea what to do with her treasure. In the end she hid it under her veil to cause as little offence as possible, but even so, several of the other women were barely polite to her for the rest of the service and one or two simply cut her dead. There were a few sarcastic remarks too, just within earshot, like 'Of course it's a Roman coin. A fine thing for a Jewess to be wearing anyway' or 'It's not real gold, of course, but some people are easily fooled', which you could see hurt Rachel's feelings even more.

When we came out of the Synagogue, it was obvious that some of the women were spreading the story as fast as they could and Rachel was stared at by both men and women.

To everyone's amazement, she stared back and let her veil slip back far enough to show that her forehead was completely bare. She had no pockets and nowhere to hide the coin, and her hands were empty. For all that, she was obviously dreadfully upset and James took her home as soon as he could.

After they had gone, Salome showed me the golden coin in her own hand. 'I told her to slip it to me and I would hide it,' she said. 'Deborah, you take it and run back to the house when you can. No one will look for it on you. But be careful. Don't let anyone see it.'

Salome's kindness over the golden crown earned her a gift from Rachel, who promised her the string of four silver coins, which she used to wear herself, as a gift for Salome's own wedding the following spring. Salome was pleased. She had long coveted those coins and, having heard the unkind comments of the other women, had the sense not to hanker for a golden crown instead.

'There's the good again,' said Imma, when we told her the story. We knew she would not be angry with us for trying to help, even if it were, technically, against the Law.

Some events though, made it hard to see the good. Deaths, especially of the young, bad harvests, robbery—and the Roman occupation of Judaea. Yeshua once said that it sometimes took a long time for the good to become obvious, especially when what looked like evil had been caused by man's own greed, anger and stubbornness, but that the Lord worked slowly and all things came right in the end. The problem was that we were all too impatient. I could understand what he meant in theory, but that didn't help the people who were suffering at the time. Patience was no virtue of mine, nor of most of our people, who moaned long and hard about the Romans and the injustices of life.

'Well, at least the Romans give us something to moan about,' said Abba, who had brought us a consignment of fresh fish from Gennesaret and was enjoying watching us eat our supper with relish, almost as much as he enjoyed eating his.

'What do you mean?' we asked as Imma burst into one of her little peals of laughter at the thought.

'Well, people like to complain. And if they have something to complain about, they don't have to get angry about what's going on in front of their faces in their own homes,' he said. 'Think about it. The Jews are far more united now in opposition to the Roman rule than they were before. It has given us a common goal. It's always useful for a race to have someone else to hate.'

He chuckled into his abundant beard as he thought about it. 'They say that if you ever have two Jews together, you have three opinions,' he went on. 'Look at us. The

Nazarenes squabble between themselves on interpretations of the Law. We disagree with the Pharisees, when it suits us, and they disagree with the Sadducees who disagree with the Essenes. And the Essenes seem to disagree with everyone. The Pharisees live in their own communities where they say there is life after death and the Sadducees live in their aristocratic homes where they say there is no life after death. The Essenes say you come back and live on the earth again. Does that mean the angel of death has to take them all to different places?

'From one end of the Jordan to the other we quarrel about interpretations of the Torah, and the food laws and whether you can eat an egg laid on Shabbat, but all these quarrels are not the things to fight wars about when you have a common enemy.

'Mind you,' he added. 'Most of us spend hours disagreeing on the amount of resistance we should give. But even so, the most fearsome Zealots, who fight the Romans tooth and claw, are still Jews and everyone turns out religiously to show moral support against the oppressors when one of them is caught and crucified.'

'Joseph!' Imma did not like talk of death or rebellion at meal times.

'Well it's the truth, wife,' he said seriously. 'But you are right. Let's talk of more cheerful things. How about another blessing on this delicious fish?'

It was soon after that that a Zealot was crucified at Sepphoris, not far from us. He had been leading a band of brigands in the hills and fighting the Romans off and on for years. Once they caught him, he was executed as a public warning, but feelings ran very high about it for weeks afterwards.

Imma went to the Synagogue to pray for his speedy death and for the Lord's mercy on his family. I asked Abba how long it would take a man to die if he were crucified, and he told me it could take three days, unless someone broke his legs. 'If your legs are strong, you can carry your weight on the nails they stick through your ankles,' he said. 'I know that sounds terrible, but it's what happens. If your legs are broken, you can't breathe because all your weight is on your arms and the pressure just kills you. It's harsh, very harsh, and it's not the sort of thing a maid wants to think about.'

He was right, I went out into the evening air and was sick, as I thought of that poor man's agony.

'Please, Lord, let someone break his legs so he dies fast,' I begged. And that was the first ever real prayer that came from my heart.

It was answered. I hung around the edge of the village to see the return of the group of people who had travelled to the crucifixion, either to comfort the man's family and friends, or just to have a good stare at something so momentous. They said the man had been crucified at dusk and had been dead by dawn, which was a mercy. I took a sharp stone and stuck it into my hand to see what it felt like to suffer like that, intending to keep it there all day. By noon, I could bear it no longer.

*　　*　　*

Yeshua returned to us, older and more serious. He was happy to see us all, and he and I had as many good games as we had always done, but you could tell he had left his heart with the Essene community. Almost as soon as he was home, he asked when he could go back.

That was when Abba and Imma, the most loving of parents, began to quarrel with him and nothing was ever quite the same again.

After James's wedding, it should have been only a matter of time before Yeshua was betrothed, but they had allowed him an extra year to discover what he really wanted. Once he had been to the Essene settlement in the south, they hoped he would settle down, but he refused outright.

'Yeshua, it's your duty,' his father said sternly. 'It is the will of the Lord for us to marry and have children.'

'The Essenes don't think so,' said Yeshua.

The Essenes were beginning to have quite some influence in Judaea, with their knowledgeable and radical interpretations of the Torah. Everyone knew of someone who had lost a son to their sect, but so far no one from Nazara had gone.

Imma's cousin Elisheva, who lived to the north, had a son, Jochanan, a celibate and an Essene, and his father Zachariah, himself a learned and respected priest of Abia, had supported his son's choice. When people heard that, they said that Elisheva and Zachariah were eccentric people anyway and that Jochanan had been spoilt.

The Essenes lived in what were mostly men-only communities on the edge of ordinary villages and although there were rumours of women actually being included in some branches of the movement, these were generally discounted. Everyone saw that idea as being just as much of a scandal as the idea of men being celibate, when one of the Lord's first commandments to man was to multiply.

From what Yeshua told us, the Essenes did not even seem to agree within their own groups about it and some groups allowed wives while others did not. None of them, however, had women in the inner courts of learning or, if they did, no one ever heard about it.

After Zachariah's death, it was said that Elisheva had joined the group at Qumran, by the Dead Sea, though most people believed she just lived nearby it, not as a part of the Essene community.

'Some of them have travelled all over the

known world studying all forms of religion and comparing them with the Torah,' Yeshua told us over supper. 'I should like to know more of other faiths and why people worship in different ways.'

He knew better than to say this anywhere but in our own small family group. Even so, Abba was angry with him.

'Son, if you want a religious life, become a scribe,' he said. 'Even a Pharisee, if you must. But marry. Be a son of Israel and raise children of Israel. It is your holy duty. You cannot be a priest of any kind without a wife to tend the women's needs. You must know that.'

The local pressure on Yeshua was enormous. Every relative was trying to interest him in their daughter, but he was polite and distant to all.

The first big argument came three days before Salome's wedding, when Abba and Imma invited a young girl round specially to meet Yeshua.

She was a pretty twelve-year-old girl called Martha and her parents were obviously keen on the match. Yeshua was pleasant to her and to her family, and agreed that she was all that was delightful. But he turned her down flat.

'Son, you will marry. It is your duty,' roared Abba after they had left. I hid behind the loom. I had never seen him so angry.

'Honour your father and mother, Yeshua. That is the command of the Lord. Your cousin

Jochanan may be a celibate, but his parents, may the Lord forgive them, condoned that. I do not. You *will* marry.'

Yeshua stood very tall. He was pale and shaking but full of dignity.

'I am obeying the Lord,' said Yeshua. 'I am sorry if it causes you pain but I will not take a wife. The Lord has sent you James as your son. He is a carpenter and he is married. I am meant to do other things.'

Imma said nothing, but she looked so unhappy that I wanted to run over and put my arms around her. I knew she was torn between her husband and her son.

Abba actually beat my brother for his disobedience. It was the first time he had ever raised his hand to one of us. I know Imma cried herself to sleep that night and Yeshua sat on the roof of the house, watching the stars and praying until dawn. I crept up to be with him for a while, taking the little pot of salve that Rosa had given me for my leg. He let me dab a little onto the bruises and I held my breath with the effort of trying so hard not to hurt him any more. Then he held me tightly, rocking me back and forth, his lips moving in continual prayer, until I dozed off in his arms.

For Salome's wedding the matter was put on one side. I was amazed at Yeshua's willingness to be loving to his parents, for I found it hard to forgive Abba for what he had done and I was sulky with him for days. But all the fun and the colour and excitement of the wedding banished everything else from my mind, and I was so proud of my beautiful sister in her wedding clothes with the silver coins on her forehead.

'You're so beautiful. You don't need to wear gold!' I whispered to her and she gave me a nervous little smile. Salome, for all her flirtatiousness and grown-up ways, was a little afraid of the prospect of married life.

While James and Rachel lived with us, in a kind of annexe room that he and Abba had built for them, Salome left, to live with Zachariah's family. We still saw her every day but I missed her warm body in the bed, her brightness and her sharp wit.

Even worse, the quarrels with Yeshua began again. He stood firm in his decision and was beaten twice more. Not once did he cry. Not once did he treat Abba and Imma with any less love or respect. He just would not relent.

One day Imma joined the argument. Abba was speechless, but she said she was sorry but she now knew Yeshua was right. She cried as she said it, and it seemed as though a great grief had come on her heart overnight, but she was adamant, even in the face of her husband's anger.

'You have always known, as I have, that he would leave us. That he had a greater destiny,' she said. 'It is right that you should ask him to be one of us and to marry, but it is his right to refuse and follow the Lord in the way he sees fit. It breaks my heart too, Joseph. Don't think that it doesn't.'

She offered a compromise: Yeshua should join the Essenes who lived on one of the hills outside Jerusalem, instead of the larger group further south. Then we would still see him on the holy days when we travelled to the Temple. She also asked that he would promise to reconsider his vow not to marry, when he had completed the two-, or three-year trial period that the Essenes imposed on anyone who wished to join their ranks.

'It would be a kindness to us to give us that promise,' she said.

Yeshua looked at her with love. I could see that they both knew the truth, that he would never marry, but that this was the best way the matter could be decided. 'I will do what you ask,' he said. 'I am sorry my stubbornness has hurt both of you. Thank you for all the love you have shown me.'

Cousin Jochanan came to collect my brother ten days later. Abba had washed his hands of the matter and was away with James on a building job in Japhia. I am not sure whether he said goodbye to his son.

Jochanan was a fierce boy even then; full of anger at the ruler of Galilee, Herod Antipas, and at the Romans, and at people who did not follow the word of the Lord. He was only fifteen, a year older than Yeshua, but he was already bearded and his body was muscular.

As he strode up the street towards us, his rough voice bellowed out the Greek name that Imma called her son, not the name we were used to giving him.

'Jesus!' he roared. 'Jesus. The time has come. Are you ready?'

I thought my heart would break as they walked away from Nazara together. I knew Yeshua would be back regularly and that we would see him if I were willing to go to Jerusalem, but I held onto Imma's skirt and buried my face in the cream linen so that no one would see my tears.

Imma put her arm around me. 'I know,' she whispered. 'I feel the same. We must comfort each other, Deborah, and look for the good that comes to us from his leaving.' There were tears in her eyes too.

At that moment Yeshua—Jesus, bright-eyed and already on his way to a new life, turned round and saluted his mother and me.

'The Lord be with you,' he called.

'And with you,' we replied. Trying to be brave, I bleated out my own blessing too.

'Shalom,' I called.

'May the Lord bless you, Deborah,' he called back. 'Don't forget. The Lord is your Lord. The Lord our God is one. Listen to Him. *Talitha Cumi!*'

The two young men turned the corner and were gone from our sight.

*　　*　　*

Abba was never the same after Yeshua had gone. He felt shame that he had been defied, though he did try to understand.

'It is the Lord's way of showing me how James's father felt when his son left for a life he could not approve,' he said sadly. 'I must accept it, and hope that he will come home when he is ready.'

The days were longer and drabber without my brother. Rosa's garden was my greatest solace and she brewed teas for grief and loss for all of us. Imma drank hers with gratitude, but Abba said he did not need any help.

I know that both Abba and Imma had a hard time dealing with friends and relatives. The Nazarenes told them repeatedly that they had reaped what they had sown by indulging the boy too much. I think Abba believed them.

I spent some of my spare time with Salome, but she was very busy with her new life and there were so many other people and children in her new family that her home was always bustling.

Rachel was kind to me, knowing I felt lost without Yeshua. She was still a little unused to us, particularly our way of discussing things so openly over meals. Abba was always talking about the Torah or the different factions in Judaism or about whether or not it was right to work in ritually unclean Tiberias even if you went to the Mikvah afterwards.

Her own family was not as interested in such things, and I used to like to go to her parents' house with her because everything there was simple and ordered, and nobody talked of anything important. Sometimes that was as good as a rest.

Rosa too was restful, with her habits of grumbling and her kind heart. I could see that it would be easy to live in a house where nothing really mattered very much.

But everything mattered to me.

Yeshua had explained many of the old stories that I had not understood in the Synagogue. Although the Hebrew scrolls were translated into folk stories in our own Aramaic, and discussed by the Rabbi in his sermons each Shabbat, the language was usually still too complicated for me to understand. Imma took over when Yeshua left and she laid special emphasis on the women in the stories. She would always smile at me whenever the reader mentioned Miriam, Moses's sister, or Deborah, the prophetess, my namesake.

She told me the story of Queen Esther, who saved the Jews, and her version was so different from my blood-mother's that I could hardly recognise it. This Esther truly was a heroine and I preferred her to the Vashti I used to know. Imma laughed when I said I thought it unfair that all of Haman's family had been executed as well as him, just because they were his children.

'I wouldn't say that outside our home,' she said. 'Purim is important to us and Haman is much hated. Just think how many would have been killed if he had had his way, and if his family had been spared they would have planned to kill us all as well, in revenge.'

I was especially interested in why Esther, a Jewess, had married the King of Persia, when we Jews were forbidden to marry a Gentile. The answer 'so she could save us' did not make sense to me, but it was the only one available.

I once piped up at a neighbour's house, asking if it would not be a good idea for a Jewess to marry the Roman emperor so that we would be freed from oppression here in Judaea. There was a terrible silence, and they looked pityingly at Imma, who changed the subject.

'But what did I say wrong?' I asked afterwards, genuinely bewildered. 'Why is one thing right for Esther and not for us?'

'Esther was a holy woman. We are just ordinary Jews,' was the best answer that Imma could give me. But Esther was just a normal Jewess until she married the King.

She also tried to calm my indignation at the blame given to Eve for the fall of mankind, by saying that yes, it did seem unfair, but Eve had disobeyed the Lord and she was not willing to take the blame on her own for her transgression. Instead, she had given her husband the fruit too, so that he would sin as well.

'Perhaps if she had been very brave, she would have saved him and stood up to the Lord herself,' Imma said. 'It was being afraid and wanting to hide behind her husband that was the worst thing she did.'

I thought about that long and hard. But I did not understand.

I wished Yeshua were still here to help me, and I sometimes talked to him in my mind as though he could answer me.

'Why? Why? Why?' were the questions that went round and round in my head, while I was weeding at Rosa's, sitting in the Synagogue or grinding corn for the bread.

Sometimes I would hear Yeshua answer me, but it was always in the same words. 'Listen to the Lord. Listen. He has the answers.'

But I did not try to listen to the Lord because I was still afraid of him.

4

The years passed and the little donkey that had carried me to Jerusalem became a full-grown, sturdy and valuable beast. He carried tools and wood for Abba and James, and we rode him both on errands and for fun. Imma rode him to Jerusalem each festival time, unless Salome or Rachel were pregnant or carrying a nursing baby.

I loved the dusty, warm scent of his body and the soft, fuzzy muzzle, which would explore my face and arms to see if I had brought him a treat. He knew his name— Zoresh, after his owner—and would twitch his ears when I called out to him as though he understood everything I was saying.

As he grew stronger and sturdier, even I realised that we were in great debt to his original owner. I asked Abba and Imma to send a message to say how grateful I was, on one of Abba's and James's work trips, but they would not. They said they did not know where he lived.

The mystery was cleared up only after I had niggled about the matter for weeks on end. At last, Imma told me that the man was a Samaritan and his gift had put them in a very embarrassing situation. 'If they knew, people would say we should not have accepted the beast,' she said. 'It was a blessing from the Lord, but it's one of those things you have to keep quiet about.'

By then I knew why Jews did not associate with Samaritans, so that explained why Abba and Imma were so uncomfortable. The Samaritans had been Jews, but they did not recognise the holiness of the Temple and, instead, worshipped on a mountain that they said was holy. Their sacrifices were made there, so no animal was ever in danger from them if they visited Jerusalem.

The man had been so kind to me that I would have liked to have done something in return, but all I could do was pray for him. I was not good at prayer, but once I had got over my stubbornness about not even addressing the Lord of the sacrifices, I asked Him each Shabbat to bless the man, to send him my thanks and give him an equivalent gift. I didn't dare do it in the Synagogue, even silently, in case anyone sensed my disloyalty in praying for a Samaritan; I could only say that kind of prayer out in the open, where if there were any Divine displeasure for my wickedness in praying for an infidel, it would not embarrass me in public or affect the rest of the family. Praying simple prayers in the open felt different from the rituals in the Synagogue. When I saw how beautiful the world was, and my heart was full of good wishes for others, I could almost believe that the Lord was like Yeshua said He was.

Once Yeshua had left, it was only a matter of time before I changed my mind about going to Jerusalem. He came home twice a year, but I was desperate to see him as often as I could. I had to harden my heart and turn my head away from the animals taken into the Temple and I prayed that they might not suffer, but it seemed pointless staying home and missing my brother when the same amount of animals were sacrificed, whether or not I was there.

In spite of the stink and the bustle, I grew to like Jerusalem over the years and would spend hours exploring both inside and outside the city wall. Each trade had its own location, with shops in front and craftsmen behind. You could choose which carpenter, which sandal-maker, which wool merchant you wanted to go to and you could select the best fruit and vegetables instead of having to make do with what there was. There was a whole street devoted just to cheeses, and another to dried foods and herbs. The languages too were fascinating. Most trading people spoke Greek and, as time passed, I began to understand quite a few words.

I liked the street of fabrics best, with its bright blues and greens and reds and even, occasionally, rich, rare purple. Many of the cloth merchants came from Babylon or beyond; they had rings in their ears and oiled, curled hair and they knew how to flirt with the passing women in a way that thrilled a wide-eyed girl, who would never dare to talk to them.

The Upper and Lower Markets were the two main streets of shops, with different foods and spices coming in every day. Sometimes I would just sit inconspicuously in a doorway and watch the people about their business, noting the beautiful clothes and bangles and the hennaed hair of the rich women and wondering what it would be like to walk with the jangle of coins in bracelets on my ankles.

Whenever we could, Yeshua and I would escape to the olive groves to the east of the city. There it was peaceful and quiet, and we could talk for hours of things that would have outraged the rest of the family and perhaps even his Essene tutors. The trees rustled comfortingly in the shade and, as the wind usually came from the east, there was no distressing scent from the Temple.

Yeshua grew lanky, as I did and I teased him about his scraggy beard and his white Essene robe. They all called him Jesus—just as they called Jochanan by his Greek name of John—but he was still Yeshua to us and he liked it that way.

'I'm so happy here, Deborah,' he would say, over and over again. 'I know no one at home can understand except you, and maybe Imma, but this is what I'm meant to do. The teachers and the inner group are as stern as the Rabbi in Nazara. Fire and brimstone are their favourite subjects. But the amount of knowledge they have! And they love to argue so I can ask as many questions as I like and nobody gets offended. I can study the Torah and all the other writings as much as I want and there's always someone to help me with the interpretation. But it's the oral teaching that's best. All the legends and things that most people never get to hear about, let alone understand. It makes so much sense when you put it all together.'

Personally, I doubted it. I only really wanted to hear about his travels.

Some of his group had travelled to Ephesus and beyond, exchanging information with other religious groups. Most of the Essenes took no notice of other cultures and faiths, but Yeshua was interested in everything.

He had been to the legendary Temple of Artemis, where they worshipped a goddess instead of the Lord. Inside the gigantic building (not as large as our Temple, Yeshua said, but prettier) was a huge statue of Artemis and Yeshua said it both fascinated and repulsed him. Other religions, apparently, were allowed to make graven images, for there were plenty that the Romans worshipped in Jerusalem if you knew where to look for them. Good Jews never did.

I had never seen a statue but what Yeshua described did sound both beautiful and frightening. Rosa had spoken of women gods, but I had never taken the idea seriously before. Because it was Yeshua, I was not afraid to ask question after question about her, but once I found that sacrifices were made to Artemis as well, I lost interest.

Yeshua would spend plenty of time with Abba and Imma, and the others, and it was good to be a whole family again. But it was obvious that he was very suited to the celibate life he had chosen and we grew used to living without him. When it came to the time for Yeshua to choose whether he would become one of the inner circle of celibates in the Essenes, not even Abba could protest.

'I'm surrounded by grandchildren,' he said affectionately, sitting James's youngest son on his lap. 'It would be churlish of me to ask for more.'

I could see how much Yeshua appreciated his father's words. Nothing more was said between them, but there was respect in Abba's eyes when he looked at his natural son, and unwavering love in Yeshua's eyes in return.

In fact, he told me, he would never fully become an Essene, but would live on the edge of the group until it was time for him to carry out the Lord's plans.

'There are things even the Essenes do not know,' he said. 'Some knowledge has only been given to the Pharisees, and I need to be able to learn from them as well. I have the best of all worlds, Deborah. I couldn't ask for more.'

That visit to Jerusalem, for the festival of Tabernacles, coincided with Salome's visit to the Temple for cleansing after the birth of Sarah, her second daughter. For eighty days, the rule for mothers of girl children, she had not been to the Mikvah or the Synagogue, though I don't think she really cared about that, being immersed in her children and (she told Imma) glad to have a rest before even thinking about conceiving again.

No one would talk to an unmarried girl about sex, so I had to pick up little bits of knowledge here and there. In Jerusalem, as at home, the married women always walked separately from single girls so that we could not overhear their discussions. But Imma had told me the basic facts of life—and they were obvious all around us every spring. The idea of sex itself did not interest me, but something did. I still went fluttery when Judah passed Rosa's garden, but the feeling felt darker and more mysterious than it used to, and lower down in my body.

Even by the age of fourteen I had no menses and Imma had warned me that the damage from my fall probably meant they would never come. Seeing how Salome suffered and how even Imma could be sharp-tongued once a month, I was not sure I wanted the monthly spilling of blood known as the curse of Eve. But without menstruation I could never be normal or accepted as a woman. Already all the other girls of my age were married or at least betrothed, and using the Mikvah in the traditional way. I had no call to go there, and I couldn't help feeling left out.

At Jerusalem I often bathed in the Pool of Siloam and, although I knew it was vanity, I would turn back after climbing out and secretly take a look at myself in the still water, hoping to see an attractive woman's face looking back. The face that did look up at me was always the same: plain and pale and surrounded by unruly orange hair, which would not be confined no matter how hard Imma and I tried. Comparing myself with my blood-mother's red beauty, with Salome's dark grace or the simple attractiveness of any young, nubile girl, I would cry tears of resentment.

Imma knew how I felt and often tried to talk to me about growing up. But what words of comfort can you give an ugly girl who will not marry or have children? She was practical, and talked to Rosa about what could be done for me. Together, they managed to get me work at the Mikvah in Nazara, helping out the Rabbi's wife, who supervised it.

'I know,' Imma said, when she told me and I reacted with horror and resentment. 'It will be difficult for you at first, but you have two choices. You can pretend the rest of the women here don't exist and wallow in your pain, or you can face up to it and help them with their problems.'

'What problems?' I couldn't believe they had any. After all, they were nubile and loved by a man.

Imma sighed. 'Quite a few of the women will envy you in secret,' she said. 'You may

110

think you have troubles, but they have far more. Many women love their husband and are eager to return to the marriage bed, but some have been damaged inside by having children and their husband's demands hurt them. Some simply dislike their husband and don't want to return to his bed. Some are afraid of yet another pregnancy when they already have more children than they can cope with. You know how tired Salome gets with two young children—imagine what it must be like with five or six. It may be unorthodox and impious, but we are human, and women with problems like those will see going to the Mikvah as the end of a blessed time of peace.'

I listened open-mouthed. It had never occurred to me that marriage was anything other than pleasant. Abba and Imma were so fond of each other and my blood-parents had been very much in love. I knew the majority of marriages were arranged and I'd heard the women grumbling in the Synagogue, but I never really thought people were that unhappy with their lot.

There was worse to come.

'There will also be some women who have broken the rules of impurity and who are in great need of kindness,' said Imma. 'The Law is set in stone, but people are human. Laws do get broken and those women will be in fear of their life.'

Imma was right. Of the sixty-two women in

Nazara who used the Mikvah, less than one third, in that private place, seemed truly happy.

Two weeks after I started work, Dinah, wife of David, died in childbirth and the whispers started at once.

'She broke the Law. It is written. Break the Law and you will die when giving birth,' said Miriam, the Rabbi's wife, sternly to the young women gathered at the bath the following day.

'She may not have done,' ventured Michal nervously.

'Then she would not have died.' Miriam drew herself up to her full height. 'Let this be a lesson to you all to obey the Law.'

Miriam was not a kind woman and her rule at the Mikvah was absolute. I did the menial tasks and she decided when the women could come, and oversaw their ablutions. She obeyed the letter of the Law but she did not add any gentleness to it. She was just the kind of servant I thought the Lord wanted. I was polite and willing and did my best to please her, but I could sense that she saw a rebel in me and she discouraged any attempt of mine to talk to her about any of the issues affecting the women who came.

The older women were all calm and disciplined and all I had to do was help them with the bathing preparations, but I could see how often the young ones were desperate for answers to questions they were too afraid to ask. Even if I had dared, I was so ignorant that I could never have helped them.

Very few of the women disobeyed the Law, but just a handful of those newly and happily married found it very hard to refuse their husbands if they became passionate in the forbidden times. I knew nothing of love, but I could sense that there might easily be a moment when all thought of the Law would vanish. The excited whispers of some of the younger ones gave me strange feelings inside.

Shy little Abigail was the next. She had been married for only two months when her husband was openly chastised by the Rabbi for touching her in public during her menses. From then on, Miriam was watching out for Abigail. Whenever she came for her bath she was verbally beaten for the guilt that was written all over her.

I could do nothing under Miriam's fierce eye, but the third month, after she had said her piece, and Abigail shrank back even smaller and more vulnerable than before, I followed Abigail when she left. Once out of sight of the Mikvah, she ran into the wild grass at the edge of the village. I hesitated, then went after her.

We hardly knew each other, but my sympathetic face was enough and she snuggled into my embrace like a lonely puppy. 'I'm going to die,' she wept. 'I want to have a baby, but if I do I'll die. I'll die because I obey my husband instead of the Law. But what am I supposed to do, Deborah, when he climbs into my bed and holds me down? What do I do?'

'You won't die,' I said, horrified at what she was telling me. 'The Lord will see that you want to be good and will forgive you.'

'No, he won't,' Abigail shook her head. 'He doesn't make exceptions. And I'm not a good woman. I'm so weak, but I can't stop him.'

'Then you must get stronger,' I said, hardly knowing what I was saying. 'The Lord is telling you to stand up for yourself more. Do you love your husband?'

'No,' Abigail sniffed. 'He's all right, but I don't love him.'

'Well, stand up to him. Ask one of your family to come and stay with you, so that there is someone else in your room at the forbidden times. Or tell your father. He'll help you.'

'I couldn't. I'd be shamed.'

'Your parents chose your husband for you. They are the ones who should be shamed. Abigail, it's better to be shamed than dead.'

I don't think she did anything. She was pregnant within the next month and so did not have to come back to the Mikvah. There was nothing I could say; nothing I could do. She just faded away and died six months later with her unborn child still inside her.

*   *   *

I did try to see the good in life. I could

understand that the Law gave many women a welcome respite from their husband's attentions. I tried to concentrate on those who were happy, or at least dutiful. But it is always the one who falls by the wayside that affects us most. I was so angry with the Lord that I had to run out of earshot of the village and shout at Him with all the pent-up fury of years of not understanding.

I cursed Him and shook my fist at the sky and wept with anger at what His rules had done. 'How can You be merciful when You allow this?' I shouted. 'How do You expect me to love You when all You do is hurt women?'

I waited for the retribution, expecting a thunderbolt or some terrible skin disease to befall me. But nothing happened. Life went on just as before.

I talked to Rosa about Abigail but she could see nothing that could have been done. In Japhia, she said, they had used herbs and oils to help the women with their fears and worries, and so that they would not conceive. 'Yes, child, it is done, in spite of the Law!'

It was the first I had heard of it and I wasn't sure whether to be horrified or not.

'The breaking of the Law is serious,' said Rosa. 'But the need to preserve life and health is the greatest of all the Laws. Sometimes I wonder if people in Nazara even know that. You can practise many things in Japhia but you can't get away with them here—at least, not openly.'

I was puzzled. 'But the Lord sees you just as much in Japhia,' I said. 'Why would that make any difference?'

'Bless you, child,' said Rosa. 'The Lord didn't kill that little girl; it was her own fear and guilt that wore her down. She was too weak to stand up for herself and you know what happens to any animal that is weak. It gets eaten by the others.'

Is that true? I thought. Is it as much up to us as it is to the Lord? It was a comforting thought and I decided I must talk to Yeshua about it next time we met. Technically, I was a weak animal, but nothing was going to eat me!

I joined the women mourning for little Abigail but I would not speak to her husband. Then something happened which took all thoughts for others straight out of my head.

Our beloved Abba was more than forty-five years old when he married Imma, and James, Salome and I never knew him as anything but grey and lined. But he was always so full of life and we all thought he would go on for ever. One morning, while working on a house at the far end of the village, he uttered a strange cry and fell down.

By the time James reached him, he was gone.

He was spared any pain or weakness and we were, at least, glad of that. But as the bustle of death took over our lives, all I could see was

Imma's white face.

With Abigail's and my parents' deaths, there was anger; with Abba's there was, at least, a kind of fullness and fairness. He had lived a long and happy life and had known how much we truly loved him. The grief for this giant of a man who had brought me security and so much happiness was painful, deep and thorough, but it was not destructive because, even if I did not understand the Lord and His ways, I could believe Imma when she said that she knew that Abba was safe and had gone to a higher home.

We buried him on the hillside, where others of his family already lay and, thanks to Rosa's garden, his grave was covered with beautiful, scented roses. In orthodox Nazara even that caused comment, as some people said that graves should be left bare. But this anonymous mound of earth was all we had left of our beloved Abba and we wanted to cover him in everything that was beautiful, to say 'thank you' for the love, security and knowledge he had so willingly given to us.

The days of ritual mourning froze time for all of us. We did nothing but sit in the house and grieve. It is a good system. James, Salome and I wanted to be brave to support Imma but as members of the family came and went, came and went, rocking backward and forward and wailing their grief, the shame of tears vanished and we allowed ourselves to mourn our dear friend and father in full.

We sent word to Yeshua, but he could not be expected to get to Nazara in less than a week.

Before then was the Shabbat Eve. We had been invited to our half-brother Jonah's home with the rest of the family, but we wanted to stay in our own cosy little house and feel the comfort of familiarity.

Just like every other Friday night, we prepared the bread and wine and water and gathered, holding hands before the unlit candles. As the sun began to set James handed the flint to Rachel, instead of to Imma. As the wife of the eldest male in the house, it was now her right to sing the woman's blessing and light the lights. But she was too overcome with emotion.

James hesitated, then passed the flint to me.

It was the first time I had ever been charged with the duty of public prayer to the Lord. Maybe any other time I would have refused, but no one else was strong enough, so I got up and stood before the candles.

I began to sing the prayers of preparation and, as my voice rose, the walls of our home faded around me; time stood still and I was standing in space, among the stars.

'And thou shalt call the Sabbath a delight and the holy day of the Lord honourable,' I sang, wide-eyed and afraid, hearing the sound of other voices, angelic, silvery, just audible, echoing in my ears. The feeling of rising up and out into some celestial dome made me dizzy and light-headed, and I closed my eyes, trying to concentrate on the words of the prayers.

'Be gracious unto us and cause Thy presence to dwell among us,' I sang. 'Keep Thou far from us all manner of shame, grief and care, and grant that peace, light and joy ever abide in our home. For with Thee is the fountain of life; in Thy light do we see light. Amen.'

With shaking hands, I struck the flint and, without knowing what I did, raised it above my head.

'From Thee comes all Grace,' said my voice, which was not my voice, and I lit the candles.

The lightning hit, through the roof, searing down in its unbearable white light and heat and crashing into the table before me. I fell back with a yelp of terror, throwing my arms up to protect myself and landing awkwardly on my back.

For a moment all was hustle and bustle, then, seeing I was not badly hurt, the family picked me up and dusted me down and waited for me to complete the ceremony.

Somehow I managed to speak, not sing, the final words. My mind was reeling. There was no hole in the roof. No damage on the table. No burns. Nothing. Nothing except a great, white zigzag of light burnt into my eyes, so that

I saw everything through a lightning flash of silver.

Even when I closed my eyes it was there. Not shadowed, as though I had looked too long at the sun, but brighter almost than I could bear.

No one else had seen anything at all.

They must have put my action down to burning myself with the tinder box, for no one mentioned it. Only Imma, her eyes reddened by grief, noticed something amiss and asked me gently, when the meal was over, if anything was wrong.

I shook my head, not willing to talk in this family group and knowing she had enough to cope with at that moment. The flame in my eyes would be gone by the morning, I thought. As it was Shabbat and I was in mourning, I knew I could stumble along behind everyone else on the way to the Synagogue that evening and they would simply assume that grief had made me even more clumsy than usual.

I slept surprisingly well but even before I returned to consciousness in the early morning, the light was there. It was as though my entire being were filled with that jagged, searing flame. After the initial despair, my first thought was to keep on hiding it for as long as I could.

It was terrifying, but apart from the flash itself, I was amazed to find that I could see much better than I ever had done before. I had

120

always squinted and found objects further away than a few yards difficult to focus on, but now the village was bright and everyone's face looked as clear as if it were right in front of me. There was no need to frown and strain to see anything.

Imma noticed my bemusement and how I kept shaking my head all day to try and dislodge the brightness. As soon as the Shabbat morning service was over, she took the first chance she could to have quiet words with me in private. Her kindness moved me to tears. She had just lost her much-loved husband and yet she was still taking time to notice and care for me.

I told her, rather shakily, what had happened, not expecting her to understand. I asked her in a small voice if it could be the Lord's retribution for shouting at Him over Abigail's death.

'I don't know,' she said slowly and thoughtfully, when I had finished. 'Such things do happen, but you say you were in a beautiful place as you sang the prayers, and your sight is better, not worse, so there has been no punishment. It could have been a warning, but I think it was something very different.'

'Like what?' I was so relieved at her understanding that I was prepared to listen to anything.

'The Lord spoke to me once,' she said. 'And to your father. Don't ask why, Deborah, that is not your business. It was frightening; very frightening, but it was good. It's quite possible this is a message for you.'

Then she asked me to show her what I was seeing in my eyes.

Jews never draw—for fear of making a graven image—but Imma said this was important, so I broke a twig from the olive tree and scratched the lightning flash in the dust of the garden.

'It looks a bit like a tree,' she said, puzzled, as we examined the pattern at our feet. 'I think you had better rub it out, Deborah, before anyone else sees it. And I think we need some help to interpret this.'

I wouldn't hear of it. 'I'm sure it will go,' I said. 'It's a bit painful because it's so bright, but I couldn't bear to tell the Rabbi about shouting at the Lord. He'd only see it as punishment.'

'Then we won't tell him that part,' said Imma, with spirit. 'Maybe that's wrong, I don't know, but I won't have you frightened unnecessarily.'

I was as stubborn as I could be, but this was one of the very rare occasions when Imma could be even more stubborn. By late afternoon I had agreed to see the Rabbi as long as Imma would come with me. We waited until after the evening service then followed the Rabbi back to his house.

Rabbi Simeon was a bent, little man, who at

first seemed as ruled by his fearsome wife at home as we were ruled by her at the Mikvah. At the Synagogue, however, he had charisma and Yeshua had often spoken of his sternness at school.

He and his wife invited us into their home and, haltingly, I told them the story.

'What do you see in your eyes?' The Rabbi was hardly interested in what he saw as two hysterical women in mourning.

'A zigzag of light,' I replied, nervously.

'She drew it for me,' said Imma. 'Deborah, draw it again.'

All I did was draw the lightning in the air before me, but Rabbi Simeon stared at it as though he had seen a ghost. For a second, he was still, then he leapt up from his chair.

'Lilith!' he shouted at me. 'Get out, you accursed woman!'

His voice rose to a scream of outrage and Imma and I ran, in confusion, from his house. People in the street turned to look at us and we drew our veils around us in terror.

We did not go home; we did not dare. It was not until we were safely outside the village precincts that we looked at each other and fell into each other's arms, shaking with shock.

'Oh, Deborah, Deborah,' said Imma. 'I'm so sorry. What on earth shall we do?'

We sat, holding each other and weeping, for what seemed like hours. Imma wrapped her cloak around us both and we felt safer as night fell in earnest and the darkness around us increased. We talked a little but there was nothing we could say that would not frighten us further.

'Who is Lilith?' I ventured once.

'I don't know,' said Imma. 'And I can't ask Joseph. Oh, I wish he were here.' Her tears fell steadily and I took some comfort in holding her and trying to calm her. But all the time my eyes were seared by the dreadful, dreadful light.

After a while, Imma sat up resolutely. 'We will pray,' she said. 'I won't believe we have done wrong, but if we have, the Lord will still help us. Whatever we have done, we have done in innocence.'

She prayed fervently, her face becoming steadily more serene in the starlight as she received the grace of certainty that she was heard. I did not pray. I did not dare.

Finally, Imma relaxed and opened her eyes.

'We will tell Yeshua,' she said. 'He will understand. Now we must go home.'

The family had started supper without us and we were glad we had not inconvenienced them too much. Imma helped herself and me to some stew and then busied herself with the children. Both James and Rachel seemed slightly nervous of us and although everyone was polite, it was not a relaxed meal. I could hardly eat at all. At last Rachel spoke up. 'Deborah,' she said, 'Miriam the Rabbi's wife came round and she said to tell you that you're not to help her at the Mikvah any more. What on earth has happened?'

'Nothing to worry about,' said Imma swiftly. 'It's just a misunderstanding between Deborah and the Rabbi. It will blow over.'

Both James and Rachel looked at me questioningly but I could not explain. Instead, I picked up my plate of stew and excused myself.

'I'll eat outside,' I said. No one tried to stop me.

Once alone, on the roof of the house, I huddled in a corner and tried hard to swallow down some morsels. What had I done? What was going to become of me?

Then, in the lightning within my eyes, I saw a picture of my brother. 'He's coming!' I whispered and, leaving my supper, slipped down from the roof and walked as fast as I could to meet him.

Yeshua was less than 200 paces from Nazara and as soon as I saw his figure ahead of me, I began to run, calling his name. He held out his arms and the pent-up shock of the day burst from me as I fell at his feet in supplication.

Inside, I knew he would be tired and would want to see his mother before talking to me, but I could not help myself. Selfishly I blurted out my story as soon as he had picked me up and greeted me with a bear-hug so like Abba's that it stirred the other grief as well.

Yeshua stood still as stone when I told him. For a second I thought he too would judge me as evil. Then he shook his head in amazement.

'I wouldn't have believed it,' he said. 'But I'm glad. Yes, very glad.

'Deborah, your time in Nazara is over. I can't explain just yet, but believe me, those who know what you have seen will find it hard to understand this. It's all right. You have done nothing wrong. You have been blessed. Blessed beyond all reason, but you will have to leave. You have a lot of work to do.

'You must come back with me. I don't know how we will manage it, but I expect the Lord will sort it out. If He has stamped His mark on you so firmly, He will know what to do. We won't talk of this again until we go. People could overhear and that would be dangerous. It is too important to risk. Can you put up with that?'

I could. As he spoke, the flame in my eyes died down, leaving only an echo of the image before me. If I had needed a sign that what Yeshua suggested was right, that would have been more than enough. As it was, the relief of his support and the knowledge that he wanted me with him were so strong that I would not have complained had the light continued. I could have put up with almost anything as long as we were together. I cried a little and he hugged me and then we walked peacefully into the little town.

Imma had sensed he was coming too and just as we approached the house, she slipped out in the dark and ran into her son's arms.

* * *

Yeshua stayed for ten days. Even if he had considered staying longer, it was obvious that he was not needed.

Although the inner grief goes on, people adapt themselves outwardly, whatever the situation. James and Rachel were now the elders of the family and their three children the heirs. Salome was settled and pregnant with her third child, and Imma was a devoted grandmother.

That only left me. Whatever it was that I had done, the village felt it swiftly. Simeon and Miriam cut me in the street and no one but immediate family talked to me at Synagogue. I don't think anyone knew what was going on, but they followed the Rabbi's lead like sheep.

I went to work in Rosa's garden and she was as kind as always. I even dared to draw the lightning flash on the ground to show her, but it meant nothing to her. She also thought it a good idea for me to go with Yeshua.

'There's something different about you, Deborah,' she said. 'There always has been, but now there's a light within you. If your brother thinks you must follow it, I expect he'll be right. I'll miss you. Maybe one of your nephews or nieces would come and help me out instead.'

It was not hard to arrange for James's oldest daughter to take my place and for the last few days, when I went to the garden, six-year-old Joanna came with me and stared, as wide-eyed as I had done, at the glories around her. Rosa clucked over her like a broody hen and I knew that I would not be missed so very badly.

I hung around each day, hoping to see Judah, to say goodbye, but when he did come, he pretended not to see me. The story had reached even him and I knew there was nothing left to keep me in the village.

Yeshua had got straight to the point when he told Imma he wanted to take me with him. We were all three in the garden picking figs and it was obvious that he was restless to go back south.

'Deborah is not menstruant, so no one here regards her as a proper woman,' he said. 'She has had a vision—everyone is saying that, though no one knows what it was. What they do know is that the Rabbi disapproves of her vision. You were right; it was a gift from the Lord, but—as far as I know—it's not something a woman has ever seen before. I can't explain any more, but I know that you of all people will understand. Deborah has no future here. The knowledge she has been given will outrage the people and, having been given it by the Lord, she cannot refuse to use it.'

'She has no future with you!' Imma was indignant. 'I can't allow my daughter to live with a bunch of celibates. They wouldn't have her there anyway.'

'We are not all celibate,' said Yeshua gently. 'Some of us choose to be, but many Essenes come to study after they have had families. There are dozens of men who have wives and children and some who marry while they are studying. They are not in the inner circle, but they live good lives and their women are an asset to us. Deborah can keep house for me or work at the Mikvah. There is no problem about that. Why don't you come too? I'd love you to. You could learn along with Deborah.'

'No, my place is here,' said Imma. 'As for Deborah,' she turned to me. 'Well, it's up to you. I'm not sure it is right for you, as you have never been a particularly religious woman. But I won't stand in your way.'

I thanked her, tears springing to my eyes. I would miss her dreadfully.

Imma's own sadness made her want to challenge her son.

'Are you saying you want Deborah to study?' she asked. 'She's a woman; she can't read or write. She has enough problems coping with the faith here. Even if she could study the Torah—even if they would let her, which they surely won't—she'd hate it.'

'I don't think so,' said Yeshua. 'Somehow, I

don't think so.' He looked at me with his dancing smile and I knew he was right. Strange as it might seem, I did want to learn and to understand our faith, as long as I could do it with Yeshua. I knew I would be safe and could ask as many questions as I wanted.

It was hard to say goodbye to Imma and Salome but at least I knew I would see them at the festivals. With Rosa it was worse. She never travelled to Jerusalem and it was more than probable we would never meet again. Without Yeshua I could not have done it. As it was, there was a happiness within the grief, and the knowledge that I would be with him, even if the life were harsh, was enough to keep me strong.

Imma insisted that I took Zoresh, the donkey. James objected, but she said the animal had sired enough offspring around the village for James to be able to get a colt for a good price.

'Deborah brought us that donkey,' she said. 'And he is her dowry. Even if he were not, Deborah can't walk all the way to Jerusalem.'

She was more right than she could possibly know.

The day after we left for the south, I began to feel dizzy and weak and heavy in the stomach. Embarrassed, I had to ask Yeshua to halt so that I could have a drink to try to stop my head spinning. Passers-by called out to us in good humour as he helped me down and fetched me water. They only saw a fond young couple and assumed that I was pregnant. I was doubly embarrassed but Yeshua was not bothered.

'I think I know what's happening,' he said. 'I shouldn't, I know. You would be best to travel on if you can, because we will need a woman's help and a place for you to rest.'

I held on tightly to the little donkey and by the time we reached the inn, though my insides hurt in a way I had never felt before, I was smiling. Against all the odds, I had become a woman.

When we stopped for lunch, my brother, knowing my state, held out his hand to help me dismount. I hesitated. New laws should now have bound me, but he took my arm with a smile.

'The Lord is compassionate,' he said. 'You need help and support and the commandment of love is greater than the Law of Purity. Lean on me, Deborah. We must help each other as much as we can.'

5

We travelled slowly because I was feeling quite weak, but that gave us more time to talk. We only discussed everyday matters on the road, but Yeshua constantly pointed out the beauty around us and I was never happier than while looking at everything and loving the colours, shapes and sizes as the landscape changed.

The Jordan River was wide and deep and sunlight made the sweeping water so bright that it was hard to look at it. Fishing birds swooped across the water and called out to each other and to us.

On the group migrations to and from Jerusalem for festivals, we were used to taking our own food or buying bread from the inns we passed. But every Jew bakes extra bread, and leaves fruit on the tree and the vine for the passing lone traveller or pilgrim. As the sun stood high in the sky, we would sit in the shade of an olive tree sharing the fruits we had gathered or been given along the way.

Yeshua always blessed the food and thanked the Lord for the abundance that surrounded us and now I joined in with enthusiasm. I had not realised the extent of the generosity and kindness of our race. Every place we stopped, we received gifts and every time I needed any help, a woman was kind to me and we would smile at each other, sharing that intimacy of knowledge of womanhood that I had never understood before.

People were so sociable that it was not easy for Yeshua and I to have much time alone together. Many of those who live on the route to Jerusalem love to pass the time of day with travellers, and others on the road would join up with us, or come across to sit in the shade with us, exchanging food, gossip and news.

Yeshua never said anything that would draw attention to himself, but somehow people knew they could ask him for advice or his opinion on matters that troubled them and he would always answer them kindly.

'It is the spirit of the Law that is important,' he said, again and again. 'It is only pure if it is kept with love. If the Law is kept with anger, prejudice or so that others can see how holy you think you are, it is tainted.'

'But, Rabbi,' said one man. 'How are we to know if we taint the Law?'

'Look inside yourself,' said Yeshua. 'Find the Kingdom of Heaven within. That is the place where you let go of your own opinion of how things should be and allow the Lord to bring your true happiness. That is the place where blessings start.'

I was quiet as we began our journey again. My brother was being referred to as Rabbi; people were seeing him as a man of wisdom. For the first time in many years, I felt shy in his company.

He saw how I felt, of course, and teased me until I laughed with him again, but something had changed and some of the enormity of what I was doing, going with him to the Essenes, hit me like a heavy weight.

I saw everything through new eyes. When I picked more figs than I needed to eat, in case

133

there were none the next day, they were mouldy when I woke the next morning. Then the story of manna from heaven from the Exodus became real. Like the Israelites, I could have as much manna as I needed, but no extra. If I took too much, it was wasted and it implied I had not trusted the Lord to feed me the next day.

I talked to Yeshua about this and he understood. 'The Lord may have planned something better for you than figs,' he said. 'And you would miss them if you were still eating yesterday's food.'

'But what about Joseph and the famine in Egypt?' I asked. 'The Egyptians saved corn to feed themselves. And Joseph's family were fed by that corn too.'

'Joseph's task was to feed a nation of unbelievers,' said Yeshua. 'We are meant to have come out of Egypt into a new land, a new life and a new perception. If each man and woman believed in the goodness of the Lord and worked for Him in joy, each one would receive manna from Heaven. That's what happened to the Israelites. There were thousands of them but each one received exactly what he or she needed. You do if you love the Lord. Look at us. Do we lack anything?'

I had to admit we did not.

That lunchtime we picked olives and figs to eat with our bread and corn. Both were plumper and tastier than any others I had ever eaten.

'How are your eyes?' asked Yeshua. Although the scorching image in my head had faded, there was still a touch, a memory of it, which was with me every moment.

'Draw it for me,' he said, so I bent down and drew the pattern with my finger in the dust.

'Now put the Sephirot on,' he said. I looked at him, perplexed. Sephirot? I knew 'sephirah'—it was Hebrew for circle or sphere. So sephirot would be the plural. What circles? Then I bent again and without my mind knowing what I did, my hand drew circles at the top and bottom, at each angle of the lightning flash, and one in the middle for luck.

'You've missed one out,' he said, with a smile. 'That shows it came from Ehyeh Asher Ehyeh. It's only mankind that requires the final circle. The non-sephirah—the veil that once was the Tree of Knowledge.' I lifted my head and stared at him. In the middle of this strange, incomprehensible talk he had spoken a name that I did not know, but which I sensed was something so forbidden it was unthinkable. Jews never spoke the name of the Holy One. However it was spelt in the Torah it was always pronounced 'Adonai'—Lord.

I could say nothing. I just shook my head at him in disbelief.

'Look at the pattern, Deborah. Do you know what it is?' Yeshua's eyes held mine.

'No, of course not.' But a fear began to settle on me and my neck felt cold and prickly. Perhaps I did know. 'Is it . . . ? No, no, it can't be.'

'Yes, it is. It is a reflection of God.'

In horror I swept my hand over the terrible pattern, the graven image, obliterating it and scrubbing at the ground, as though to erase the record of its existence from the very soil. Then I covered my face with my hands and began to moan, begging forgiveness for what I had done.

'What do you see?' asked Yeshua as I shook my head and rocked back and forth in distress.

'I still see it,' I said. 'It's in my eyes. I don't want to. I don't want to. I did not ask for this. Lord, help me!'

He took my hands from my face and began to speak. Each word was more terrible than the last. I felt as though my hair was standing on end and my body was screaming with discomfort.

'Deborah, what you see, and what you have drawn is the knowledge given to Adam in the Book of Raziel, after he and his wife were expelled from Paradise. What you see is the teaching Melchizedek gave to Abraham, and Abraham gave to Isaac.

'What you see is what God, yes, Deborah, God gave to Moses on Mount Sinai because the children of Israel had forgotten it. It has been taught only to men. Only to those mature

136

enough to handle it and it has never been allowed outside the priesthood—even in the Essenes.

'I was given it in the Temple that time I stayed behind when I was twelve. That is why I stayed with the priests. I had to know what it was and why. I'm sure you can understand that now! And you, Deborah, have been given it too.'

'What does it mean?' I stuttered. 'Why? What am I to do?'

'Learn about it. Teach it,' said Yeshua. 'You are a sign to me. I know my Father wants me to teach this outside the priesthood, so that all men can learn the truth of the Kingdom of Heaven and the Kingdom of God. Now I know the teaching is for women too. At last. Your vision has made my life clearer, Deborah. Thank you.'

I would like to say that I felt lifted and enlightened; that I had seen a magnificent path carved for me by the angels; that I felt the love of God settle in my heart, but I did not. I made several very sarcastic remarks about how wonderful it was that my life was ruined so that Yeshua's could be sorted out, and burst into tears.

We began our journey again once Yeshua had fetched me some water and bathed my brow to help me calm down.

'I won't say much more today,' he said. 'You have had quite a shock. But one of the reasons why we don't speak the Name is because there are ten names for the Lord which speak of His Wisdom, His Understanding, His Mercy, His Justice and other equally great attributes, and to speak only one of them, other than the Greatest Name of all, is to deny the rest of God.

'Those who would speak the Greatest Name, Ehyeh Asher Ehyeh, must only be those who understand it, and what it means for us. Otherwise it might be profaned.'

'Stop!' I put my hands over my ears in confusion.

Yeshua walked on, leading Zoresh, and I sat, slumped on the donkey's back with my brother's words echoing around my head. Slowly they began to make sense. And knowing the meaning behind a law was a wonderful thing.

'Yeshua?' My voice sounded very small.

'Yes?' He looked up and smiled.

'It's . . . difficult.'

'Of course.'

'Yeshua?'

'Yes?'

'What . . . what can we call the Lord God if we cannot use the Greatest Name because we do not understand?'

'You will understand,' said Yeshua simply. 'But I call him ABBA. It makes it all much simpler. I'll tell you why if you like.'

'No. No, I think I know enough for today . . .

but . . .'

'Yes?'

'The Tree of Knowledge?'

'Hmm?'

'We're not supposed to eat from the Tree of Knowledge.'

'No. That's what caused the black hole in the picture. The space. The veil. Our distance from ABBA.'

'Oh, I see. I think. Well, no I don't.'

'You will. What was the name of the other tree in Paradise?'

'The Tree of Life.'

'And what did Imma tell you the image looked like?'

'A tree.'

'Well, that's what it is. The Tree of Life.'

*   *   *

That was the beginning of the time of beauty. We arrived in the village on the north side of Jerusalem on the fifth day. Emmaus was not only an Essene community, but a village in its own right. The celibate brotherhood lived alone, away from the others, but the married men who studied on the edge of the community were a part of normal village life. Yeshua told me to wait with Zoresh where the village proper ended and the simple huts of the Essenes began, while he went to find the community's leader. What he said I'll never

139

know, but he was gone so long that I worried myself sick. Men and women walked past me and greeted me curiously, but I did not encourage them to stop and ask what I was doing there. I fiddled with the donkey's halter so much that I had to re-plait the ends. When Yeshua returned, he was with another man; tall and very dark, with stern, hooded eyes. His size and colouring dwarfed Yeshua and made me realise how young he still was.

'This is Joseph Barsabbas,' said Yeshua. 'He has agreed that you can stay, but he wants to ask you a few questions himself. Don't worry. It's nothing to trouble yourself about.'

I looked up at the towering man before me and he looked down.

'Well, Deborah,' he said kindly. 'We have never had a single woman here before and there may be some who find that difficult. But Yeshua says you are a hard worker and willing to learn and I believe him when he says you need to be here. Everything we have is shared. No one has anything they can call their own. Will you be able to cope with that? Do you have jewels or special things you would want to keep for yourself?'

'I have nothing but my clothes, sir,' I said. 'And my donkey. He is my dowry and I am happy for anyone to use him, provided they are kind and they allow me to give him treats sometimes.'

Joseph Barsabbas smiled. 'He will be used

well,' he said. 'You have my promise on that. And he is very welcome. We do not eat meat here and we do not make sacrifice or hurt any living thing.'

'Except plants,' said Yeshua.

Joseph Barsabbas looked at him with affectionate exasperation. 'Yeshua, if your sister is anything like you, the two of you will drive me into an early grave,' he said. 'Very well, we do not hurt creatures. A plant is not a creature—be quiet!' he added, as Yeshua looked as though he was going to speak again.

'Deborah, if you can keep your brother under some kind of control, we shall all be very grateful to you. Now, as we share everything, each of us has to give our talents and our hard work to the group so that we may live. Your brother says you are a gardener and you can run a Mikvah. Both those talents will be well received. The donkey you can leave with me. I'll ask one of the brothers to take him to the stable.'

He nodded at me, and the interview was over.

I felt rather lonely leaving Zoresh behind and he brayed mournfully as I walked away.

'Don't worry,' said Yeshua. 'If anything, he'll be loved to death and you can see him whenever you want. People here are stern in many ways, but they do love animals.'

*   *   *

The first week at my new home passed in a daze. Many people assumed I was Yeshua's wife, but they accepted me just as easily when they discovered I was his sister. Because the Essenes and their followers had come from so many different parts of the tribes of Israel, there was an air of acceptance of strangers in the outer group, which was completely different from the atmosphere in provincial, nosy Nazara. Apart from being expected to go to the place of worship (we did not call it the Synagogue) every day, whether you were male or female, and the delightful rule of taking regular baths in the wonderful wash-houses, the customs were no more severe than at home, so I had little trouble settling there.

Yeshua worked as a carpenter when he was not studying or teaching and had a work-room that he shared with one other man, Nathaniel. He was able to give me his old sleeping chamber and put a rush mattress in the work-room for himself so that no one was disturbed by my arrival. The little house was very basic, but it was a cool roof over my head in the summer, and there was a fireplace for the winter and for cooking, so there was no hardship.

In the daytime I worked in the pastures that belonged to us all. There were plenty of the basic fruits and vegetables, olives, garlic and figs, but I thought the local knowledge of the more unusual vegetables and of herbs was surprisingly scanty. I was able to be useful at once and within five days of arriving, I went out into the countryside with my fellow workers Judith and Leah to search for wild comfrey, thyme, lavender and rosemary.

Without knowing it, I had brought more of a dowry than just the donkey. When Imma helped me pack my few clothes, she had hidden twists of bark containing seeds from many of Rosa's vegetables and flowers. I fell on them with delight and nurtured them with fierce determination. And there was more abundance to come. Each time the family came down from Nazara, Rosa would send more seeds, and even bulbs, cuttings and rose plants, so our garden blossomed over the years into a place of beauty as well as being our larder. One man did complain about the roses because he thought they were frivolous, and when I explained that I hoped to infuse and sell valuable rose water, he was outraged that I did not know that the Essenes and their followers never used scent on their bodies.

'It's for sale to those who do,' I said meekly. 'We can sell it to buy what we do need.'

At that he calmed down a little. He was still not sure he approved and he was not going to apologise, but he would let the matter be.

Quite a few of the Essenes were like that. Rosa would have called them pretentious, but for a long time I was too new to think they were anything other than perfect.

At regular intervals I helped Judith at the Mikvah. Unlike Nazara, the women felt free to come to her with any problems and Judith gave counselling and teaching to anyone who asked for it. She was delighted to include the oils, herbs and essences that I provided to help with the women's griefs or aches and pains. When I grew confused over what the man from the inner circle had said, she laughed. 'The inner circle is the inner circle,' she said. 'They may study the mysterious inner knowledge, and sit for hours in devout conversation with the Lord and His angels, but it does not seem to teach them much about everyday life and even less about women and our needs. The knowledge has been handed down by mouth from man to man so there is nothing there for a woman. If any of them ever had to have a life as a woman, they would certainly think again!'

I liked Judith, for she had a way of bringing everything down to simple, practical basics and of bringing laughter into our work.

As time passed, and my knowledge of remedies became tried and tested, I found myself with a reputation as a medicine woman. Sometimes even men and women from the outside world would come to our Mikvah to ask for advice, but we kept that quiet, and just did what we could to help.

Ten days after arriving at the Essene village

I used the Mikvah myself, for the same reason as the other women did and that felt very good. However, my cycle was always far from regular; I could go for months without bleeding, so I was always a little separate, but that suited me. I was naturally a loner. The other women's menses were drawn together, as often happens with women in a small group, so some times were extra busy and others were peaceful.

It was delightful to see women treated with so much respect, both by each other and by the majority of the menfolk. We were expected to be knowledgeable as well as hard-working and our efforts were recognised as being invaluable. The family men could not study without our help and backing and the celibates depended on all of us to support their learning. In theory they too practised a craft, but apart from a few scribes and craftsmen, few of them had any specific skill apart from prayer and worship. They were very particular about not defiling themselves and did nothing that could possibly make them ritually impure. They also prayed alone in a place higher up the hill from the rest of us, but for all that we still felt a part of the whole, in a way I had never done at home. Joseph Barsabbas was one of the celibates, but as the community's leader he would also take as many of the main services for the rest of us as he could. Each time he would talk to and about the women, as well as the men, and mention every new thing that had been achieved. If one of the women were sick or pregnant, or gave birth, we all prayed for her.

The Essenes had a particular routine of worshipping the Lord through His angels. Each morning and evening there was a separate aspect to learn from and appreciate and, along with this, we acknowledged the Earth as our Mother, as much as the Lord was our Father. So every night and morning the devout would go to the place of worship and invoke the power of the angel of that time in helping us to serve the Lord better. The Angel of Love was more popular than the Angel of Creative Work—but we were only human after all!

We were also encouraged to spend time in silence, either in the place of worship or during our daily life, thinking about the angels, the Heavenly Father and the Earthly Mother, and just being still within our minds.

'That way you can listen to what the Lord has to say to you alone,' said Joseph Barsabbas. 'To pray is to praise or to ask. To be still is to listen for the answer.'

I began to see that how you worship the Lord affects your perception of Him. Here, it seemed, He did appreciate our efforts of service, and although He was still a stern master, He had compassion and understanding. In Nazara we were always being told that we were evil and had to do better.

I tended Rosa's stumpy rose bushes with love, expecting one or maybe two strong blooms in their first year of transplanting. But both bushes put out a dozen great, heavy buds as soon as the rains ended. They blossomed on Shabbat and the scent of the flowers flowed into the place of worship. Joseph Barsabbas thanked me directly for the beauty of the Lord manifested in our home and, behind the women's veil I shed a tear of joy. Later nearly everyone from the outer group took time to visit the roses, smell them and give praise.

My own faith began to grow stronger in this atmosphere of acceptance and peace. I thanked the Lord every day for Rosa and the knowledge she had given me, and for Imma's wisdom in making me work at the Mikvah in Nazara. Even for fierce Miriam the Rabbi's wife, whose thoroughness had made me an efficient and observant bath attendant. All the Essenes were rigorous in personal cleansing and the inner group seemed to take it to almost ridiculous lengths, bathing in ice-cold water several times a day to cleanse their souls and psyches, as well as their bodies.

I also thanked the Lord for my plainness and for my limp because, without them, I would never have come to live with the Essenes. Even though the woman in me would have liked marriage and children, I knew how lucky I was. So, when Imma came down to

Jerusalem for the first time since I left, I knelt at her feet and kissed them in thanks for all she had taught me and the strength and possibilities she had seen in me.

'You were right,' I told her. 'Without my lameness, I would never be here, and now I can thank the Lord for being so damaged. Thank you for helping me to see that I would be grateful one day.'

Imma glowed with happiness, her face transforming her back into the beautiful woman I remembered. She had seemed older and less filled with joy since Abba's death and though her natural grief was part of that, I thought perhaps she missed Yeshua and me more than she was willing to admit. The two of us felt keenly the lack of Abba's dear presence within the family but Yeshua and I had new challenges and a different home to fulfil us. Imma now had no one with whom to share the depth of her faith and, though her grand-children were obviously very dear to her, there was not one of them who carried the same light as she did.

Yeshua asked her again if she wanted to join us, but she refused. 'I will ask each year,' he said. 'Perhaps one day you will come.'

'Perhaps,' she answered, smiling at him. 'But not yet.'

*   *   *

Apart from the hidden dimension of knowledge that surrounded us, the Essene wives and daughters were just like women everywhere else. Some were genuinely interested in what their menfolk were learning while others just lived their own lives. They bickered with each other and each thought her own children were the best in the world—and some of them always had to know better than others. But all of them had faith of some kind, and all of them were cordial towards me as long as I remembered never to take sides in an argument!

The celibate Essenes, who learnt the innermost knowledge, ate together in the long hall and spent most of their time secluded from the others. The married men in the next circle ate with their families for much of the time, and studied the Torah during the day. Some of them worked in the fields for their keep but most taught the new recruits to the group, or copied out religious texts. They never charged directly for their work but money and gifts came in as thanks. 'Some groups won't accept gifts in return for the Work,' said Yeshua. 'They think they are too holy! But the Lord joyfully repays anything you do for Him and it is rejecting Him to reject His abundance.'

The system worked well and the manual workers among us were proud to support the learned men. It was always made clear to us that we served the Lord as well as they did.

Other Essene groups refused to have any women near them, as they said we were a distraction and would cause quarrels. 'Perhaps they could look into their hearts and see where they have distractions and quarrels within that they want to blame on others,' said Joseph Barsabbas. 'Celibacy is a fine thing if embraced voluntarily, but hating women is hating an aspect of the Lord.'

If one of the women had a problem, we were encouraged to go to Joseph about it instead of getting our husbands or brothers to do so for us.

'That teaches you equal responsibility,' he said. 'It is easy to hide behind others, but if you have a grievance you have to have the courage to look at it yourself, not ask others to take it away from you.'

It was many years before I realised how enlightened our leader was, but in our group at least he was right. Any bickering between the men was more about interpretations of the Law than the distractions of women.

It might have been because he was my brother, but it seemed to me that Yeshua stood apart from the other men. He was already teaching groups who were ten or more years older than he, and he wore the traditional white robe of the inner circle. But, unlike most of the others in that select group, he would not set himself apart. He spent time each day working in his carpenter's shop, saying it kept him in touch with the earth. Sometimes he ate with the other celibates, but more often we ate together or with friends.

'I am blessed,' he would say. 'I am allowed to learn the inner teachings, but I can live in the everyday world. It is not always good to be cut off from ways of living the knowledge in an ordinary human life. How can you have compassion if you do not know how people live and understand their temptations?'

Even though he was such a misfit, and would argue long and fiercely over some interpretations of our faith, no one disliked him for it. Some of the elders complained at his youth and cheek, but it was with amazement, not anger.

Just watching him was a lesson in living. The more he did, the more time he seemed to have. When you were with him, time stood still, so just a few minutes seemed an abundance.

Every night, from the very beginning, he took an hour or two to devote to my education. He had been right in suspecting that I had a thirst for knowledge and I looked forward to the evenings with a longing far deeper than anything I had felt for Judah, or for the strange mysteries which led the married women to whisper among themselves in private.

In the first years I learnt how to read and

write in Hebrew and Greek. To start with, I would devour the letters in fascination, willing them to change from a meaningless jumble into words that I would speak and images I could see. Sometimes I got so frustrated that I would lose my temper and storm out. But when I had recovered myself and come back, apologetically, my brother would always be calmly involved in something else. He had never let my tantrums bother him.

Here, my stubbornness was useful and, even in the difficult times when Hebrew seemed an impossible torment, I kept going. I was determined to be a good scholar so that I could read some of the scrolls he often brought home with him. A whole new world was staring me in the face and nothing was going to stop me getting there.

I read the Song of Deborah first. Then the story of Judith. Then the Book of Ruth. Oh, the joy of having a story to myself! To be able to take time to stop and start, and go over the difficult bits. Of being able to read out the passages that confused me, instead of having to describe them. Of being able to discuss the books and the way they were written. The only jarring note was the lack of any copies whatsoever of the Book of Esther. When I asked why, Yeshua shrugged. 'They say it is because the Lord God is not mentioned once in the Book of Esther,' he said. 'Without the Lord, it is not thought to be relevant.' I pondered that deeply, but whatever I thought, I had to be content without Esther. One day, I promised myself, I would find a copy of her story and read it for myself. There was something important for me in there, whether or not the Essenes valued the story.

I avoided talking to Yeshua about the Tree of Life for as long as I could. There was more than enough in my mind to keep it at a safe distance, and even the identity of Lilith seemed less important than reading and learning what was in front of my face.

'There is plenty of time, Deborah. The beginning is always a good place to start,' said Yeshua, smiling, when I became slightly apologetic about being more interested in the delight of exoteric knowledge than in the inner teaching.

Time slipped away in that little village and I felt more secure and at peace than I had ever thought possible. Yeshua too continued to grow stronger and wiser, and his bright and cheerful face shone with the light constantly flowing into him from the Heavens. He often left us to travel south to Qumran and as far as Alexandria in Egypt, but there was plenty to do and enough good company to fill the void when he was away.

Our good fortune was never more apparent than when the two of us met up with the rest of the family for festivals in the city. It was quite difficult to work out when they would be coming, because we lived by a sun calendar, not the lunar one used by the rest of the Jews, and our festivals were always on different dates from the celebrations in Jerusalem. In many ways that was a help, because we could celebrate with clarity and meaning in our own little community, and see our blood-family at a time when we did not have festival duties to attend to.

It was always a joy to see Imma and Salome, but there just seemed to be more and more children, wives and husbands adding to the group; people milling around with no real purpose in life and no interest in anything, but who married whom and whether they had been cheated in their last deal. They had nothing new to talk about and no knowledge of anything outside Nazara unless it affected their taxes.

Among the Essenes, we picked up news quite swiftly. There were groups of us all over the country and some as far away as Alexandria, which sounded like the most wonderful place in the world—filled with libraries and groups dedicated to learning. Yeshua had been there many times and loved it. He told me that people there also had knowledge of the secret we shared—the Tree of Life—but I was still not ready to hear any more about that.

Men from all the different Essene groups regularly came and went and the stories they had to tell from the outside world swept through the group like wildfire.

The celibates thought Jerusalem and its Temple were places of darkness, but the women, and the men who were not in the inner core, went regularly into the city to trade and to enjoy the sights and hear the news. Judith and I sold the herbal essences I made and our rose water was always snapped up within minutes, giving us plenty of time to wander round and enjoy the sights of the city.

*　　*　　*

I had seen Herod Antipas and his wife Herodias. I had seen the prefect, Pontius Pilate, and his beautiful wife Claudia Procula. I had seen the High Priest, Caiaphas, in his everyday clothes, haggling over a piece of cloth. I had seen dozens of rich Roman women carried in litters by slaves. We used to laugh at them a little, as they seemed so chubby and pink and petulant. 'Thank the Lord that we have our own wonderful water system,' said Judith. 'If we did not have the opportunity to bathe as much as the Romans can, we would probably envy them. And I'd hate to be carried like that. I'd rather go on my own two feet so that I can look in all the shops and see everything around me. They have slaves to do that for them, of course. Do you know, Claudia Procula is said to have more than five baths a day? She can't have anything else to do!'

'Be careful,' I said. 'Some of our own inner group do the same!'

Judith snorted. 'But they, at least, do it for a spiritual reason,' she said.

'So may Claudia Procula!' I teased her. 'We don't know anything about the Roman religions.'

There were hundreds of Romans in, and around, Jerusalem. To start with, I hated them cordially because Judah had done so and because it was the fashionable thing to do. But slowly some of them became good acquaintances and even better customers for our herbs and oils and fruit. Their efforts to speak Aramaic could be comical and they enjoyed teaching us bits and pieces of their own languages. Most people in Jerusalem spoke Greek but the soldiers came from all over the Empire and they spoke in a mixture of Greek, Latin, slang and other strange dialects. The soldiers themselves were always scary because you knew they could be friendly one day and under orders to kill you the next, but the other Romans were human beings like the rest of the Jews although they were often better mannered!

Feelings ran high now and again, especially if there were crucifixions of Jewish rebels, and we would lie low on those occasions when people would riot or throw stones at the soldiers. Terrible things did happen, mostly after the Romans had insulted the Law in some way, and they were impossible to predict. We learnt that if we were in Jerusalem and heard the sound of shouting, or even just a rumour on the wind, then it was safest just to leave at once without further questioning.

Many of our group hated the Romans and believed that their expulsion should be carried out by force. Joseph Barsabbas and Yeshua taught us about inner peace, but there were plenty of people who believed that spiritual thought excluded the Romans. However, it was the Pharisees who seemed to hate them most and who suffered the worst of their purges. They believed the Lord would send the Messiah to throw the Romans out of Judaea, and we often heard rumours of one promised Messiah after another. None of them seemed to come to anything at all.

I could not feel the same unreasoning prejudice against the Romans as my fellows in the community once I realised that most of their slaves were better off than the hundreds of Jewish poor people who lived from the gleanings after the harvest and whatever itinerant work they could get. The Zealots blamed the Romans for the homeless people's poverty too, but they blamed the Romans for everything. I still thought slavery was wrong, but I thought sacrifice was wrong as well, and that didn't make me hate the Jews.

One day, after I had been with the Essenes for five festivals, Yeshua brought me a scroll containing the first book of the Torah. Before that, I had only read texts from the Prophets. He said he had Joseph Barsabbas's permission but that I should be careful not to tell anyone else for now.

'You are ready to start the Work,' he said. 'Read and ask me about everything you don't understand.'

'Everything? I'll never stop asking questions!'

'How else can you learn? And how else can I learn how to teach you?'

It was difficult work and Yeshua became a hard taskmaster. Slowly I made my way through the stories and he explained the esoteric meanings behind the words. To do that, he had to talk again about the lightning flash, the Tree of Life, and all the things he had learnt at an esoteric school in Alexandria and at the great Essene centre at Qumran. To read that what I had seen in my vision actually existed—and to decipher the reality behind the symbolism of the Menorah, the seven-branched candlestick in the the heart of the Temple and in Moses's Tabernacle—moved me to tears. I also re-read and understood a little better the story of Ezekiel's vision, the dream of the fiery chariot representing four worlds and mankind's link to the Holy One. Yeshua taught me that what I was beginning to comprehend was generally called the Merkabah—or Chariot—tradition, as it was so well described in Ezekiel's dream. With my brother's perseverance and my own insatiable curiosity I began to glimpse the inner workings of the structure known as the Tree of Life and saw that it could be used not only for worship but to help me understand more about my everyday life. The pattern of the Tree of Life itself was depicted on the Menorah in the Temple, and there were ten of these candlesticks in the Holy of Holies. Understanding their significance meant unravelling the meaning of life itself. If the Tree of Knowledge was the symbol of mankind's fall from the Garden of Eden, the Tree of Life was the route back.

Yeshua told me that the image of the Tree was not of the Lord Himself, but of Adam Kadmon, the perfected man, made in the image of God. Each one of us, man and woman, was a part of that potentially perfect being and, as each of us became all we were meant to be, we would hasten the day when God beheld God.

'But if the Lord wishes to behold Himself, and this image helps us to grow so that He can, why doesn't everyone know this?' I asked, perplexed.

Yeshua sighed. 'Not everyone would want to,' he said. 'Too much knowledge too soon can hurt people, and what good would it do to give it to those who don't care about anything but their own wealth and power? They would only use it to wield yet more power over others. That's not what it's for. You can see too that it is not something which can be written down. It is too complicated and too personal. This is the oral tradition of the Lord and it must be taught person to person. You can find it in the Torah, as you know, but the truth that can be defined in writing is not the eternal truth.

'The reason I'm here is to tell people as much as they are willing to hear about it. The priesthood has held this secret too long and they have hidden its true glory behind a veil. It's time people had the chance to learn if they want to. When the time is right, I will teach it, but in stories, so that it doesn't frighten people as it frightened you.'

'You are going to teach this to everyone?' I was incredulous and, I have to admit, slightly resentful. I liked to think I was rather special.

'Yes. That's what I'm here to do. Most people will only hear the stories and very few will actually understand. But those who have ears to hear and eyes to see must have the knowledge now. It's God's will that our eyes are opened to His Kingdom. It has to be made available to everyone so that everyone can be their own Rabbi, their own priest.'

'The Temple priests aren't going to like that.'

'I know. I won't be teaching for long, Deborah. There will be plenty of opposition. But it has to be done. It's my Father's work and it is necessary. How can mankind be free if no one knows how to listen to God in his or her own heart? Fighting battles against the Romans is no use if we are still slaves to our own prejudices and hatreds. We will not be freed that way. It has to be done from within.'

He showed me the significance of each sefirah on the Tree of Life, and encouraged me to search for them in my everyday life. He showed me what was balance and what was not. He helped me see where my own faults and strengths were and where I needed to work on myself. He taught me how to live in the sun and not in the moon—the moon aspect of each of us being where we react to situations instead of responding to them. And so much more, just from one little diagram!

The image of the lightning flash could be repeated four times, so every pattern fitted neatly on top of the others. Each one represented a different world in its reflection of the Divine essence and the base of each one was called Malkhut—the Kingdom.

'Look,' he said, drawing it out again in the dust of the floor. 'Azilut, Beriah, Yetzirah, Assiyah. The world reflecting the Divine, the world of Spirit, the world of the Soul (or the Psyche), and the world of the Physical.

'That spells ABYA or ABIA—you know about the priests of Abia, Jochanan's father was one.' Zachariah had died some years ago and our fierce cousin Jochanan (now called by his Greek name of John) was now travelling up and down the Jordan River, baptising people and calling them to repent. So, Zachariah had taught this knowledge as well—did Elisheva know it? I wondered.

I could grasp the concept of most of the Four Worlds spoken of in the Merkabah tradition—the world of the Lord, the world of the Spirit and the Physical world were simple enough, but Yetzirah, the world of the soul and the mind, confused me.

'It is the world of your thoughts,' said Yeshua. 'It is where you make pictures in your head after you have had an idea. The idea comes from a spark in Beriah, the world of Spirit, and you make pictures to start understanding it and planning how to make it happen.'

'But it makes my head hurt to think about thinking!'

'Let's see if I can make it easier.' Yeshua thought for a moment. 'Deborah, look at your hand.' I obeyed.

'Now close your eyes. Can you still see your hand?'

'No. Well, I can imagine it. I can see what it

162

looks like.'

'Then it is a form in your mind. That's Yetzirah. It's still real, because you can see it in your mind. It is not actually in the physical world, but it merges into it as thoughts turn into reality.'

'Do they?'

'Of course. What you concentrate on, you create in the physical world.

'If you constantly think of depressing things, you are using your mind to look down and expecting difficulties in life. If you do that, you will find them. If you think of blessings—like we used to play that game of looking for the good—you use your mind to look up. Do you see?'

I did. The way the worlds merged meant that the kingdom of the world of Spirit or Heaven was in the centre of the world of the mind. If you were conscious of what you were thinking, and free from anger and prejudice, you were at the place called the Kingdom of Heaven. If you looked up from there, by thinking of blessings instead of being resentful, you could see the Kingdom of the next world, the Divine. The Kingdom of God.

'So suppose you change the name of the world of the soul to Beracha, the world of blessings,' said Yeshua. 'That would mean you were always looking up to the Kingdom of God and you would be closer to the Divine. If you do that, the Trees spell ABBA. Father. I think that works well, don't you?'

'But you can't just change things like that—can you?'

'I can change my perception—it is the same world. I'm not changing the structure of the tradition, I'm just choosing to look for God, not for misery. Maybe that is what I am here to teach!'

'But if you are always looking up, won't you fall over?'

Yeshua stared at me. I pushed the point.

'I mean, how do you live if you are looking for God all the time and aren't involved in the real world?'

'But you *are* in the real world in the Kingdom of Heaven. That's the whole point. It's the crown of the physical world. You are in control of your life in a way that doesn't hurt. All that you need comes to you with ease. You get manna from Heaven. Only when you have achieved that can you truly look up to see God. Most people can only touch *that* Kingdom for a few minutes here and there. But just doing it, even for a second, changes everything.

'If you *don't* look up, you are constantly worn down by your physical needs—worrying about where to get your food and money and shelter. It's all meant to be easier than that. You never need lack for anything if you can touch the Kingdom of God, even if you are still living on the earth.'

That sounded rather unlikely to me but, slowly, Yeshua taught me what he meant.

He lived it. He lived a life of worship and he loved all that he did. The inner circle did not have to help with the dirtier jobs and never had to do anything that would make them ritually impure. But Yeshua did. He joined in with all of us. He touched the sick, carried the dead and shovelled the dirt. But he did it all with such joy and love that working with him made it a pleasure for others. He said that nothing could make you impure if your spirit was clear.

He was looked after, too. By us, certainly, but by the Lord as well. People he met outside the group said he made them feel better and, just for the pleasure of his company, they would give him gifts, which he shared with all of us. Birds flew down to sing to him in the morning and if ever an animal in our care was injured, it would find its way to Yeshua to be healed.

One day he and I were in Jerusalem together going to see the family. A riot blew up, right in front of us and, before we knew it, dozens of Roman soldiers were catching hold of all the Jewish men in the street and dragging them away to be interrogated, or worse.

I caught onto Yeshua's sleeve in fear.

'Don't worry,' he said. 'This is none of our business. Don't react, respond. Think of the

Kingdom of Heaven. Think of the Kingdom of God. They won't even see us.'

I tried to calm myself, and his arm around me helped. He just kept walking, looking straight ahead, and the soldiers completely ignored him. It was as though a light shone around us to keep us safe.

'You see, the lower half of Yetzirah and all of Assiyah are about basic emotions, such as fear,' he said afterwards. 'Fear draws fearful situations. If you lift your heart to God, you draw down His protection. That is, if you are not responsible for the trouble you find yourself in! If you are, you have to deal with it yourself. That's only fair. But even then, ABBA will help if you put yourself in His hands and trust to His mercy.'

Looking back, it seems those were the golden years of peace, knowledge and beauty. I was safe. But safety does not test the servants of God, and the servants of God must be tested to prove their mettle.

One day, after I had been with the Essenes for so many years that my life in Nazara seemed like a dream, I was taking the children's morning lesson in one of the lower fields. We were talking about looking for the good in life, when I saw a stranger walking up the slope to our village. We were always welcoming new members to the group, but this man's walk and his blue-and-white-striped Pharisee robe caught my eye. He passed by, looking across as the sound of the children's chatter and laughter attracted him. He started when he saw me, and I put my hand to my chest as shock made my heart contract.

'You!' he said. 'What are you doing here? Lilith!' And the angry gaze of Judah turned my stomach with fear.

6

That night I finally asked Yeshua to explain who Lilith was and why she was so hated and feared. In answer, he fetched me the first book of the Torah and told me to re-read the first two chapters, concentrating on the story of the creation of man and woman.

'So God created man in His own image, in the image of God created He him; male and female created He them,' it said in Chapter One. But in the following section was written that it was not good for Adam to be alone, so Eve was created from his rib.

'What sense do you make from that?' asked Yeshua. I read the two chapters again.

'Adam had a wife, and then was alone, so Eve was created. It doesn't make sense at all, unless there was someone else before. Was there someone else?'

'Yes. Eve was his second wife. Lilith was the first.'

'But it doesn't say anything about Lilith.'

'No. The Torah doesn't say a lot of things. But it gives you all the clues, if you have eyes to see. If you want to know more about the ways of God you have to find the oral teaching —as you have done. As I want to teach all people to do. Lilith is only in the oral teaching.'

'So what happened?'

He told me that Lilith refused to bow to Adam to acknowledge his Divinity and power. She had thought nothing of her own power and wanted his as well.

I already knew the story of Lucifer, the most beautiful of all the angels, who refused to bow to Adam as the Lord's greatest creation. Lucifer in his pride preferred to break away from God and lead his own legions of fallen angels, rather than bow to the puny little man.

So woman had done the same.

I sat hunched, a sense of despair welling up within me. It was hopeless. How could I fight the story of Lilith?

Yeshua put his arm around me. 'Wait before you judge yourself,' he said. 'Remember that Lucifer, who became Satan, punished himself the most. He loved God and his pride turned his face away from Him for ever. Can you imagine the pain of that?'

I nodded. The Lord was still a mystery to me, but whether I understood Him or not, I would not have been without the knowledge I now had.

'Another thing to remember is that Satan still serves the Lord, even without wishing to,' said Yeshua.

I looked at him, my brow furrowed.

'No one comes to ABBA without their merit being tested. Everyone meets the tempter somewhere along the way. That's Satan's job. He tries to stop others reaching God because he is jealous of those on the path to the Divine. You cannot reach the Kingdom of God without Lucifer testing your courage, your will or your faith. He is essential. What are not necessary are the pain and grief and anger we go through when we meet him. But that is our responsibility. We know the ten commandments.'

'Sometimes it hurts to keep them,' I said. 'Telling the truth can get you into trouble. Standing on your own in a group that wants to go on a different route can cause you to be outcast, or even physically hurt.'

'Yes. I don't deny that. But it's God who matters, and if we follow His will everything else works out. Not necessarily immediately, but certainly in the long run.'

'Even if you die for it?'

'Even if you die for it.'

My brother and I looked long and hard at each other. His face had a deep serenity in it, which made it impossible for me to doubt him.

'I can see that for the person who dies, it is

simply going home to God,' I said. 'But how can others who love them see that? Surely it's too hard?'

'It's very hard,' said Yeshua. 'No one said it wasn't. But it gets simpler, the more you know about our Father in Heaven. If you can understand some of His ways it does become easier. If you don't know and trust Him, then it is almost impossible.'

We sat for a while, in silence. I knew he was right, but I did not know if I was strong enough to follow him.

'And Lilith?' I asked, knowing she was the Lucifer of women.

'She left Adam because he would not give her his power to add to her own,' said Yeshua. 'What she didn't realise was that if she had acknowledged Adam, he would have bowed to her in return to acknowledge her Divinity and her power, which were different from, but just as great, as his. Remember, I told you about that country of dark-skinned people to the east where I went to a year or so ago, where people worship male and female gods and have their images all over their temples?'

I nodded.

'Well, the people there always bow to strangers to acknowledge the Divinity within them. They treat you as a visiting deity. They do not wait to see if you will bow to them first. If Lilith had been less proud, she could have seen that whoever bowed first to acknowledge

170

God in the other, was the one who was the greater of the two. But she threw away her power.

'And then, later on, Eve was created from Adam's rib—not from the cosmic dust as he was. Lilith's action made woman lesser in the eyes of man. And that's the way it has been ever since.'

I sat, head bowed, filled with shame and anger. 'So any woman who searches for the true teaching is thought of as trying to steal Adam's power?'

'Yes. If they take it from men that is so. But the daughters of God have every right to the power that was first given to Lilith. Their own power, not Adam's. Your vision of the lightning flash was to show you that. God has always been willing to forgive woman for refusing to acknowledge her own power. Can you see, Deborah, how wonderful that is? And how important it is that you should learn about the Tree of Life and use it to teach this to others?'

'But I'm going to be called Lilith!'

'To start with, maybe. But you must use your knowledge as a woman not as a man. You must listen to God yourself and get the teaching of women for women. Look at Imma. She has always held true power and Divinity within our home. She has no feeling of being lesser than a man, so she is not. But she is the exception.'

171

He got up and began to walk around the little room, fired with enthusiasm.

'Many women steal power from the man in the home,' he said. 'They have no power in the outside world and the power within themselves has been suppressed for so many generations that they don't know what else to do to have any influence or effect in the world.

'They begin as mothers, by not teaching their sons how to take care of themselves, so they will be dependent on a woman for their food and clothing. They teach their daughters to do the same as they do. But if they knew how to take their own path to our Father, they would not need to be the tyrant in the home.'

'But they are loving parents!'

'Yes, and I am not blaming them. They are doing their best in a world that calls them inferior and their natural rhythms impure. So many women say they do not mind or feel the pain, and for some of them that may be true. But you know a person's true heart by the fruits that grow from them. Resentment and sickness are the fruits of not knowing or feeling your own powerfulness.

'Men are just the same. We are all playing a game of stealing power from each other. So much of what we call love is tainted with the need to control. It captures children instead of setting them free. It wants the children to grow up to be what the parents think they should be, not what God wants them to be—whole and beautiful beings in His image.'

'But, Yeshua, you and I are not married. We are not parents. How can we know what it is like to be in those positions? Who are we to judge?'

Yeshua smiled at me. 'Forgive me, Deborah,' he said. 'I had no intention to sound as if I were judging people. Please do not think I am doing so. I am looking with the discernment of the impartial observer. It is easy to see things from the outside. That's why I am unmarried and different. So that I can see with the clear eye of the stranger.'

'It won't make you very popular!'

He sighed. 'I know. But being popular isn't what I'm here for.'

I was about to ask what he meant, but he went on speaking:

'Now the world is changing and expanding. We can travel to places we never knew existed and talk to all kinds of people from all races of men. The Romans have done that for us— though I won't say that too loudly! The time has come for women to have true power and Divinity in the world. Men have been worshipping the masculine in God and so have women. That's out of balance. Here, the Essenes try to redress the balance and understand the feminine, which is why we pray both to the Heavenly Father and the Earthly Mother. But outside, in the average home— and remember, you and I did not come from an average home—there is no acknowledgement of the true female power at all. What we have to do is swing that balance back for everyone. God is far beyond sexuality, but to deny the feminine in Him is as bad as to deny the love within Him.'

'You truly think God has a feminine part to Him?'

'Of course. God is neither male nor female, but there are essences in God that are of both sexes. The feminine is the Shekhinah; the breath of God, the life-force if you like—the very essence of God in the world—nature, growth and decay, death and rebirth, these are all parts of the feminine. You've learnt that over the years, surely?'

'Yes, but it seems different here, as though we worship a different Lord.'

'Yes,' Yeshua looked serious. 'I know what you mean. And you have a point. It is harder outside our community. Worshipping God in a way that is unbalanced is not a true and inspiring faith. It's very easy for the men to disregard the women.

'I call God my Father; ABBA. I am a man. I relate to the male aspect of God but my wife is the Shekhinah, so I love and appreciate Her too. You are a woman. Can you not make IMMA the Divine name? Let the feminine come into you and teach you the God within yourself. Then you can take the masculine in God as your husband! Knowing this, you can teach men and women that you respect both the masculine and the feminine in God and in mankind. What a gift, Deborah! What a duty! What a joy!'

For a moment I was fired with his enthusiasm, but something else nagged at my mind.

'What happened to Lilith?' I asked, knowing I would rather not hear the answer.

Yeshua looked at me with love, and moved closer so that he could hold my face in his hands. 'There are many legends,' he said gently. 'But most of them have been created by man, not God. Lilith never ate from the Tree of Knowledge, so although she is human, she is not mortal. They say she married the King of the Demons. They say a thousand of her children die every night. They say she preys on the children of Eve. They say she does every wicked thing a woman could ever do.'

I took a deep breath. 'And could she have put the lightning flash into my head? Is what I know from the world of evil and not from good?'

'No, it cannot be. Lilith was never given the Book of Raziel. That was given only after the fall. It comes only from God.'

Then he held me as I began to weep.

'Deborah, do you trust me? Do you believe what I teach comes from God?'

How could I answer that? That he could doubt my faith in him!

I did not have to speak, for my face said it all.

'Then if you trust in me and in my Father in Heaven, and I trust in you, how can the knowledge you have be wrong?' he said. 'But I can't convince you, Deborah. Only God can do that. You must listen. Listen to Him yourself. I don't want you to believe me. I'm just a messenger. You can only believe for yourself.'

'But why me?' I burst out. 'Why me? Why have I got to stand up and be different? Why?'

Yeshua laughed. 'I know what that feels like!' he said. '"Why not?" is the answer. Why should it not be you?'

Suddenly there was nothing else to say. We sat in silence for a few moments, then Yeshua bid me good night affectionately and gave me his blessing.

After he left I must have put myself to bed, but I was barely conscious of my movements. My mind was overloaded with thoughts and feelings and I slept fitfully that night, afraid of the demoness; afraid of the Lord; afraid of myself.

*   *   *

Just before the dawn I got up and slipped into the work-room where Yeshua lay. I did not want to disturb him, but I hoped some of his faith and strength would linger in the air to give me peace.

176

He was fast asleep, spread across the mattress, looking young and vulnerable. Moonlight shone down across his body, dappling it with silver light.

But there was no moon that night. No stars, no light at all. Nothing but this strange, iridescent beam which turned my brother into unearthly spirit.

I wanted to be afraid. But here there was nothing to fear. Instead, I stood, quietly, watching and waiting.

'There should be angels here,' I whispered to myself. And words slid into my head: 'There are. Sit, Deborah, and listen.'

I never knew whether I slept and was dreaming, but in my dream the room was filled with forms of light, and a strange, strong song of silver and violet filled my body with the scent of wild sweetness and brightness.

I listened, and I heard who my brother was and what he was on earth to do.

I heard too what my own task was, and wept with repentance when I saw what I had done to women myself in past times when my soul was young.

'But I can't do it,' I said. 'It's too much. I'm not strong enough. I'm lame and imperfect.'

Then I was wrapped in light and comforted, but comforted with white fire, which would take no denial. It was made clear as icy water, clear as the brightest crystal, that there was no return.

The voices swelled, the scent and touch of silk and wildness became unbearable and the fire and ice expanded within me. For just one moment I felt the Glory of God within me—His daughter; *Her* daughter, daughter of The One.

When I woke, it was before dawn and Yeshua was staring down at me.

'Deborah! Did you fall? Are you all right?' He leant over to pull me up. As he lifted me the world tilted and I stood dizzily with all my perspectives wrong. The room looked different, something had happened.

Yeshua stood, calmly, looking at me.

'Well?' he said. 'And how is your leg?'

'Painful.' I was angry at such a mundane question when he must have known what I had been through.

'Try walking,' he suggested. I looked at him askance. Hope—unbelievable, but still hope—slipped into me and I stepped forwards. For the first time since I was four I walked equally on both legs. No swing, no groan from the hip, no drop onto the shorter leg, no twist in the foot. Not perfect. No, not perfect. Still painful; still weak; still unbalanced, but good enough. I cried out with delight, running my hands down my body and feeling the symmetry of the line where before there had been crookedness and strain. I was tall. I was straight. I burst into tears.

'Now don't let me hear you doubting the

Lord again,' said my brother cheerfully and, beginning to whistle, he set off for the morning prayer of the sunrise.

*   *   *

Three days later, I passed Judah as I walked, straight-backed, to the Mikvah. Everyone had been commenting on the miracle of my new posture and though it still hurt to use the muscles in a different way, I felt filled with life and song. Even with this man who had been my friend when I was a child, and who had judged me without thinking, I could no longer be afraid.

He had called me Lilith, and I remembered that Lilith had refused to use her own power or to bow to the Divinity in Adam.

'Good morning, Judah,' I said with a smile as he walked past without acknowledging my existence.

'The Lord be with you.' He turned back and looked at me and I bowed to him.

For a few seconds we both paused, our eyes linked by fire. I walked on, my cheeks burning and my back straight. I had stood in my power and not been shamed before him. I held my head even higher for the rest of the day.

The next afternoon, Judah walked past me again. He said not a word, but he stopped for a second, looked me in the eyes, and bowed to me before walking on.

179

Judah was a Pharisee, used to life in the town, and as he was only a visitor to the Essenes to decide whether he wanted to come and learn, and maybe take their path to God, he could spend as much of his time as he wished with the rest of us. His wife had died the previous year and his children were all grown and married and it was time for a new start.

When Yeshua told me he was coming to eat supper with us, I felt terrified again, but my brother was so enthusiastic about his visit I did not have the heart to wish him away.

Yeshua and I did not speak of the night of my miracle. There was no need. There had always been an unspoken bond between us and this was simply heightened. But Judah must have heard the talk that raced through our community and noticed my new straight posture. He was naturally curious.

He was courteous to me when he arrived but it was obvious that he wanted me out of the way so that he could talk to Yeshua alone about what had happened. He made one or two clumsy references to wanting to talk in depth, one to one, but my brother merely laughed and served him with more bread and vegetables.

'You want to talk about Deborah,' he said. 'What happened to Deborah is Deborah's business. You should ask her. Or are you afraid of a woman who understands the word of God?'

Judah stiffened at this direct challenge and that lock of hair, which used to attract the young Deborah so, fell forward into his eyes. He thought for a moment and took a mouthful of food. Then he obviously made a decision.

'Yes, I am afraid,' he said, looking at me. 'I have been taught that a woman's place is in the home, creating beauty and serving her husband. Not learning the Law or doing men's work.'

'I have no husband,' I said. 'And, apart from this place, I have no home. What would you have a childless and unmarried woman—made unwelcome in her own village—do with her life? I live with my brother who can take care of himself. I do the work I am fitted to do in the fields and the Mikvah. What would you have me do with the hours that another woman might give to her husband and children? What better can I do than learn to understand the Law and to serve the Lord?'

I spoke gently but firmly and looked Judah in the eyes. He stared back at me with anger, but I managed to smile and hold my hands as though offering him myself, to show I had no enmity. No need to fight or disagree. Inside, I wanted to fight, to spit angry words at him, and I was proud that I had the strength to respond and not react.

You could see how hard it was for him to accept me. A great struggle was going on behind those deep brown eyes.

After what seemed an age, he said, shakily, 'I don't like this, but I need to know more. Something strange is happening and I want to learn. I know I can be wrong.'

The three of us talked until the early hours. Yeshua and Judah grew heated at times and it was hard for me to hear Judah's prejudices and criticisms and his long-held views on how men should pray for women, and women should accept that they were unsuited for a life of worship.

Yeshua did not mention the lightning flash that had changed my life, but talked instead of compassion, of a time of change, of allowing the Spirit of God to come through in different ways; direct contact with God for everyone, instead of relying on priests or Levites or men to do it for us.

'What good is a Father you are too frightened to talk to?' he asked. 'God is love. God is justice. We need knowledge of God to come to wisdom and understanding.'

'But not for women!' said Judah.

'There is a new world coming,' said Yeshua sternly. 'Believe it. You will see it. This old, out-of-date creation will pass away and be replaced by new thought, new realisation. It is happening now. It may take thousands more years before men and women truly forgive each other but we will make a start. We three, together with others, will make a start. Now.'

At the end of the evening, Judah thanked me gravely for the hospitality and my company. 'I'm not convinced,' he said. 'But there is something about your brother which has such—would splendour be too strong a word?'

'No,' I said. 'It would do very well.'

*   *   *

Two days later, Joseph Barsabbas called me over and said that Judah had been asking questions about me.

'I have told him you were given the inner teaching by the Lord,' he said. 'He knew you had been taught by someone and he thought it must have been Yeshua. I thought it best to tell him the truth straight out.

'I also said that you carried out your work here faithfully and modestly without bragging about your knowledge. However, your secret is out now, Deborah, and you will have to handle any backlash there may be.

'You know, Yeshua and I are unusual. People don't like change—even the Essenes! —especially when it seems to go against the written teaching. They don't realise that the oral teaching is not written, for the simple reason that it needs to grow and adapt the written word to the world we live in.

'My advice to you is to keep your head low and continue just as you are. Don't get drawn into any arguments of right or wrong. If anyone asks you, just say you were taught by the Lord and get on with your work. They may not like it, but they can't argue with that.'

Dear Joseph Barsabbas. I did not appreciate then how great and kind he was. Or what a good friend. Perhaps he was sent by God to give us rest and calm in the beginning so that we could learn in peace. Without him, everything would have been so much harder.

He was right. Word spread like wildfire. Not only was I walking straight, but I knew the hidden teaching! Such a scandal would rock the most balanced of communities.

I felt like one of the strange animals sometimes brought into the Roman theatre in Jerusalem to entertain the crowds. It was hard to tell if it was my perception, expecting to be rejected, or whether people did begin to avoid me slightly and to look at me as if they had never seen anything like it before.

Dear, honest Judith came straight to the point: 'The men say you've found out the inner teaching,' she said. 'They're quite outraged of course. So am I really—surely that's only meant for them? Why do women need it? What do you want it for?'

'I don't know,' I said, lifting the pitcher of water and getting on with my work. 'All I know is that the knowledge was put into my head when I did the Sabbath blessing when I was fourteen. I didn't ask for it. I didn't know it existed. It wasn't my own choice.'

'Oh well,' said Judith sensibly. 'Least said, soonest mended. I've liked you for more than ten years now and if you've had the teaching all that time without even talking about it, there's no point in getting upset with you about it now, is there?' She picked up her own pitcher and followed me. After a couple of minutes of silence she gave a deep sigh.

'If you think it's appropriate, it might be nice to talk to you about it,' she said. 'I don't need to know of course, but, well, if the Lord gave it to you, perhaps other women could know a bit too? That is, if it's approved by Joseph Barsabbas.'

'No,' I said. 'Joseph has nothing to do with it. It's whether *you* want to learn, not whether a man is going to allow you to do so.'

'Phew!' Judith had to think about that one. 'You mean I shouldn't tell my husband?'

'No, of course not. The teaching is all about honesty and clarity. But I think the whole idea is for us to work out our own worship with it, not to steal any of the men's ideas or do what they do. It's to make faith more fulfilling for us—and for our daughters.'

'Is this what you've been teaching the children when you take them down to the fields once a week?'

'Not really. I teach them what Yeshua taught me when I was their age—to look for good in all things and to be true to themselves.

185

I suppose once you know about it, you always teach it, but most of us know about it instinctively anyway. It's generally just good sense.'

Dear Judith's honest face creased up with laughter at that. 'Yes!' she said. 'That's what we really need. Good, clear common sense. Good for you, Deborah. I'm with you on this.'

Before the week was out there were six women wanting 'just to have a little talk about things' with me and, despite all my confident words, I ran straight to Yeshua to ask him what I should do.

'You don't teach them the Tree of Life,' he said. 'Not yet. You just talk about what you know from your own life—about balance and strength. If they keep coming to listen to you and really, truly want to know more, then you may teach them, but the inner knowledge is never to be readily available. It has to be earned. It could be misused too easily.'

I was still too scared to hold a group—and afraid that some of the men might be angry. None of them had mentioned anything to me, but that did not mean anything.

'We'll hold a gathering for everyone on the hillside after the Shabbat morning service,' said Yeshua. 'Anyone from the rest of the village can come too, if they want to. I'll talk to them about the Kingdom of Heaven, just as I do anyway, and then we can divide up into men and women and all you have to do is try and answer any questions they have.'

'What if I don't know the answer?'

'You probably won't,' said Yeshua cheerfully. 'But God does. Let Him speak. Just offer him your faith and open your mouth. That's what I do and it works.'

The plan spread like wildfire but I was so frightened that I hardly slept the two nights before Shabbat. After the morning service, a group of thirty of us walked down to the far pasture and my stomach was a knot of nerves.

Most of the people were families intending to have a good time, but several of the more forbidding celibates had come along too, to see what we were up to. It was quite likely that they might complain about us afterwards.

Then Yeshua began to speak.

We listened spellbound as the sun rose and then dipped in the sky. He spoke of love and understanding. Of finding the beauty in ourselves and our lives. Of loving others and seeing the Divinity in them.

It was not just what he said. As we sat there, a kind of light came down over all of us, helping us feel what he was talking about, as well as hearing it. We felt like a family. God's family.

Yeshua spoke of the Kingdom of God, saying that it was time we moved on from our cosy aspects of worship to hearing God directly in our lives. Just listening to him, you knew it was possible; that the world was a place of hope and beauty.

Then one of the men spoke up.

'What about the Romans?' he asked. 'Don't tell me we are meant to love them and see the Divinity in them as well!'

Yeshua turned to him and it was not just my brother speaking, but someone far greater. Someone carrying the love of God within him.

'And why not?' he said. 'Do we affect them by our anger and resistance? No. Could we affect them by love and by setting an example to show them there is one true God? Yes, we could. Remember, anything outside of you that angers you is a part of you that is not acknowledged. We must find the invaders against the Truth in our own hearts and minds and then, perhaps, the Romans will leave of their own accord.'

The man made a gesture of disgust and walked away.

I held my breath. Two others hesitated, then followed him. The rest of us sat tight.

'Go on, Rabbi,' said Judah. 'I don't understand you, but I want to know more. Tell us.'

We finally broke up the meeting at dusk, and everyone trailed wearily but happily back to their houses for supper and to talk over the day. Yeshua and I embraced. I was so proud of him.

It was only as we ate our own meal that I realised I had not spoken at all—there had been no need, and for that I was very grateful.

*   *   *

My own work began after that magical afternoon. It started with answering the little everyday questions of my fellow women that followed on from Yeshua's teaching. Many of them came up to me for days afterwards and each one began, 'I know it's silly but . . .' and I knew they would never have dared to have asked a man what they wanted to know. I could help, and that felt like the greatest gift of all.

Judah, too, became steadily more supportive. He spent much of his time with us, and I grew to love him again for the kindness within him, which sat so uncomfortably with his fiery temper and his inbuilt beliefs.

He worked so hard and studied so fiercely that he almost wore Yeshua out with his questions and arguments. I would have to break them up in the early hours of the morning and suggest they rested so that they could begin another bout the next day!

But Yeshua thrived on this volatile friendship. 'Once Judah is your friend, he's a friend for life,' he said. 'It is wonderful to know someone I can trust to the end. And I will be able to trust him.'

I trusted Judah too, for all his explosions of indignation and temper. They only mirrored my own and I could sympathise with his struggles to get his fiery nature under control.

Sometimes he would touch me, very lightly, as he said goodbye and I would waste a little time wondering what might have happened if . . .

The thirst for knowledge grew in the outer group, but rumblings of dissent reached us from the inner core. Many of them were not pleased that some of the mystical teachings, which they had spent years trying to be worthy of, were going to be taught to all and sundry.

Joseph Barsabbas supported us wholeheartedly, but I think Yeshua and I both knew that our days with the Essenes were numbered.

To my surprise, I did not mind when Yeshua and Judah set out on a long journey together to the north. They planned to be gone for several months and to end up seeing John (now called The Baptist).

Although the wanderlust in me had often made me wish that I too could go on these journeys of exploration, I was so enjoying my life of discreet teaching—and the fellowship of the little group who wanted to know more of the truths Yeshua had taught me—that I was content to stay behind.

I knew that once the men had gone, the people would come more often to ask questions of the Rabbi's sister. It would be a challenge and an honour, and I was happy to meet it. With hindsight, I might have been enjoying it too much . . .

The questions brought to me were always simple matters about how to live a life of happiness and the answers came easily into my head. Before I knew it, a small group, mostly of women, set itself up, meeting weekly to talk over the things Yeshua had said. I was always the one appealed to for any meaning that was misunderstood. Slowly I began to teach them the very basics of the inner teaching and you could see their faces grow intent and bright as they began to understand the words they had been speaking by rote.

I loved the feeling of being someone they looked up to and could turn to with any problem. Perhaps my head began to swell.

It all ended one autumn afternoon when I was working with the older children, picking berries and talking with them about their lives and little troubles.

I must have been blind. I should have taken note of the rumbles behind the happiness surrounding me. I should have realised that teaching when Yeshua and Judah were not around to shield me was different from simply helping them. I should have noticed the groups of celibates growling in the background. I should have realised that some of the women were avoiding me. I was enveloped in my own little world.

The first I heard was a shout, and then pain

struck me in the back. One of the children gave a howl of fear and they all began to run. The stones pelted down and before I fell, dizzy with the shock and the pain, I saw, with anguish, that one of the children was hit too.

7

Three of us and the donkey set out on a bright clear morning as soon as the trumpets blew to open the gates of Jerusalem. We were travelling south and east to the Jordan, near Jericho, where we could wait for my brother and Judah to return from wherever they might be, and see John the Baptist preaching repentance and baptising all-comers.

Zoresh the donkey was very old by now, his muzzle and eyes brindled with grey. But he carried me willingly enough, and the others kept a watchful eye out for me in case I fainted from my injuries. The cuts and bruises were anointed with myrrh and firmly bound where necessary.

I felt battered and shaky, but the prospect of seeing both Yeshua and Judah again was enough to keep my head high—and the pain was no worse than I had been used to as a child. And this time it would heal again, so I had no reason to fear. Joseph Barsabbas had carried me back from the field where I lay unconscious, believing me to be past help. But Judith and Joanna, well versed in the healing arts, were able to revive me sufficiently with aloe and lavender to convince him that I might live.

They knew I could not stay with the group another day. Once such lack of control had been shown, any one of the people who supported me could be in danger. Judith and her husband Aaron arranged for me to be taken swiftly from the community to a place they knew in Jerusalem where no one would look for me. Joseph called a meeting of the Essenes to decide what was to be done and to discuss whether a group that could foster such lack of understanding and communication could continue to exist and call itself a community.

I had woken, slowly and painfully, in a dark, hot place filled with the scent of human sweat overlaid with perfume. A woman, veiled and with her hands covered with intricate tracings of henna, was bathing my face and neck.

'Be quiet!' she said firmly as I tried to speak. 'You are safe. You will live. No bones are broken. You don't need to know anything else.'

I kept mouthing words but she ignored me, muttering to herself in irritation as I winced at her ministrations.

'She will want to know what happened to the child,' said another voice behind her as a second woman, also veiled and hennaed, appeared like a shadow in the darkness, the sound of bangles and jewellery tinkling as she moved.

My eyes widened in the shock of realisation. I was in a brothel! I tried to sit up, exclaiming, but the first woman pushed me back roughly.

'Shut up, if you know what's good for you,' she said. 'You haven't been sold into slavery. You're not tarnished. You needn't judge us, just because you're so cursed holy. We're trying to help you. We're about the only people who will, so think yourself lucky. The child will be all right. It was just a glancing blow for him. You will take longer. Now lie still.'

'Thank you,' I murmured, my head spinning and allowed myself to fade away into half-consciousness.

It was seven days before I was well enough to stand up or walk. The women and their servant, Ruth, ministered to me as though I were a baby, feeding me bread and broth, taking care of my physical needs and telling me news of the outside world.

Ruth and the second woman, Sophia, were quite friendly but the one I had first seen remained aloof, veiling her face and answering questions without warmth.

I was acutely aware that both prostitutes were plying their trade in the upstairs room as I lay below. Embarrassment and misery were my bedmates throughout the day and evening, though I tried not to show it to the women and I tried even harder not to be angry at the destruction of yet another happy life. Plenty of heart-searching went on during those pain-filled days as I lay in the dim cavern. I knew I had been on the verge of becoming arrogant and thinking I was impervious to all harm because of my knowledge. I had almost begun to flaunt it and to think myself better than those who thought differently.

At last I was able to see that it was simply the end of yet another stage in my life. That perhaps I should have trusted myself enough to ask to go with my brother, instead of taking the coward's way out and staying behind, where I could become a big fish in a small pond.

I thanked God that I was alive and would recover—and that the child was not badly hurt—but it was harder to come to terms with where I had ended up.

Judith came on the third day. She had come before, but I was sleeping. As I looked up at her, the distaste for my situation must have shown in my face.

'I know,' she said. 'I know, my dear, but this was the safest place. It had to be somewhere where you could not be sought if you had been declared a witch—and that could easily have happened—and where the people would agree to care for you. Mary has long been known to me and has often talked of wanting to leave this work and start life again. She may seem brusque to you, but that's just her pride. She is terrified of you. She sees you as a celibate holy woman—everything she believes she is not. Her heart is good and perhaps, as she takes care of you, you can teach her by example that there is another way to live.'

'What kind of example am I?' I said bitterly, trying to raise myself on the pillows. 'Look at the mess I'm in now. It's not exactly inspirational, is it?'

'I think you should go to your brother,' said Judith diplomatically. 'Even if he had not gone north with Judah, he would not want to stay with a group who could do such a thing to one of its members.'

She sighed, and I wondered what was going on in the community I had so loved.

'I want to go home,' I said pathetically, feeling as though I were a child again and being torn away from Bethsaida.

'Well, you can't,' said Judith. 'Honestly, Deborah, we're doing our best.' Her dear, weather-worn face crinkled in distress.

'Oh, Judith, I'm sorry.' I took her hand. 'I know you love me and you've probably saved my life, but everything has fallen apart. Again! I don't know what to do or what to think. I should apologise to you for the mess everything is in.'

We hugged each other, rocking backwards

and forwards and crying a little. Her touch was painful but I wanted the comfort so much that I did not care.

'Who was it?' Judith asked. 'Who threw the first stone?'

'Don't you know? Has he not admitted it?' I was amazed.

'No one has said exactly who it was. There are about twenty who say they support what was done; that you were debasing the teaching and that it's heresy for women to have the inner wisdom.'

'But they say women are equals in the Essenes!'

'Equal on the outside with the married men, who are also not equal,' said Judith heavily. 'As long as we don't rock the boat and try to be really equal, they'll tolerate us. The group can't go on like this. It is already dividing up. Some of us will go to the area around Qumran, where families are still welcome. The celibates can look after themselves. If they want to become more ascetic and exclusive, they can. We don't want to, so it's up to us to leave. It's the only thing to do. About thirty of us are going. We don't know when yet. The others can have fun with their holiness while we get on with living. They may find it harder than they think.'

'Did I cause this? Oh God forgive me!' I hid my face in my hands and wept.

But Judith was made of sterner stuff. 'Pull

yourself together, Deborah!' she said firmly. 'You must not let it stop you from teaching. You must give women a chance to learn about the received wisdom. You must go with your brother and teach. You will have to take the greatest care, but it's what the Lord wants for you, without a doubt. I hear Jesus is back from the foreign lands and he's been baptised by John in the Jordan. Now they say he has gone into the desert to fast before beginning a new ministry to the people. He certainly won't be coming back to our community once he hears about what has happened. Something big is happening and this is all just a part of it. Who knows, we may all end up with Jesus. We may be going to start a new world.'

'Come with me then!' I begged her.

'No, for the children's sake I can't. Not yet,' she said. 'But who knows what will happen in the future? Your brother is a prophet, Deborah, have no doubt about that. He's an angel! But he needs strong people around him. Judah is there and other men will join him, both from our group and outside. Go too and represent the women. Please. For the sake of our children and our children's children, if not for us.'

She came again to visit me, twice, and each time her resolute character strengthened me. We shed bitter tears on parting the last time, not knowing if we would ever meet again.

*   *   *

On the twelfth day when I was up and testing out my battered body and limbs, Joseph Barsabbas arrived with Zoresh, the donkey. Mary had said I was strong enough to ride and Joseph had promised to escort me to the Jordan. There we would find a band of people already waiting for my brother's return. All this made me feel rather odd. I was too used to having Yeshua's company to myself to relish joining a group of people I did not know, who were hailing him as a prophet. But I had no choice.

To my surprise, Mary, for once bare-faced and with no covering on her hair, brought me fresh clothes for the journey.

'Are mine ruined by blood?' I asked, wincing a little as I turned my body and looked at the yellowed bruises and closing scars all over my flesh.

'No,' she said. 'They're in a bundle here, but you can't go dressed in the cream of the Essene women. You're in hiding, remember? You got stoned because you are a woman carrying knowledge, remember? Do you really think the rest of the world is any more tolerant?'

I had forgotten that our familiar robes were like a signal of light, saying who we were. In Jerusalem it did not matter, but Essene women rarely travelled further afield.

It was very strange to wear colours again, after so many years. And what colours! 'There's no need to turn your nose up at them,' Mary said as I looked, amazed at the way her finely woven cast-off greens and blues seemed almost to float on my arms and my breasts. 'They're perfectly respectable, even if they did belong to a whore.'

'I'm not turning my nose up!' I snapped back at her, sick of her continual defensiveness. But, before I could alienate her further, I remembered to step out of the moon's reaction and into the light of the sun, as Yeshua had taught me.

'Mary,' I said, touching her arm. 'I don't care if you're a whore or what you are. I have no judgement of you. Why should I have? You have protected me, housed me and clothed me, a complete stranger. I owe you my life. You also have grace and beauty, which I have not. Just remember that I have lived a long time without the colours you are familiar with, and it's all very strange to me.'

'You've never been a whore,' she said aggressively, taking no notice of the rest of my speech.

'No,' I admitted. 'Look at me.' I gestured at my long, scrawny body and her plump, soft one. 'How could I be? I haven't your beauty and I haven't your experience. I would be a terrible failure as a whore!'

She was shocked for a minute, but then she

burst out laughing, showing teeth as white and small as a child's.

'You'd be as bad a whore as I'd be a hopeless holy woman!' she said.

'Oh, I don't know!' I was so pleased she was beginning to thaw. 'I think it would be a lot easier for you to study the teaching than it would for me to learn your arts of love. At least I can sit quietly and pretend when I'm not managing to pray properly, and then only the Lord knows the difference. You can't do that!'

'You'd be surprised,' Mary said wryly, eyeing me through her long, black lashes. 'Maybe one day I'll tell you.'

We looked at each other as if for the first time. She was small with a rounded, luscious figure and dark hennaed hair in long, oiled ringlets. Her eyes were huge and outlined with dark pencil, dominating a smooth, oval face of clear olive skin. Mary was very, very beautiful. But she was older than I and the years were beginning to show.

'Come with me,' I said, on impulse. 'Come and find the one man who really will change your life. Who won't want you to be anything but what you truly are. Come and learn the teaching for yourself.'

'I couldn't!' She took a step back, aghast.

'Why not?'

'They tried to stone you! What would they do to me?'

201

'What are they doing to you now?'

She looked at me long and hard and I could see the battle going on in her breast. She had four or five more years of desirability when she would still be rich and sought-after. She might well have saved for a retirement of semi-respectability, perhaps in some distant city to which her notoriety had not spread.

'I'm offering you the Kingdom of Heaven,' I said, holding out my hand. 'It won't be easy. But the rewards are eternal.'

'Ah, but when do you get them?' she asked. 'When you die, so if they fail you can't complain?'

'No, now. Can't you feel it already? You don't have to be judged on what you do any more; you can be who you are. It's different.'

She stood there, irresolute, biting her lip.

'Well?' said Joseph Barsabbas, knocking on the door. 'Are you ready?'

I saw Mary quail at the thought of facing his opinion of her and made a quick decision.

'Yes, and Mary wants to come too,' I said. 'We are going to find Yeshua together. You don't have to come if you don't want to, Joseph. The two of us will be safe together.'

He smiled at me and then directly at Mary. 'Of course I'm coming,' he said. 'It's a new life for me as well. Hurry up. We haven't got all day.'

For a long moment Mary Magdalene hesitated. I held my breath—it had to be her own decision, not mine. Then she nodded. 'I'll be just a moment longer,' she said. 'I have to sort a couple of things out before I go.'

*   *   *

It was a strange feeling to leave Jerusalem amid the bustle of people queuing up for the gates to open. For so long I had been separate, and now I was going back into the world. Mary was stared at by several people who thought they knew her, and she drew her scarf around her head and hid her hennaed hands in the folds of her cloak. Joseph was still wearing the white of the community, but I could have been any Judaean woman, sitting on a donkey and being escorted by her sister and her brother.

Joseph was wearing sandals and had brought extra pairs for us. In the community we usually went barefoot.

'Judah made several pairs for anyone who needed to go on a long journey,' he said, noticing my look of surprise. 'I didn't think I'd ever wear them! It feels most strange.'

Mary had her own shoes, but they were delicate slippers and before we were many miles along the road, she had to admit that they were not helping her feet. She made a grimace of distaste when tying on the sandals, but once she realised that the leather was well tanned and supple and that it stopped the stony ground hurting her, she fell in love with them. She was like that; she would often refuse something automatically, then see its worth and change her mind. Then she would be as fierce with others who did not see her point of view as she had been with those who had suggested the innovation in the first place.

We exchanged life-stories as we made our way east. Joseph began by telling of his childhood in Alexandria. His mother, a Jew from Ramathaim, had married an Egyptian man, and he told us wonderful stories of the great city and how all the religions and races could live there in harmony.

'I was raised as a Jew,' he said, 'but I was taught to be tolerant of other religions. My father worshipped the one God as well, but in a very different way and he told me all the stories of the Egyptian gods he had been raised with. He had changed his religion when he married my mother but he still honoured Isis, Osiris, Horus and the rest.'

Then he entertained us with stories about the Egyptian deities. 'You can see that each one represents one part of the true God,' he said to me. 'If you look at the names of the aspects of the Lord on the Tree of Life, you can see that each of the Egyptian gods represents one of those.

'Once you know that, other religions are easier to understand.'

'You mean the Tree of Life works for all religions?' I was curious, and very happy that

Joseph was willing to talk with me of things that were known only to the inner circle.

'Of course,' he said. 'There are plenty of people in Alexandria who spend their lives looking at the roots of all religion. They are the same at the source, but are just looked at from what often seem to be very different directions.'

Joseph had joined a group of Essenes who lived on the fringes of Alexandria and had decided to move to Jerusalem when our community was set up and needed experienced men to help it grow.

Mary was half-intrigued and half-repulsed by our religious discussions. She desperately wanted to know what we were talking about but, as she admitted, she did not want to commit herself to anything that she would not like later on.

'I'm always changing my mind,' she said. 'One day I want to be holy and the next I want to be wicked. You can't do anything for that with your religion, can you?'

Joseph was very patient with her. 'It isn't really a religion,' he said. 'We are Jews, of course, but what we believe—and what Yeshua believes—is that there are many true ways to worship the Lord. We do think it makes life better to worship Him somehow, and perhaps if you did too, you might not change your mind so much!' Mary snorted rudely and made a face, but Joseph did not react. After a minute of glaring, her mouth curved into her ready smile, she tossed her head and forgave him. Life was far too much of an adventure to bother with small offences any longer.

Mary was born Miriam but, like many Jewish women, she preferred the Greek version of her name. Her father was a merchant in Magdala and her brothers and sisters had all married well. Mary's husband, however, had been a proud man who wanted heirs above anything else. When she had miscarried her third child after mourning two born alive, but who died within weeks of their birth, he divorced her and married a young widow, known for her fertility.

'My family was ashamed of me,' she said. 'An infertile woman is no woman at all. I was a disgrace to them.'

As she spoke I realised again how lucky I had been to be raised in a family who regarded me as a whole person no matter how crooked my body.

'They had no wish to take back such a failure, but they would have done if I had thrown myself on their mercy,' said Mary. 'I'm not going to tell you I took the only option I could that meant I wouldn't starve. I didn't. I took the option that left me some independence and which, if done well, could earn me a considerable amount of money, if not respect.'

She threw her head back as if waiting for

our judgement. Joseph and I remained unperturbed. Mary was always looking for offence to be taken, but we did not want to play that game.

'Most women would say they had no choice,' I said. 'I really admire you for knowing that you did.'

'Humph,' said Mary.

Life had become difficult for her in her home town when an increasingly large group of orthodox families began to take steps to stop her plying her trade.

'They were going to start stoning me pretty soon,' she said. 'They had already set fire to my home twice. So I moved to Jerusalem. There's plenty of willing trade in Jerusalem, for all it's so holy.'

There, she set up home with her servant, Ruth, and later another prostitute, Sophia, and became known as The Magdalene. There were many Marys and Miriams in the city and people could easily get confused. 'And in my trade, you can't afford that!' she said. 'Anyway, I think Magdalene is much prettier than just Mary. I expect Ruth and Sophia are glad to see the back of me,' she added, striding out in her unfeminine sandals and taking deep breaths of the fresh air. 'I was always far too picky for them. I used to refuse to sleep with a man if he didn't appeal to me. Some days we didn't eat when I was in a bad mood. But on others we had plenty of meat. If you are exclusive, you eventually become sought-after!'

We should have been shocked rigid by the stories with which she regaled us, but for all her bravado and prickliness, Mary Magdalene had such a good heart that no one could take seriously against her. We knew she had handed over the deeds of her home to the other women unconditionally, keeping only what money and clothes she thought the three of us would need. I don't think I could have been so brave or so generous. Her generosity along the way was just as heart-warming. 'I love money,' she said. 'It can do so much good—for me and for other people.'

Dear, celibate Joseph, who had lived a life mostly without money in the hallowed halls of the Essenes, took all this in good part. Many of the celibate Essenes thought that money was a wicked and evil thing and that we should do without it. Yeshua used to laugh at that. 'Money was invented to make things fair,' he said. 'If people choose to make it evil, it is not money's fault! You can make it holy just as easily. Then you can bring great good through it and, after all, bringing good is what we are here to do!' He also used to say that people who boasted of their poverty were just as arrogant as those who boasted of their wealth.

Joseph coped too with Magdalene's coarse tongue and her bawdy stories though he often blushed and took it upon himself to talk to other people along the road when she looked at us sideways, her generous mouth curved into a smile and began a sentence with 'There was this man from . . .'

I stayed and listened avidly, and laughed and was amazed. I had never shared secrets with a girlfriend because there had been nothing to tell, but Magdalene assumed I was celibate by choice and she said it would do me good to know a little about the ways of the world.

I found her fascinating. I was profoundly envious of her beauty and I believed that Yeshua and Judah would love her on sight, for her spirit as well as for the bright attractiveness that caught every male eye we passed. Part of me knew that would be hard for me, and a well of jealousy often threatened to open up beneath my feet. Looking at Magdalene, I could see that she eclipsed me in every way—and she would learn swiftly too, so not even my knowledge would be superior for long. I would have liked to have hated her in my own defence and, to my shame, I did allow myself to try, but she was too open and too captivating. Magdalene seemed prepared to love me from the moment we left Jerusalem and in the face of such affection, I could not long feel anything but friendship in return.

She respected my knowledge too, and often asked me to talk about God and the Kingdom of Heaven, so I was not even given a chance to dislike her for her arrogance.

I taught her about living in the light of the sun and not in the shadow of the moon, and she had fun working out which was which in her life. Most of it seemed to be reaction after reaction, but as she said, with wisdom far beyond what she had been taught, 'Maybe that's how it had to be then. I wasn't living the kind of life where anything else would have kept me alive.'

I had to admit she had a point.

'What about now?' I asked.

'Who knows?' she replied. 'I'll see when I meet this brother of yours. I may just turn round and go back.'

But we both knew that, whatever happened, she would not do that.

The game of finding good in all things was her favourite. It gave her a wonderful excuse for reliving the whole of her life out loud yet again. Some of her conclusions were so outrageous that Joseph and I choked. Then she would laugh at us and bounce ahead of us for a while to give us time to collect ourselves. We would watch her glowing with the joy of life itself, in her bright colours and veils, while Joseph, the donkey and I stepped carefully behind her.

*   *   *

After two days we reached the banks of the Jordan, where John was baptising. There must have been about forty people there in makeshift camps stretched along the waterside, and most of them were gathered in what shade there was from the fierce heat of the sun. They had come from all over Judaea—Jews who were sick of the routine of the ritual cleansing at Synagogue and Temple, where no prayers were said and no one really cared about anything except whether you followed the letter of the Law. When you were baptised by John you knew the meaning of ritual! You felt as though you had been turned inside out and could start anew. Little wonder he had become so popular.

John himself was an even more fearsome sight than I remembered, with his long, tangled hair and ever-open mouth bellowing, 'Repent, repent!' as he pushed yet another supplicant under the silver waters.

People hovered around him and his group of disciples as though they were a magnet, simultaneously attracting and repulsing people in waves.

Judah was there. I saw him sitting with a group of men just removed from the Baptist's disciples. His face lit up in surprise and pleasure as he saw Joseph and me and he came running along the edge of the water to greet us. I felt my heart jump and was glad to take his hands and feel his kiss on my cheek. 'Oh, Deborah!' he said in concern as he saw the bruises on my temples and arms and I gabbled out an explanation. 'We should never have left you. I should never have left you.'

I blushed and looked up into his deep brown eyes, loving their fierceness and sincerity and the laughter lines etched into the skin. His hair was beginning to turn grey.

He hugged Joseph like a long-lost brother and then we all turned to Magdalene, standing rather stiffly behind us, holding the donkey. We introduced her simply as a friend from Jerusalem who had saved my life and who had come to join Yeshua with us.

Judah greeted her courteously and thanked her on both his and Yeshua's behalf for taking care of me. He could be excused for turning back to me immediately to exclaim at what had happened and ask for the full story, and I was woman enough to be glad that his eye was not caught by her beauty. The next time he looked at Magdalene, it was with a slightly suspicious look and she was well aware of it. You could tell she thought he had recognised her, but it could just as easily have been his old antagonism towards women followers of the teaching.

I thought, wryly, that yet again I had challenged men's belief in what was right. Most Pharisees—and that's what Judah was raised to be—would never consort with a prostitute. Then I laughed a little to myself. They might not consort in public, but the women's clients had to come from somewhere.

Perhaps the men we met would be more afraid that Magdalene might recognise them than concerned with judging her.

Even in that bunch of people wishing to repent and renew themselves, Magdalene drew nearly every eye. She veiled herself as soon as she realised what an effect she was having but her inner grace would have shown through the thickest cloak.

The effect of the henna on her hands and feet was lessened by the violent orange colouring that she had insisted on painting all over Joseph's feet, and my own too, as we set off on our journey. 'It keeps you cooler,' she explained to Judah and the others, when she saw how startled they were—and she was right. Once the initial heat of the plant's application in hot water had worn off, the scorching of the sun on the tops of our feet had been greatly eased. We all made a joke of it and Judah asked if she had any more, in case Yeshua wanted some when he returned from the desert.

She blushed and said she did, and I was grateful to him for his courtesy.

'Why do you wear it on your hands?' I asked as the men walked ahead of us, talking about old times. She looked at me sideways. 'So it feels as though you are not really touching them with your skin,' she said quietly.

For the first time I could see the harsher truth behind Magdalene's brash talk and jokes.

Virgin though I was, I thought I could understand what she was telling me and we shared a look of friendship.

We stayed by the Jordan for three days and each one of us was baptised by John. When he first saw me, he roared at me in recognition of the little cousin he had seen so many years before and we exchanged a few pieces of family news, but that unnerved me more than if we had never previously met. It took me two days to approach him again, but he gave me a crooked smile of greeting before shouting at me to repent and pushing me vigorously under the water. Not for John the niceties of wondering whether a woman were fit to touch. If she asked to be baptised, then baptised she was. Male and female were all scum of the earth to him, unless we were willing to repent!

I thought it might feel a little like that first time when Imma had taken me down with her into the Mikvah at the Temple, but it was very different. There was certainly a feeling of power and of shifting reality, and I opened my eyes under the water and saw the cloudy silver and gold of the light above filtering down. This was baptism by water, not light as Imma had given me. It was strong and cleansing but not sublime.

Afterwards, I found myself a quiet place to wring out my hair and brush the water from my shift. The other women gathered together in camaraderie, but I wanted to be alone to savour the experience, and to think about repentance.

'To repent, of course, simply means to think again,' said a quiet voice behind me, as I began sectioning my hair to plait it.

I turned in delight.

'Repenting can be fun. It doesn't always have to be full of regrets,' said my brother, smiling at me. 'I've been doing a lot of repenting these past few weeks. How about you?'

With a yelp of joy, I threw myself into his arms and we hugged each other tightly. All my cuts and bruises shrieked, but I ignored them, the joy making nothing of the pain. When we let go, to take a good look at each other, we laughed at how disreputable we were. I was still damp, with my hair cascading everywhere. He was filthy, bone-thin and brown as a berry, with clothes that were a disgrace. But through that you could see there was something new and strong about him. Something even more powerful and brighter than before. Whatever it was, he was still my beloved Yeshua and I was his beloved disciple.

We walked down to the others together, hand in hand. I think my face must have been split in half with the broadness of my smile. Judah's face too lit up at the sight of his friend but then he looked at me and his expression froze. Shot through by a bolt of lightning, I realised that my hair was still tumbling like a wild woman's all over my shoulders and breast. Hastily and clumsily, I began to gather it up and plait it, and fell back to recover my modesty as Yeshua went on to greet his friends and disciples.

He spent a couple of days talking with John and teaching some of those who had gathered to see him. Many said they had seen the Spirit of the Lord descend onto Yeshua when John baptised him, and John had told them it was Yeshua who should be the teacher and he the pupil.

'John baptises with water,' said Yeshua, when this was related to him. 'I shall baptise with fire.'

He spent time with Judah and with Joseph alone, that first week, and both of them seemed to change in stature. Judah aged with a kind of responsibility, but Joseph became younger.

Yeshua had looked on Magdalene with love from the first moment he met her, but he did not call her to him, instead waiting as if she were a frightened deer. Nervously she inched a little closer to him at each meal time until, at last, after several days, she found herself sitting at his bare feet. Yeshua smiled at her and she dared to ask him if he would like her to use the last of her henna to cool them.

He thanked her and watched carefully as she heated the herbs in water and ground them into paste before washing the dust from his feet and applying them with love.

When it was finished, she looked up at him and he laid one hand on her head. I can't say she was never impatient or awkward again, but beautiful, proud Magdalene became an easier woman to be with and one more at peace with herself.

Of course, Yeshua saw only good in the reason I had to leave the Essenes.

'It was terrifying. It hurt!' I said indignantly, wanting his sympathy, but there was a new, harder edge to my brother, which would not allow such diversions as self-pity.

'You must have drawn the experience to you,' he said and I hung my head, acknowledging that fact. 'What's more important is whether you have forgiven the man who did it and those who condoned it,' he said. 'Have you?'

I had not thought about it. Too much had happened. 'Pray for them,' instructed my brother. 'Then you will know.' Then he relented a little at my outraged face and took my hand. 'Deborah, we have a lot of hard work ahead of us,' he said. 'We won't have the space in our hearts to hold onto past hurts.'

I looked at him and it felt as though his touch was full of light. 'I forgive them,' I said and somehow it was true.

They said later that he did the first miracle at the wedding in Cana, but there were others before that which were not spoken of, because they were inner miracles and we did not wish to talk of them to others.

Just as he took my hand that day and I spoke of forgiveness, not only did the lingering aches and pains from being stoned fade away, but my still-weakened hip strengthened yet again and heat shot from my head to my toes. Others too seemed revitalised after spending time with Yeshua, as though a light shone through his presence.

We travelled north together, Yeshua, Judah, Joseph, Magdalene and I, and I was always grateful for that time. Several of John's disciples had decided to follow Yeshua (with John's full approval) and we were to meet up with them again after visiting Cana for James's daughter's wedding. So many other people too were to come into our life that it would have been even more difficult to handle, without that quiet time of travelling and talking to each other about what we had learnt since we were apart.

One night, I noticed that Zoresh the donkey was stumbling; looking older and more tired than usual. We camped early and I gathered him some fresh grass and brought him water in my hands, but he would not eat or drink.

My heart sank and I excused myself from the others' company to sit with him in case the end was near.

In the heart of the night, Zoresh lay down, and I was strong enough to lift his head and place it in my lap so that I could stroke his dear, silky ears and whisper words of love as I felt his strength ebb away. He whickered gently and nibbled at my sleeve, as he had always done since I was a child.

He had been sent by the Lord to carry me for as long as there was need and, now that I was whole, he could go home and rest.

At sunrise Judah found me, weeping, bent over his dear grey body.

'What shall I do without him?' I asked. 'He's been the only thing I had who was always there. I shall miss him so much.'

Judah lifted me and held me in his arms. 'You have me now,' he said. 'If you need to be carried I will carry you. But you don't need to be carried. You need someone to stand by your side. Marry me, Deborah.'

'But what about children? I can't have children,' I said stupidly, my eyes blurred with tears and my heart pounding with shock.

'I've got quite enough children!' he said. 'Four of them will be meeting us in Cana. And we don't need children if we are following Yeshua, do we? If the Lord sees fit to give us any, so be it, but I don't think that's anything to worry about, do you?'

He smiled down at me and touched my tears with one finger. 'I think there have been enough of these,' he said. 'You have spent long enough as the overlooked one and the weakened one. You're a woman, Deborah, and

219

you are ready to take up that challenge. I would like to be the one who stands by you as you do it, if you will have me. Let's look forward now and see where the Lord wishes to take us.'

As he spoke, the sun slid between the early morning clouds and showed, far below us, the glittering waters of my beloved Sea of Galilee. I had not seen her since the day I left Bethsaida more than twenty years before and the perfection of the moment was sealed. My heart and throat felt so full I could not speak, so Judah and I just held each other, looking down at the bright, silvery sea and thanking God for this sight, for the morning, and for each other.

*   *   *

It was wonderful to see Imma, James and Salome, and all the cousins and children again as soon as we arrived, footsore and thirsty, at bustling and festive Cana. Rebekah, the bride, was James's second daughter and Jonah, her husband, a distant cousin of both ours and Judah's. James looked tall and distinguished in his best clothes and greeted us in a way so similar to Abba's that it brought tears to my eyes.

We had no smart clothes so we stuck out like a sore thumb amid all the wedding finery, but Jonah's family was more than hospitable and did everything possible to deck us out as best they could. Joseph and Judah took their cue from Yeshua: if he wanted to be ascetic and refuse finery, they would too. But my brother was always happy to receive love as well as give it and that included a willingness to wear the bright and beautiful colours offered to him in honour of the wedding celebrations.

'God created colour and festivals and beauty,' he said. 'I honour all those from the bottom of my heart.'

Judah and I had spoken to him about our decision before we told Imma and the others. His dear face lit up with joy and he gladly offered to officiate when Judah spoke his vow to me in the name of God.

Imma, too, was delighted. She told Judah sternly to be a good husband to me, but I could see that she liked him immensely. The mother in her was happy to see another daughter safely married and she introduced me to those I had never met with an extra pride, which I had not felt in her before.

Judah's family was polite but reserved—but that was all I could expect. The last they knew, their father had left to embrace a celibate lifestyle with the Essenes. To have him arrive back with an unknown woman who seemed to be a female Essene struck them as a little odd, to say the least, and it would take some getting used to. I thought we would probably have little to do with them anyway and I was too happy to worry about whatever concerns they might have about our marriage.

We did not encroach on the young couple's wedding, but held a quiet service of our own as everyone else was ending the three-day feast. Because Judah was a widower and I was past the age of being a blushing bride, no one thought it odd that we had waived the traditional year of betrothal. Judah had a perfectly serviceable copper ring that he could give me—and it was enough. Together with Yeshua we had worked out words we wanted to say to each other before the wedding to mark our union. There was a deep feeling of peace in my heart as we stood under the bridal canopy and Yeshua blessed us and prayed for our happiness. However, there was a surprise for me as soon as the ceremony was over. Somehow, my dear husband had found time to get me a bride-present to make up for the lack of a betrothal gift. As we were just about to sit down and eat, he made me close my eyes and wait as he went to fetch the surprise. I fidgeted, excited as a child. Then there was a gasp of delight from Imma and Magdalene and, in my cupped hands, Judah placed something small and rough. I looked down at a carrot, but the baby donkey's nose got there before I could react. The tiny creature gobbled up the treat and shook its head up and down, as I laughed out loud with delight.

'I thought *you* were going to take care of me!' I said.

'Well,' Judah looked sheepish. 'I just wanted you to have her. Just in case.'

And the lightning hit me again.

For a second, the world spun around me and in a flash of knowledge I understood that there would not be many years when Judah could take care of me. The road ahead would be lonely. And it would not just be Judah that I would lose.

I must have swayed and fallen, because anxious hands helped me to sit on the beautiful coloured cushions. I looked across at Yeshua, in confusion, and saw that he already knew.

8

They ran to fetch me wine, but there was none left. Rebekah and Jonah's wedding was nearly over and there had been many more guests than expected, including ourselves.

It was Imma who asked Yeshua to help, asking an impossibility as though it were as simple as day. I protested that I was fine and that water would do, but she and my new husband were all concern and prepared to be angry with the wedding hosts if I could not have the best.

No one knew what Imma was talking about when she sent the men to fill the wine skins with water, and she was obeyed only with great reluctance. Even those in our little family group thought she was being stupid and were embarrassed to be the cause of such a scene.

I watched from what seemed to be a different place. I was there and conscious, but not a part of that world. It was as though yet another layer of darkness had been lifted from my eyes and I could see as clearly as Imma could that, should he wish to, my brother had the knowledge and the power to change the laws of the physical world at will. I could also see that he was reluctant to do so—he wanted only to work for God, not to please mankind. But he honoured his mother, and listened to her, and he knew my need. For a moment he sat asking within himself whether such a miracle would be appropriate but before he had even finished talking with the Lord one of the men came back into the room with the skins and poured the liquid within them into our cups. It was red as rubies, fragrant as sunshine on autumn berries and it shone in the candlelight as though it were alive.

I burst into fresh tears, but these were tears of joy, that I had seen this manifestation of Yeshua's power and that it had been done for his mother and for me.

Until then, everything we had been a part of could have had a simple explanation.

Everything he had taught us could have been a comfortable illusion. Now we had to look again at this man who could move between the worlds at will and understand that he carried the power of God.

When James and some of his friends outside our immediate circle saw and tasted the wine, they were shaken to the core. James had to face the congratulations of the rest of the guests, who seized the chance to celebrate anew. He had no choice but to accept their compliments but, in his confusion, he avoided us for the rest of the celebrations. It was understandable.

For one moment, at the end of that long, long day, as the men still danced and the women began the long process of clearing up, Yeshua stood alone by my side. We looked at each other and I found there was no need to speak.

He knew, with a deep inner sadness mixed with an even deeper joy, that he was going to die—and how. Even before I formed the question in my head, I knew that he had always known, even Judah's part, which was integral to the whole.

'But why him?' I asked out loud, feeling my own grief over the strange calm that had descended on me since the miracle.

'I won't be able to trust the others,' he said. 'Those who are here already or those who are to come. Dear men and women all, and each one with his or her own great destiny, but the one who should deliver me to the glory that will come will not have the courage to do it. So, it must be Judah. And if not him, Deborah, it must be you.'

He left me, shaken to the core, needing time alone, which would be almost impossible to find on my wedding night.

I slipped away to the stable, where I could hide for a while and hold onto the little donkey with its soft coat and questing lips.

Yeshua had spoken to us before of destiny —not fate, which affected only ourselves, but destiny—our tasks which would affect the whole world. He told us how, when something had to be done, three people were lined up by the angels so that there would be no mistake. Should the first fail or back out, the second would be brought in. And if he or she also refused, then the third was prepared.

On one level, I could accept that he had to die. He had told us enough of the unreality of death—that it only meant the sloughing-off of the coat of skin and the physical world, so that we could see the worlds of Spirit and of God more clearly. It seemed only logical that he should demonstrate the glory of eternal life by showing people the way to God and that there was nothing to fear. Mentally, I could accept that; emotionally, the thought of losing him, and the pain it might involve for everyone, was quite a different prospect. A simple, peaceful death with his Spirit being lifted by the angels before our eyes was perhaps bearable and right. My ego could cope with that elevation to the higher light. But it might not be like that . . .

It would not be long before we would be followed by spies from the Sanhedrin, the priests of Jerusalem, looking out suspiciously at this new prophet in case he caused trouble. It was known that those who threatened the established order tended to vanish, or be handed over to the Romans on a trumped-up charge for execution. Once they knew the extent of Yeshua's miracles, and that he intended to teach their inner knowledge to workmen and to women . . . I shuddered.

'But you could save him!' I pleaded with the Lord. 'You are all powerful. Why must he die?'

It seemed as though a light shone around me in that tiny stable and, looking up, I thought I saw a star above. An answer, in pictures, made itself inside my head, showing me thousands of years, or more, in the Pargod—the heavenly image of all that was and all that would be—looking like a tapestry of threads all woven together; each one making the rest of the picture strong. Every thread showed a life and every life was relevant, making its own contribution down the ages. New threads came in, casting their weave over a hundred generations, and old ones went out, having fulfilled their purpose.

In the centre of the Pargod were those who had carried the mantle of the Messiah and, where I stood, there was a gap, filled with light for the time that was now. I saw the plan of his life and of the future, and the absolute necessity for his death to be public, planned, shown to be the miracle it was, in the midst of so many other miracles. I saw Judah's life and mine—but only to the point where Yeshua died, because there, the whole structure of the tapestry seemed to offer choices for us. Either to remain the same and learn nothing, or to live with a knowledge that death could be overcome. I saw that when all the Four Worlds met up in one supreme sacrifice, everything was possible. From that moment on, the tapestry would have a million possibilities as everyone throughout the lands, whether Jew or Gentile, would have the opportunity to see the truth for themselves. And I saw how difficult that choice would be.

*   *   *

Then it was gone, and I was alone in the cool, dark air and my husband was calling my name.

It was a strange marriage by most standards, but I had nothing to compare it with, so I was satisfied. I was not the kind to worry that Judah and I would have no settled home but would spend most of our time on the road or staying with friends and relatives. I had no expectation of children so there was no need to find myself a nest, and, as Yeshua, Joseph and Magdalene stayed in Cana for a short while after the wedding, I had their company to help me feel that things were not so different after all. Judah's eldest daughter Dinah and her husband lived in the home that had belonged to Judah and his first wife and we built a little room there which had a partitioning curtain, its own hearth and a lean-to attached for the donkey. For a while it was fun to live there, playing house and getting to know my step-children and their sons and daughters, but it was not long before I was impatient to be back on the road again. I knew the time with Yeshua would be short and I wanted to be with him and to learn as much as I could. Strangely, once the initial shock was over, the knowledge did not upset me—it was as though that part of my soul was protected and cocooned so that I could go on living normally. I spoke of it to no one, though I knew that one day Judah and I would have no secrets.

It was hard to be a wife. I was not young enough to adapt easily to everything that was new and I was so grateful for Magdalene's earthy wisdom and advice about many things. Judah was always kind and loving—though he could be very firm at times—and I felt a strange loss of freedom and innocence as my body adapted to the physical pleasures of marriage. I knew now why Yeshua was celibate. Part of you merges with the other when you lie together and live together, and there are subtle changes that make it more difficult to be truly yourself. I had to remind myself constantly that I was Deborah, and not just Judah's wife. I did not always manage that very well.

Yeshua always gave us space to be together when we needed it and he enjoyed being with us when we did not. He said it would be very useful to have a married couple with our group, as we could counsel others where he could only teach. We always had our own hearth, even when we were travelling, and Yeshua enjoyed sitting with us to get away from the almost constant bickering of the other disciples as to who should have the honour of sitting next to him. With us, he could lapse back into the old days, when we had sat in our tiny home near Jerusalem and debated philosophy without anyone expecting any more of us.

Judah and I stayed in Cana for two months. Joseph Barsabbas too stayed in the little town, where he had a sister and nephews and nieces. Yeshua left us after two weeks when John's disciples came to join him. Together with them, and Magdalene, he travelled east to the coast of the Sea of Galilee. It was hard to be left behind, even if I did have a new life to get used to. I so wanted to see the beautiful waters of my lake again and to feel the wind on my face. I was grateful for Joseph's nearness as well as Judah's, and the three of us spent many pleasant evenings together discussing the knowledge we had, as well as everyday things and the news that traders brought to the town.

When Yeshua sent for us, I was packed and ready within minutes. My comfortable home and the simple pleasures of married life in a community were suddenly as nothing compared with the prospect of being with Yeshua again and learning more about the secrets of eternal life.

I know many others will chronicle the events of the next months and years as we travelled north, south, east and west, teaching everyone who wished to hear us. It would be easy to concentrate on the disbelief, and the questions and confusions within our families and our group as they realised what was happening and who Yeshua was—but it would serve no purpose.

It would be easy, too, to talk of the squabbles and irritations between those who wanted to follow Yeshua for the miracles and to serve their own ego, and those who simply wanted to help him teach the inner wisdom to all who were willing to hear.

The fishermen who joined us soon after our wedding were gruff and simple men and Simeon and Judah never really got on. How could they? One was a highly educated son of a prosperous Pharisee and the other a salt-of-the-earth type, who acted before he thought and had many ingrained opinions that he found hard to change. When Yeshua renamed Simeon Cephas, the Rock (which the Greek speakers translated into Peter), Judah was hard-pressed not to take umbrage. After all, he had more knowledge than Cephas then and a better way of teaching others.

Later, when Judah was thinking more clearly, he saw that we needed people like Cephas to talk in the language that the common people could understand. Once they had grasped his points, it was easier to hear of the other worlds of which Yeshua taught from someone rough-and-ready, who understood the harsh lives that many of them lived.

Attitudes towards Magdalene and me and later on, towards Imma, Susannah, Joanna, Mary, Martha and the other women, were interesting to say the least. Yeshua never treated us as being lesser than the men. He taught us all equally and often, as he explained the Tree of Life and the lightning flash to his twelve chosen men and his seven chosen women, he would often ask me to expand on a point or to put it from the feminine point of view.

Of course, as we taught others, we were often divided by our sex. It was bound to happen in Jewish lands—no one would come to us if we openly broke all the rules. Yeshua taught wherever we went but sometimes, in the

Synagogues or after he had spoken to the multitudes, we would break up into groups and those who genuinely wanted to know more would come up to us and ask questions. Women could not go up to the men to ask about matters of a personal nature, so they came to Magdalene and me.

We heard terrible and sad stories. Sometimes we could deal with them and at other times Magdalene would go and fetch Yeshua to lay his healing hands on the poor woman's head to ease the pain of her dreadful life and speak words of inspiration to her.

It was for these women and for Magdalene, divorced for her infertility, that he became stern in his teaching on marriage. 'One day,' he said, 'women will no longer feel that they are at a disadvantage. One day they will stand in their own strength, choose their own mate and marry in the love of God. Now, the woman is discarded if she does not fill the role she is contracted to play. She can make a choice not to marry—we always have choice in everything we do—but she does not realise that. The alternatives too are very hard.

'Most marriages are no marriage at all, just convenient arrangements to serve people's pockets or their lusts. In Moses's day, a woman who was divorced could find another mate. Now that is not so and she may fall by the wayside.

'Marriage is meant to be a sacred contract

of honour between two people, contracted as a partnership to serve God. If it is not that, it is simply an agreement of cohabitation, not a marriage.'

He was openly laughed at for that statement, and some of the listeners jeered at him. 'How can you know?' they cat-called. 'You're not a real man! You've never even had a woman,' (though others were even coarser about what they thought he and Magdalene were to each other).

Most of the disciples too were displeased and had plenty to say about women who ruled the home and made life hell for their husbands. Yeshua just said, as he always did, 'That was in the old world. We are trying to help both men and women see that the old ways do not work and that God's way does. Those who follow the Way, whether they are men or women, will not rule others through unkindness or misused power, but will lead them through love.'

Cephas, John, Andrew, Nathaniel and later Matthias were not at all fond of having women travelling with their teacher. They had left their own wives at home—cared for by their grown-up children and not in lack, except for their husbands' company—but they had received many stinging reprimands for their chosen lifestyle. They would try and keep us in our place by talking loudly over our remarks, and Cephas openly yawned and went to sleep one evening when Yeshua had asked me to lead the group.

It came to a head in Jerusalem. It was the time of menses for Magdalene and me and, as was the custom in the city, we walked in the centre of the street with the sick and lame and others who were ritually impure, while the men walked at the sides. Cephas started to grumble at Yeshua.

'What are we doing with these women?' he asked. 'I cannot believe the teaching should go to creatures who are weak and impure by means of their bodies. Look at them. They are walking in the middle of the road with the sick. Who are they to hear the word of God?'

Yeshua opened his mouth to admonish Cephas, but Judah beat him to it.

'I'd rather walk with the ritually impure than with someone whose mouth is foul with judgement,' he said and stepped down into the road with us. He reached out and touched us both, so rendering himself impure by the contact. For a second I shuddered, remembering little Abigail, but that was just the old fear, which did not understand the new ways. Instead I made myself hold my head high and accept his hand.

Cephas made a sound of disgust and turned his head away.

'Judah, you are acting from another kind of pride,' said Yeshua kindly. 'But you are right, for all that. After all, it is the sick and the needy that I am here to help. I too should not be making divisions by walking by the side of the street.'

Saying that, he stepped into the road, put his arm around Magdelene and walked on without another word to the other disciples. Joseph Barsabbas followed him immediately.

I can imagine the irritation and grumbling that went on behind us, but after a minute or two they were all, but three, walking in the centre of the road with us.

That night, on the Mount of Olives, Yeshua talked of purity. 'You can bathe a hundred times, but if your heart is still full of spite or judgement or unforgiveness, you have only cleansed your body,' he said. 'The Kingdom of Heaven is the place where we have mastered the physical world. Ritual cleansing is all very well, but it is in here,' he pointed to his heart, 'that the path to spiritual cleansing begins. It's about looking up to God, not looking down in judgement. When you get to the Kingdom of God you have transcended the rituals of the flesh.'

Cephas seemed to want to avoid me that evening, but I knew it was important to clear any atmosphere between us. I went and sat with him at supper and offered to serve him. Yeshua often said, 'The last shall be first and the first shall be last', to teach us that humbling ourselves before another was a way of honouring the Divinity in all things. When

236

we did that, he said, most quarrels would be resolved and we would know the meaning of the Kingdom of God.

Cephas did not like this kind of teaching, though his love for Yeshua was so great that he would have followed him anywhere. His good-natured, honest heart struggled with the new knowledge over the conditioning of a lifetime. He was not a young man and he felt rough-and-ready beside learned people like Judah and Nathaniel. The sea was his trade and he was never really happy far from his beloved Sea of Galilee.

He lived in Kfar-Nahum, but came from Bethsaida. I wondered if he had ever known my blood-father and started asking him questions of the fishermen he had known.

As we talked, his face brightened. He described the old harbour so well that I could almost see it. When I mentioned my father's name, his eyes lit up in recognition.

'Yes, I do remember him. He was a fine sailor. I was sorry to hear of his death. So you are his daughter? Well, I never . . . So you are the child of that . . .' Then he stopped.

'That what?' I asked nervously.

'Well, you know what came of your mother, surely?'

'No, I was never told.'

Whatever happened between us later, I will always remember Cephas's kindness then. He had the opportunity to tell me harshly, as a punishment for my womanhood, that my mother became a whore and died. He did tell me, but with such gentleness that I could bear the pain.

'Your mother went out of her mind with the grief,' he said. 'She didn't know what she was doing. She thought she could earn her passage —and yours—back to Petra by dancing for the travelling men at the inn at the top of the town.'

I remembered the place vaguely. Merchants came and went and I suppose it had its trade of prostitutes and dancers.

'One man took a fancy to her and maybe he offered her a lot of money,' said Cephas, putting his rough, great hand over mine. 'She was found, dead, in the morning, in his room.'

'He killed her?'

'No one knows that. There are some substances some of these men take for pleasure, which can kill someone who has never tried them. I think it would have been that,' he said, nodding his head. 'He would have given it to her before she went upstairs with him. She wouldn't have known what she was doing. I did know her. She was a fine woman. She would not have debased herself willingly.'

He patted me on the back, clumsily, in just the way Abba used to do.

'So many deaths,' I said wearily. 'So much unhappiness.'

238

'Aye,' said Cephas. 'And it's up to us to give the folk some hope.'

I tossed and turned under the starlight that night, and as soon as I could, told Yeshua what Cephas had said.

'Is she damned for what she did?' I asked bluntly. 'You teach us the rewards of eternal life. What about those who make such dreadful mistakes. Those who fail?'

'No one fails in the end,' he said, gently. 'Some take a hundred thousand years to learn and many of the lessons are bitter. In the end we will all have learnt; in the end we will all be at the place of the Messiah.'

He reminded me of God's wish to behold God; why he created mankind. So that when every one of us had become perfect, we would each be one tiny particle in the perfected human being—capable of beholding God.

'Pray for your mother,' said Yeshua. 'Those who are resting between the great lessons of life can hear us, and all ill will or pain between us can still be solved. Everything is possible with God.'

I did pray for her, but I struggled for many weeks that followed with the anger and despair at her abandonment, which had been locked inside me for so long. Many was the night I was sleepless, boiling with a little girl's grief and fury, and I knew that I had much to learn before I could call myself a disciple.

Yeshua saw my struggles and was gentler

with me than usual. He spared me some of my duties of helping the people that he healed and spoke to, and sent me off alone to think and meditate. Sometimes, when it got too much in the night, I would go and lie at his feet and draw a little courage from him. Once, he awoke and placed his hand on my head. 'Let it be,' he said. 'All is well.' And I was able to creep back to Judah's bed feeling as though he had lifted a great weight from my soul.

*   *   *

The strange, assorted group of us who were his followers travelled all around Judaea, finding food where we could. The way we fed our own group was a miracle, let alone feeding those who came to hear Yeshua. But there was never any lack—even when we thought there was nothing to hand and no hope of eating that day, someone or something would always turn up and Yeshua would berate us for our lack of faith.

'Are we not doing our Father's work?' he would ask. 'Then how can we not be taken care of? In the Kingdom there is no lack. Learn again and trust!'

Yeshua made it very clear that his ministry was for everyone when we began to travel across Galilee to the lands of the Gentiles. At first nearly everyone protested, even Magdalene; the knowledge that we were the

Chosen People with the only truth was so ingrained within us that the idea of sharing the inner teachings with heathens was horrifying. I alone kept silent, thinking of the little donkey and remembering the kindness of the Samaritan Zoresh and of my own mother, only Jewish by conversion of her grandparents and never a believer. I also thought of the Jews who opposed us and hated us for revealing the teaching to the common people. Perhaps the Gentiles would be less hostile and, if so, surely they deserved the chance of knowing the secrets of life? As Yeshua talked to us from the prow of Cephas's boat, I could see the others beginning to enjoy the idea of converting the heathen and, even though I was not sure if that was the best way go about it either, it was a most attractive feeling. By the time we arrived, the whole group of us was singing, filled with the fervour of having a great knowledge that the Gentiles would surely be delighted to receive.

When it came down to it, most of the Gentiles were exactly the same as the Jews. They all thought they were a chosen people too, and most of them hated any idea of change. Word of what Yeshua could do had gone ahead of us and, almost as soon as we landed, we were surrounded by people. At first they were fascinated and those who were sick came forward eagerly. But once the miracles were done and we sat down to talk to them, we could just as easily have been back at home with a few people listening, but many more moving away, bored or unwilling to listen; or heckling and spitting at us. The local priest, together with his henchmen, had come hastening down the path after being alerted that there was a possible wolf in the fold and watched us suspiciously. It was yet another lesson in acceptance and humbleness for those of us who had hoped to be evangelists and bring the heathens home.

You could feel an undercurrent of danger the whole time, though whether that was from the people or from our own fear of the unknown I could not tell. It came to a head when Yeshua healed the man possessed with evil spirits and exiled them to the herd of pigs nearby. The animals, driven crazy by the demons, threw themselves over a cliff. From a purely physical and financial point of view, you could understand that this would give the people of Decapolis a problem! Not only was there a sorcerer about (he was never that, but sometimes people saw him as such), but he was a Jew who did not care that the pigs should have been their food for the winter. We were asked to leave rather forcefully and had to thank the Lord that it came to no more than that.

*   *   *

From time to time we returned to Cephas's home town of Kfar-Nahum, where we would stay in extra rooms that we built on his family's homes, or we would go to the homes and towns of the other disciples for rest and recuperation. Cephas's wife, Leah, spoke out loudly against this intrusion of waifs and strays, and several of us received a lashing from her tongue for being in the way. The matter was solved for us, however. Leah's mother was prone to bronchitis and after Yeshua healed her of a severe fever, when everyone had feared for her life, Leah changed her mind and loved him as much as the rest of us did. For Yeshua, she would put up with the rest of us, as she told us all repeatedly—but he could not heal her of her sharp tongue where her husband was concerned.

'Why should I not be angry with him?' she would say if any of us winced for Cephas. 'He cares nothing for me or what I want.' She was very probably right, but she was not going to mend anything between them, even if Cephas were willing to do so!

Judah and I spent most of our spare time in Cana and I got to know Judah's sons Zebedee and Philip and their wives, Sarah and Ruth, very well. They were always most hospitable, even if they did heartily disapprove of this strange, nomadic marriage.

We needed those times of rest, for everywhere we went Yeshua was mobbed.

The sick of all ages and all types heard of his powers of healing and came from all corners of every village. We grew so used to the miracles that they seemed hardly worth comment. We knew who he was, so how could we doubt his power?

Yeshua's philosophy was simple. He wanted to teach the inner knowledge to a chosen group of all ages and professions. He wanted men and women as different as chalk and cheese to teach the Work in their own way. We learnt how to preach about the Kingdom of God and how to speak in parables so that those who really listened would find an extra gem and know that there was more to be learnt if they cared to ask.

'Why can't they all be told the whole teaching?' asked Andrew, as I had asked before.

'Because it is too much,' said Yeshua, who never tired of helping us to learn as long as we were making a genuine effort to understand. 'It takes years to live and understand the inner way unless you are taught every day by someone who knows the heart of God.

'Most people would waste or ignore the knowledge, and you don't cast your pearls before swine. Others would misuse it, because without the greater love of God, the teaching could be used for magic or even for harm.

'Those who have ears to hear will hear. Those who are ready to learn will learn.

Others will still benefit from the outer teaching if they want to—just to know of the Kingdom of God is enough. All we can do is give them the chance. We can't make them change their lives. We can't make them understand us.'

We could not make them understand us in Nazara.

*   *   *

At first it was wonderful to return to the place of my childhood. It was too late in the year for the hills to be lush and green, but it was still beautiful in its own way. I tethered the new donkey in Zoresh's old stall and looked around the old house with affection.

There had been many changes in Nazara; many births and many deaths. Simeon the old Rabbi was dead as was my dear friend Rosa. I had heard of her passing at Emmaus and grieved for her, but it was in Nazara, where her beautiful garden had nurtured me, that the sorrow truly hit home. Rosa's house had been passed on to a grandson and from what I could see, peeping over the old, familiar wall, most of the garden was now devoted to chickens and fruit. All of the plants that did not appear to give immediate yield of food or herbs had been trampled or pulled up. It was now a true Nazarene yard, functional and efficient. I gave a long sigh as I looked at it; for my own garden, seeded from Rosa's, was probably just as lost in Emmaus. I would not have swapped what I had for the past, but sometimes I wished they could be merged.

Many of the people in the village had no idea who I was. Those who did remember exclaimed at my height and my straight legs and back. All I had to do was gesture towards Yeshua and smile, but the majority of them did not believe me. I had managed to give up the need to be believed and that, in itself, was a great relief.

James was more than pleased to see us. We could see that he wanted to be a part of our group, but Rachel was not impressed and avoided us all whenever possible. She did not approve of nomadic women, who did not bear children—nor of men who seemed to have left their families to wander the world. How could she? If she had agreed with us, it might have been seen as a signal to James that he could suggest they both joined us or, even worse, that he might leave her behind.

People in the Synagogue were not impressed, either. Yeshua read from the Prophets and spoke to them and I could see they were not willing to hear. Anyone who knew or loved him, or had an open heart, could have seen his integrity; could have seen the light that shone around him; but the part of me that used to doubt the love of the Lord understood why they could not.

Not for the first time, those whose foundation was built on their lack of knowledge became hostile. Usually we knew when people were not going to listen and would simply fade away before there was trouble, but in Nazara I thought they would be glad to see that everything they had always prayed for and believed in—the coming of a Messiah from their line—had actually come to pass.

I should have known better!

Cephas, John and my brother James were with Yeshua as the crowd grew angry. Imma, Magdalene and I were, of course, in the women's gallery, helpless. We prayed. We knew by now that prayer was answered.

Almost at once there was a diversion. Another man appeared, who looked so like Yeshua that I had to look twice. The crowd turned on him and my brother and his friends just vanished.

The crowd could have hurt the man who had arrived, but luckily the people with him and his voice, shouting in alarm, alerted them that this was not the man they thought it was. 'No, I'm not Yeshua of Nazara,' he shouted indignantly. 'I'm not the so-called Messiah. Get lost, you idiots! I'm Thomas of Joppa. You leave me alone!'

That night we camped a good distance from our childhood home. Yeshua was philosophical. 'A prophet is always without honour in his own country,' he said with a shrug.

Just before we settled down to sleep we were hailed by two men and a woman making their way through the darkness towards us. It took a moment or two to recognise them and then we were amazed. Before us stood Imma, my brother James, and the mysterious Thomas.

'We're coming with you,' said James. 'Imma can make her own choice and Thomas will speak for himself. My sons are old enough to take care of their mother, and I have told her she is welcome to come too. I just know that I have to be here with you.'

Several of us felt a moment's compassion for Rachel, whose fears and resistance had created exactly the situation she did not want. Then Yeshua leapt up and embraced James heartily. 'It is brave of you to come,' he said. 'We need brave people. And you?' he said, turning to the small figure of his mother before him. 'I have been expecting and longing for you. Are you truly come now?'

She nodded, tears in her eyes, and he kissed her gently.

'Will you be in the care of my sister Magdelene and my sister Deborah, sister Miriam?' he asked and I could see the shock in her eyes as he both renamed her and took away their relationship.

'You are no more my son?' she said.

'No more,' he replied, smiling down at her.

'Be content.'

Thomas waited, looking embarrassed. Now that he was standing so near to our Master we could see that the resemblance was striking.

'Welcome,' said Yeshua with a smile. 'Thomas Didymus. Thomas the twin! And why are you here?'

'I don't know,' said Thomas. 'All this religious stuff seems pretty stupid to me. You all look as scruffy as a herd of mangy goats, but you can certainly turn a town on its head and I like that. Serves them right to have their hackles ruffled, I say! I'm willing to try anything for a laugh and with luck there might be plenty of wine and adventure thrown in. I suppose if I'm going to have rocks thrown at me for looking like you, I might as well find out what it is I'm being hated for!'

For a moment everyone was still, shocked by Thomas's irreverence. We were on a holy mission! We did not want to attract people who did not have our fervent beliefs and our dedication to the cause. Then, one by one, we saw the arrogance and stupidity of such thoughts. Yeshua laughed out loud, a great bellowing roar of laughter, and he stepped forward, clapping Thomas on the back.

'Welcome again!' he said. 'God has surely sent you to stop us from taking ourselves too seriously. Thomas Didymus, doubt as much as you like. You can only test us and make us stronger with your jokes and your questioning.'

9

We came to value Thomas greatly as the days and months passed by. He was always laughing, making jokes and lightening our mood. We could get far too serious and introspective at times.

Yeshua loved him from the start and that caused some jealousy, especially as it took Thomas months before he even began to revere anything we thought important.

'Sounds stupid to me,' he would say with a yawn when we tried to talk to him of different worlds and perceptions. 'Why bother with any world that doesn't include good wine, sunshine and all the beautiful things we can see right in front of us? Why does the Lord want to make it all so difficult?'

In vain we would try to make him see that it was easier once you were less attached to the physical world. You did not worry so much about what you wanted to do or be, but were happy to be what you were created to be, and to follow God's path for you.

'Did God ever eat a pomegranate?' asked Thomas. 'You can't have those in worlds where there are no trees or earth. Why don't we just appreciate them now and deal with the next worlds when we get there?'

He was very good for us. He taught us how

to teach and to realise that Assiyah, the physical world, was important as well as the higher worlds we were aiming for. It was all too easy to act holy and pretend that we were better than others, when the only difference was that our stumbles and mistakes looked far more stupid. We were supposed to know better! Where Yeshua was stern with us and exacting in the way he led us by example, Thomas goaded us from behind.

He knew how to poke fun at each and every one of us, and John in particular would cluck like a hen and take great umbrage whenever Thomas made a joke in what John thought was poor taste. Thomas thought John needed some of the stuffing taken out of him and would go on teasing him until John stormed out of the camp in fury.

John had no sense of humour at all, which was particularly obvious when it came to spiritual matters. He was a very young man and ardent. He was good-natured and pleasant, and willing to do his share of the work and no one disliked him, but he was such an earnest young scholar and so intense about everything we were learning that he found it hard to relax and be himself. He loved Yeshua with a desperation that half-amused and half-irritated the rest of us, though Yeshua loved him back like a son, and would tease him gently to try and bring him down to earth. Often John would scuttle to Yeshua's feet after

Thomas had been particularly vexing and Yeshua would talk to him gently but firmly, teaching him how to find the inner strength that would parry Thomas's barbs.

Poor John did not make a good teacher because he took other people's attitudes to heart so much. You could see how it hurt him when the wonderful knowledge he carried was rejected by others. He carried a precious scroll of papyrus with him everywhere, with diagrams and notes on it that helped him to understand and explain the miracles we were learning. He talked with angels and received visions of light and mystery and he taught with great fervour, but he set his sights too high and expected others to have his own vision and clarity when they did not. I even saw him throw down his precious papyrus in frustration when he had failed to get his point across to a group of itinerant workers.

'Why won't they see?' he would wail like a child, and sometimes would even run away and hide. It was tempting to try and follow him, and give him a hug and a word of reassurance, but no one tried that more than once! John was too spiky to accept comfort from anyone but Yeshua himself. He just needed to be left alone to recover. Then, with reassumed dignity and the mask of serenity back on his face, he would pick up his burden, together with his papyrus, and try again. He would always keep on trying.

You had to admire John, but you could never get close to him, particularly if you were a woman. It was not so much that he did not believe in our right to know the teaching—he did not believe in us at all! To John, women simply did not exist, except as hands that served the food. That was far more difficult to deal with than Thomas's affectionate insults.

*   *   *

Probably the best teacher we had was Levi, now known as Matthias. There had been huge opposition to his joining us because he was a tax collector. Those much-despised men lived in a world halfway between the Jews and the Romans. They collected money for Rome so that the Jews all but disowned them, but the Romans still regarded them as Jewish, so they got no special privileges. What's more, both sides usually accused them of being cheats and thieves—and often they were!

Matthias had been fascinated by Yeshua and the teaching and he was an example to many of us. He abandoned his old life completely, not even going back to his trade in the quiet winter months as the rest of the group did.

Yeshua was quite sharp with those who opposed Matthias's joining us, asking whether we had learnt nothing that we still judged by appearances. Did we think we were holier than

Matthias? he asked us. If we did, we had just fallen flat on our presumptuous faces!

Strangely, most of the people we taught were fascinated to hear that Matthias had given up his old life to follow the exciting new teacher. At the heart of every Jew there was a healthy respect for a man who had money, and this man was either a bigger fool than anyone had a right to expect or he knew when he was on to a good thing.

They were interested enough to give him enough time to say what he wanted to say, and Matthias spoke in such easy, simple language that he regularly had the largest audience of any of us except Yeshua. Some of the others found that very hard, but they had to get used to it.

Our life on the road was a mixture of inspiration and resistance, so it was very tiring much of the time. Most nights we sat around a camp fire, or in one of the cluster of homes where we would stay, and Yeshua would teach. He taught mostly by answering our questions, admonishing us whenever we needed it but helping and praising us too. Those evenings are where my memory always goes when I need reassurance. I can see his dear face, lit up by the golden flames so that his whole head was surrounded by light, and hear the clarity and joy shining as it fell from his lips. I can see the faces of the others too, some half in shadow, some restless, but mostly sitting peacefully in his light, listening and learning and loving. Those who were not of our inner group were allowed to sit with us, but for the evening hour of teaching only we, the disciples, were permitted to speak. Yeshua told the others that the days were theirs for questions but the evenings were set aside for our refreshment. Sometimes we spent part of that precious time in silence, either watching the fire or with eyes closed, striving to listen within to the voice of the Holy Spirit. It took us all a while to realise that the harder you try, the more difficult it is. If you just sit and let go, the receiving is easier.

We liked it best, though, when Yeshua talked to us. To those outside he told parables—the leaves on the Tree of Life—but to us he taught the roots and the trunk so that we could bear the leaves for others. No matter how much we learnt in those flame-filled evenings, there was always something new to know.

There were other presences there too, as though angels and the souls of long-dead people gathered around us to listen to the Master of this place and time. John felt them the strongest, and even Thomas was respectful of him at those times. John was truly a mystic and you could see the seeds of a great man within him—if he could only become more human at the same time.

Few of us had any doubts by now that

Yeshua was the Messiah, though it took Cephas to say it out loud. Once it was revealed, we all knew there was no going back. And I knew that his death was assured.

The resistance usually came during the daytime. Many of those we taught refused our message, but they were not the problem. Yeshua taught us every day that it mattered only that we spread the word. It was within ourselves that the struggle was great. It was all very well listening to the holy words and ideals around the heart-warming fire, but another matter to apply them to ourselves and to others in the cold light of day.

We quarrelled and disagreed on points of the teaching. We jostled for position, both as teachers and as pupils of Yeshua. We argued with the Pharisees and Sadducees who came to try us and, worst of all, we feared that they might be right and we were wrong. The women among us particularly suffered, for many people thought it was immoral of us to teach. We intended to do so only to the other women we met along the way, but there were times when we were challenged in public and then we were rarely allowed to defend ourselves.

Strangely, the fiercest opposition came from our own sex. Though many were interested, there was nearly always a pocket of orthodox women who heartily disliked the idea of anyone trying to change the status quo. We tried to remember that we were challenging beliefs they held deep in their hearts and that it frightened them that we showed them a precious freedom they would never allow themselves—or their children—to have. The most hurtful part was that these women would rarely challenge us themselves, but fetched their husbands or fathers to do so for them instead. The men threw the Law at us unmercifully and much as we tried to show them and their women that we were willing to listen to their point of view, it was hard not to feel betrayed by our sisters.

When the stones they threw were only from their lips, it was bad enough, but once the physical assaults began and we came back to the main group, bruised and bleeding, it was obvious that we would be in danger of our lives if we went on.

Yeshua came to sit with us one afternoon as Miriam and I bathed Magdalene's wounds behind an outcrop of mottled rock. He ordered the others to keep the people from him while we spoke—and they did their best. It was almost impossible to keep the hordes away whenever we were within sight of any settlement. So many people wanted healing or to see the miracles he brought that we were mobbed. Yeshua would heal the sick and then often leave one of the disciples to teach the crowds. What usually happened was that they slipped away as fast as they could, once the excitement and the miracles were past, leaving the hecklers and the hostile to argue and be difficult. But even they wanted to quarrel with the prophet himself, not with his henchmen. The disciples' self-esteem would be tested to the limit as they saw how uninteresting they were to the crowds if they could not produce magic or argue, so there would be a chance of a fight.

'This cannot go on,' said Miriam to Yeshua as we anointed Magdalene's back and shoulders with lavender and arnica root. 'We are in danger whenever we travel with you. People will not listen to women teaching.'

Both Magdalene and I began to protest. We wanted so much to be equal, to teach as the others did. It seemed too hard that we were persecuted just for teaching the other women.

Yeshua silenced us by putting his finger to his lips. Then he blessed us and took Magdalene's face between his hands. By now you could almost see the light flowing through him as he healed. It did not come from him, but through him from the realms of light, but it shone within him as though he too were part of its creation.

He kissed her on the lips and she bowed her head. The great, proud, fierce Magdalene, who would fight any battle and any man, would always bow before Yeshua. Sometimes when she was away from him she would rail at herself for doing so, but when the light was before her, she knelt again. We all did.

'Great and noble women,' he said. 'Dear sisters and daughters. You do not run to me like the others and demand my attention for your wounds. You use your own strengths, your knowledge of the herbs and spices and your support for each other. You serve God by collecting food and relishes as we walk along the road. You take time to walk further, even though you are more tired than the rest of us, when you see there is a clump of vegetation that will aid our digestion or the pains of the masses we meet. You stay behind to nurture the souls of those who have been healed and who find it hard to adapt to the change. You give them potions and gentle words to support them in their new life, while the men seek out new fields to conquer. You do not drain me with demands on my time and attention. You do not fight to be the ones who serve me my food, although you make it with all the love in the Kingdom of Heaven. You do not question me before thinking over what I have said. You are blessed daughters of God.'

Then he told us a story he had heard of another Messiah, a man who lived in India, who had been born a prince but had given up his worldly ways to find enlightenment. This man, too, had women followers who wanted to teach but he forbade them.

One woman defied him and fought him and demanded why. It was not because she was

259

lesser, he said. Not because she was unworthy, but because she would not be safe. The world was not ready for women to teach.

'You are as valuable as the men. You are protected by God,' said Yeshua to us. 'But you have to take care. God will not protect those who are continually reckless, for they must learn their lessons. God will not go against the ways of the world, for that would destroy the world's free will. The world is not ready for women yet.'

'I do not want to teach,' said Miriam. 'It is enough to be with you and to serve.'

'I do,' I said. 'I want to teach. You know I do.'

Magdalene seized Yeshua's hand and mine. 'We must!' she said. 'We must teach. How can we just hold inside what you tell us and not teach it? It would be like holding onto riches like a miser. You are always telling us that the rich who keep hold of their possessions poison themselves. That all wealth must flow to create health. Surely if we hold the knowledge we have inside without sharing it, we are guilty of avarice, of refusing to share the riches we have!'

Yeshua laughed. 'Oh, woman!' he said. 'You have defeated me! You are right. You must pass on the knowledge. You cannot hold it within you or it will turn sour. Yes, you must teach. But again and again I will say to you, you must teach as women. Not the way the men do by standing on hillsides and shouting. You must teach as the Shekhinah does, with the quiet voice of power. One day the world may wish to hear you shout but, until then, you must teach quietly. Wait for the people to come to you. Do not go out and seek them. Teach them as a woman when they do come. Do not teach as I do, but as you should. I cannot teach you how. You are doubly blessed. The men need only follow me, but you must listen directly to God and follow your own path. Let the inspiration of the Holy Spirit come through you in its own way. Listen to the Shekhinah, the feminine of God, but take God himself as your Divine Husband. *You will not be persecuted if you teach as women.* If you teach as men, there can be no protection because you are not teaching as your true selves.'

We wept, Miriam too, as he laid his hands on our heads, kissed us and blessed us again. As he left us, I got up and walked a little way away to be alone with my thoughts. Ahead of me, I saw Philip run up to Yeshua and gesticulate angrily.

'Why do you love Magdalene more than us?' he asked with tears in his eyes.

Yeshua looked at him. 'Ask yourself instead why I do not love you as much as her,' he said and walked on.

*　　　*　　　*

261

One day, as we were dealing with the usual bustle of people we would find outside any town waiting to see us, a man called Jairus from the Synagogue in Tiberius came racing up to us and fell at Yeshua's feet, begging him to come and save his daughter, who was dying.

'Come now, Master,' he pleaded. 'There is no time to waste.'

Yeshua looked at the others, who also had much need of him and put his hand on the older man's shoulder. 'I have work here first,' he said. 'And I am tired. But I will come. I will send my disciples Judah and Deborah back with you now, to do all that can be done, and I will follow after them.'

Jairus was almost in despair. 'Only you can save her. You must come now!' he said with all the force of authority.

Yeshua looked at him. 'Peace,' he said sternly. 'There are others in need too. I have given you my servants to go before me.'

Just what Jairus thought of that was shown by his decision not to come with us but to stay to try to persuade Yeshua to hurry. He sent us into Tiberius with his servant, together with instructions that he was bringing Yeshua as soon as he could.

We were greeted by the girl's frantic mother and her women as we arrived in the street where they lived. Mistaking Judah for Yeshua, they ran to him, almost dragging him into the house, and he was hard put to explain that he was not Yeshua. Their disappointment was shown in anger and they refused us admittance. I spoke to them calmly, but to no avail. Then a voice rose within the house, lamenting, and the mother screamed and fell at my feet. 'She's dead, she's dead,' she wept and all the others lent their voice to the ritual wail of mourning.

Judah turned to the servant. 'Go back to your master and tell him,' he said. 'There is nothing that can be done here now.'

But I slipped inside the house and found my way to the room where the girl lay, white and empty on her bed. Another girl, I thought probably her sister, sat wailing at the end of the bed.

'What is the sick girl's name?' I asked as she looked up at me, amazed.

'Chloe,' she answered in a whisper. 'But she is dead.'

'Chloe,' I said softly. 'Chloe, can you hear me?' The living girl stared at me as I looked up around the room. I knew that if Chloe had just died, her spirit was still there. It was traditional to open the shutters of a window to let it out and I might be just in time.

I sat down, holding the dead girl's head in my hands and stroking her hair.

'Chloe,' I said. 'I know you are still here, even if you are not in your body. Listen. Yeshua is coming to help you. If you want to stay, he will bring you back into your body and heal your sickness.'

Then I just repeated her name again and again, almost under my breath, while praying that I was doing the right thing. Suddenly I felt a coolness brush my shoulder and a certainty that I was right. I raised my head, but there was nothing to see but the girl's mother and the rest of the family crowding into the room and staring angrily at the stranger who was interfering with their child.

'Be still!' said my voice, with authority. 'The girl is not dead but sleeping until the Master comes.'

God be thanked that he arrived before they tore me to shreds. I held them off for perhaps a minute and then it felt as though the air around me shimmered with joy and moved in a rush towards the door.

He came in and Chloe's spirit flowed back with him. From that moment there was no doubt what would happen and I slipped away out of the room, glad to have done what little I could. It was left to Peter and John and James to see the miracle itself.

I felt, rather than heard, the rush of amazement and euphoria that washed through the house as Chloe's soul and spirit and body were reunited. Once they were certain she was filled with health and there was no further danger, they would have carried her and Yeshua all around the town proclaiming the miracle. Of course he forbade them to do so and told them not to mention the miracle outside the house. We all knew that would be impossible—the neighbours had heard the mourning rituals begin—but we understood how important it was to play down such an event.

Before he left Chloe's room, Yeshua called me to him. His instruction to her mother and to me was simple—'Give her bread'—but we received it in different worlds. For the mother it meant the nurturing of the physical body; for me, the nurturing of the spirit.

We all spent the evening at Jairus's house with Chloe, restored and beautiful, waiting on Yeshua and the whole family ready to fall at his feet. For the disciples too there was a change. This time he had raised the dead. This was different. This was a new era.

Yeshua left Judah and me behind with the family for a few days to help them with any questions or readjustments they might want to make and to pass on whatever of the teaching they wished to learn. This was by far the most difficult time of the Work, for people who have witnessed miracles can be shocked and disorientated, or they can find it hard to adapt back to normal life.

But Chloe was not like that. Although she was grateful for what had been done, her psyche had no memory of it and she did not want to know any more of the source of the miracles. She did remember seeing herself lying still on the bed and being drawn towards Yeshua as though she were floating on air—but she did not want to remember it. It made her different from the other girls and she did not like that.

Judah in particular was disheartened by her attitude. He thought she should be transformed and he spent hours patiently trying to teach her the Work. She and the rest of the family listened politely, because they felt they owed it to us, but they thought it all rather a bore and Chloe could hardly keep from yawning in his face.

Her cousin Rizpah, however, listened enraptured. When the teaching sessions were over, she stuck to me like a burr, asking question after question. We had much in common, for her parents were dead and she had been raised as Chloe's sister, as I had been as Yeshua's. When the rest of the family was there, she was silent, but she served me first at all meal times and even sat at my feet at the end of the day. Judah did not notice, for he was too involved in trying to teach Chloe to realise that the true healing had been for Rizpah. Chloe had no wish to change, while Rizpah had every desire for transformation.

I answered every question as honestly as I could, and I could see that she was desperate to leave her family and follow us to find out more.

'You are alive,' she said once. 'We are all half-dead. We walk around in the physical world with no idea that the worlds of the Lord also exist and that we can live in them. We have had proof that there is light available to us, but no one wants it except me. Please take me with you. I don't want to stay and fall asleep again.'

I asked Judah and he, reluctantly, asked Jairus if Rizpah could come with us for a while. His answer was to boil with anger and to tell us to leave the following day, without speaking to either Chloe or Rizpah again.

'I will not have my family encouraged to break the Law and become outcasts,' he thundered. 'We have been patient with you long enough.'

'Rabbi, your daughter was healed by the Master!' Judah was outraged.

'So you say,' said Jairus. 'Maybe she was not dead after all. Maybe it was a miracle. But whatever it was, we now want to get on with our own lives, living and worshipping the Lord in the old ways. We do not want any of this modern heretical rubbish you are teaching. We have listened for politeness' sake, but now you want to take one of us, and a child at that, to your sect. I will not hear of it. You will leave at first light.'

Judah was angry with me then, but I knew (and so did he deep inside) that it was due to his own fear that he might have taught badly and turned the family against all we stood for. I tried to reassure him; he was an excellent teacher, kind and clear and always ready to put a lighter point so that people would not find the teaching too serious and difficult. He could not, and did not, want to hear me.

I felt angry too. For Rizpah, who was to be held back and forced into a traditional Jewish life where she would have no further help to look into her own soul; and for myself. She would have been such a daughter to me . . .

I knew she could read a little and I took the risk of writing her a note, which I left with the stable boy together with a jar of clove-oil for his toothache. In it I told her that she must honour her guardians for now, but that she must always honour the Lord more. If He should give her a sign in future years that she was to come and join us, I would take care of her, but she must wait until that sign came.

Then we left, Judah still angry and sullen, and I watchful and nervous lest my note should be discovered and more anger heaped upon both Rizpah's head and mine.

*   *   *

All thought of these things was forgotten by the time we had rejoined the main group, for news was rife on the road that my cousin John the Baptist had been beheaded by Herod Antipas. Horrified and disbelieving, we

268

hurried on, stopping only for Magdalene, who had been left to counsel and teach a woman who had dared to touch Yeshua's cloak to heal her continual menstrual bleeding. The two women had become firm friends and when we stopped to collect her, Joanna insisted on coming with us to join Yeshua's followers. I was glad for Magdalene. Since my marriage I had not been such good company for her and it was so good to have another woman to swell our throng. Others, who came to know us, would join us whenever we were in their area but they did not feel they could stay and we were always saying goodbye.

By the time we reached the main group, it had swelled to nearly a hundred men, many of whom I had never seen before. Perhaps some were followers of The Baptist and others were from those groups that followed us fervently for a week or so and then returned home disillusioned at our lack of hostility to the Romans.

Many were honouring the rituals of mourning, rending their clothes and saying Kaddish for John's soul. Others were shouting and demonstrating, holding clubs and knives and calling for revenge.

'Where's Yeshua? Where's the Master?' called Judah to Peter and Thomas.

'He retired into the hills to pray and is not to be disturbed,' they replied. 'It is time for us to act for him. Come and join us. We must avenge this wrong!'

Judah plunged into the throng and was soon caught up in the fervour of the men who were talking open revolution. If Yeshua were the Messiah, they said, he would be their King and their task was to take arms and fight to release Judaea from the shackles of Rome. Then they could destroy the Roman-approved Herodian usurpers and a true Jew could reign instead. They were loud with soldiers' talk and big ideas, imagining the wrath of God following them into battle. The coming of the Messiah was so commonly thought to mean the end of the shackles of Rome that we were faced more and more with this kind of reaction, as Yeshua's miracles had become more widely known. When he was with us, it was easier to talk of the Kingdom of Heaven and a sword in the world of spirit, not to be used as a physical weapon; but without him, it was all too easy to be swayed by the mood of a crowd.

Miriam was standing, helplessly, half-way up the hillside and Magdalene and I took Joanna over to her.

'Why is it always the physical battles with men?' she asked wearily. 'Can they not see how they are misinterpreting his words? How often has he said that his Kingdom is not of this world? It is the conquering of the evil in our own souls that we must face.

'I suppose it is easier for we women, as we have fought the battles in our hearts and minds for so long without being able, or allowed, to find out what the physical battle is about. You cannot transform anything by meeting might and anger with might and anger. They listen to him telling them that every night. Why don't they hear? Why don't they see?'

We comforted her as best we could, but the situation was beginning to look dangerous. We now had over fifty followers of our own gathered in that spot and the outsiders were egging the others on. I thought for a moment I saw a group of Zealots whom we had met on our last trip to Jerusalem. If they took control, we could be lost.

But what could I do? I was only a woman. If I tried to speak or intercept the others, I would be knocked to the ground.

Then the story of Moses and Aaron and the Golden Calf flashed across my mind and suddenly the fear vanished. I was running down the hillside to Judah and Thomas, to catch hold of their arms and breathlessly beg them to see reason.

'Wake up! This is temptation! This is temptation!' was all I could say as the other men jostled me and tried to push me away.

Then Magdalene and Miriam were beside me, chanting, 'Hear, O Israel, the Lord our God is One. The Lord is One! Lead us not into temptation, O Lord.' Magdalene was knocked over, but she shouted even louder.

271

'Lord! Deliver us from evil! Deliver us from evil!'

My beloved husband stood still, as though turned to stone. As Miriam and Joanna tried to pull Magdalene up, I turned to him again, tears pouring down my face.

'Don't leave me,' I said. 'Not yet. Don't go.'

'Oh, Deborah!' he said, stunned; shocked back into himself. 'Thank the Lord! Thomas! Thomas! Peter! John! Step back, we are looking for the Kingdom of God, not the temptations of the Kingdom of the physical world! Listen to me. Listen!'

Five of the twelve men closest to Yeshua heard him and, as if a spell had broken, they shook their heads and looked up with eyes that were awake. As each moved away from the group, some of the others woke too and joined them. Together with our small group, they spread out until we stood in a circle around the others and then we began to say the Shemah, followed by the prayer that Yeshua had taught us. The one that brought God down through the Four Worlds from his Crown to the earth we stood on.

'Our Father,' we prayed together. 'Who is in Heaven. Hallowed be thy Name . . .'

It was the first miracle that the disciples wrought together. It was as though the Light of God descended upon us all and those who would fight were vanquished by angels.

Within moments the ringleaders had run off

down the valley, still shouting, but afraid of the power that streamed down the hill after them. About thirty of us remained, shaking a little but calm. John and Nathaniel moved into the centre, closely followed by Peter, and they began to chant more prayers. At once the men moved in, to begin a service, leaving us three women on the outside. Magdalene began an expression of disgust, that again the world of form had taken control, but Miriam stopped her with an outstretched hand.

'Wait,' she said softly.

Three things happened simultaneously: John waved to us to move in and join the men; Judah, James, Andrew and Thomas stepped back, to include us in their part of the circle outside the main group; and a light enveloped us from behind.

Yeshua stood behind us, smiling, his whole body wrapped in light and his arms held out to us.

We all turned and went to him.

10

Though we did not realise it, the final days were already approaching. Hanukkah was long over and we were passing through those last weeks of deep winter before the calls of awakened birds swelled across the land at dawn to signal the beginning of spring and the breeding season.

Cephas and most of the others were in Kfar-Nahum or Bethsaida with their families, and Yeshua, Miriam and Magdalene were staying with them. Judah and I had gone home to Cana to spend time with his children, to rest and to prepare for another year of travelling and teaching ahead of us.

We had a small group of followers in the town and held a weekly meeting to discuss the Tree of Life and the Four Worlds, and how best to apply the inner knowledge to everyday life. Sometimes I thought these were my favourite times. I missed Yeshua, but it was comfortable and peaceful to have my own secure hearth and to teach without having to move on continually.

We earned our living in these winter months. I helped at the Mikvah, as I had in the old days, and Judah preached and sang in the Synagogue in between helping his sons-in-law with the sandal-making and leatherwork business.

We were treated a little like strangers, but that gave us more precious time to be together and a respite from the continual demands on our energy and time when we were with the other disciples.

The events and miracles of the previous two years now seemed almost commonplace. Each one of us had learnt how to heal and though our results were not as spectacular as Yeshua's, we were able to link the worlds sufficiently to bring relief and the occasional miracle healing for those who came to us.

By the second summer Yeshua had already started sending more than seventy of us out on our own individual missions to heal and teach. He was anxious this should not go to our heads, and when John came back one day to tell him that he had stopped a stranger healing in Yeshua's name, because the man was not one of us, he was admonished sternly.

'Healing is God's gift, not yours,' said Yeshua. 'He who is not against us is for us. Anyone who heals in my name will not be able to speak badly of the Light.'

There were plenty of those who could and did. We were followed suspiciously by religious leaders and priests, and by spies sent from the High Priest and the Temple in Jerusalem. If that were not enough, we also attracted curious Roman soldiers who wanted to see if we were a different kind of threat, and we were haunted by Zealots who wanted to stir us into physical revolt, by madmen and sometimes by those who simply wished to stir up trouble.

Yeshua answered them all. Mostly he spoke to them with patience and kindness, but sometimes he would launch into a powerful anger when they chose to misinterpret his words or tried to trick him into going against the Scriptures.

He tried again and yet again to tell the fighters among them that the prophesies of the Messiah spoke of Kingdoms that did not involve the physical world. He said the sword he carried was a sword of light and that the judgement of the Lord lay within each one of us to address ourselves and not for us to hurl at outside enemies, who were only here to point out the turmoil that we needed to address within.

'As above, so below,' he would say. 'As without, so within. What you see in the physical world is a reflection of what you have within yourself.'

He debated the scriptures with the Sadducees and the Pharisees, with the Essenes and with members of other sects I had never even heard of. Now and again he would draw on the ground, as if idly, to show a Pharisee who understood the principles of the Tree of Life that he was indeed teaching the inner faith; that he had exactly the same source for his words as the one they should be using. This silenced many of them, but it moved others to fury.

On days when we were tired and had been inundated by crowds of clamouring people it seemed that we were wasting our time. People of all parties saw him as a threat. The common people only wanted his miracles. Very few would actually listen to what we had to say, or learn from it.

'It doesn't matter,' Yeshua would say again and again as we sat down wearily for a simple supper by the fireside. 'Those who have ears to hear will hear. All that matters is that we speak the truth and give them the opportunity to hear and to see that miracles do happen when the Four Worlds are linked together in a man's soul and spirit. If they choose not to hear, that is their right. It is not our business to chase after those who will not hear.'

Even so, he too seemed to grow more easily tired by the constant opposition and calls on him to explain himself. He began to spend more time with Cephas's family in Kfar-Nahum and even more with the sisters Mary and Martha, whose brother Lazarus he had also raised from the dead. In both places he, like us, could teach smaller groups of those who really wanted to listen and to spread the word quietly by living it in their everyday life. In future years we realised that this was where the most important work was done, not in the public domain where people did not have to make any commitment to the Work but could come and go as they pleased and watch the entertainment.

Magdalene was a little jealous of Mary and Martha (though she had no need to be) and would often stay with Judah and me or with Miriam, Andrew or Philip in Kfar-Nahum when Yeshua travelled south. She too enjoyed the peaceful times and gathered around her a group of women from the town who were semi-outcast for one reason or another. She had an eye for colour and was a wonderful seamstress who could create the most beautiful garments from almost nothing. With Miriam's help at the loom, and as much shouting and stamping of her feet as of her fabled kindness, she taught the women to create little businesses selling beautiful clothing and ornaments, as well as helping and healing others with herbs and oils.

When Lazarus was murdered by spies of the priests, who did not want the story of his resurrection to get around and start a stampede to Yeshua's way of thinking, we finally understood why he always told the people whom he had healed to keep it quiet. Those who trumpeted his works too loud were now in danger.

Perhaps people expected him to raise Lazarus a second time, but Mary and Martha did not ask him to, and he did not offer. The

278

two women were still young students of the Work, but somehow they knew (as intuitively we did too) that this death was different. Lazarus had been a changed man after his life was restored. He made reparation in many places where he had left pain and anger behind him before, and perhaps this death occurred when his soul was so redeemed that he could find his destiny in the higher worlds.

*   *   *

One blowy wintry day, when Judah and I were spending the last quiet month of the cold season in our small but comfortable home in Cana, Yeshua arrived unannounced.

He came alone, cold and tired, wrapped in an old brown cloak, which hid him from the curious eyes of passers-by. We greeted each other with joy, but behind his eyes we saw such a firmness of purpose that we were nervous too. Something important was about to be revealed. When we tried to ask, he quieted us, saying he was in need of rest and laughter and that our business could be taken care of later.

Then it was like old times at Emmaus. We laughed and joked and debated, and Yeshua seemed to relax visibly as the evening wore on. In fact there were five whole days when we were all just the best of friends and those are precious treasures in my memory. He had brought some olive wood as a gift so that he could build a small wooden chest for me to store my herbs and medicines in. He would handle and carve the wood lovingly as we sat and reminisced during those long, cool evenings just before the spring.

On the fifth evening he finished his work and placed it into my hands. Inside, he had cut and polished the words *Talitha Cumi*—maiden awake—the words he had called out to me the first time he left Nazara; the words he had used to lift Chloe back into life.

'In case you should ever forget,' he said gently. 'There may be times ahead when all this will seem like a dream and you will be tempted to leave all you have learnt behind.'

I wanted to deny it; to proclaim my loyalty, but something in his eyes stopped me.

'Now listen,' he said. 'Both of you. Draw close to the fire and let us pray together. Then I have to talk to you of great matters.'

We prayed with him and then sat in silence waiting for the moment. It was a long time before he spoke, and though we tried not to look at him as we waited for his words, the changes in his face as he battled with some inner torment moved us both to the verge of tears. We wanted to hold our arms out to him, to comfort and reassure, but we stayed still and silent and waited.

'Judah,' he said at last. 'Deborah.' It was almost as though it were not Yeshua speaking at all, but some archangel or even higher being speaking through him.

'Yes, Lord?'

'I am going to my Father. Soon. It is my time and it is necessary.'

Again, we resisted the impulse to deny what he had said; to jump up and cover over the words as though they had not been spoken.

The air took on a strange new quality and I felt a silver shiver of cold sink into me. An image of the Pargod ran through my mind, the strands of our lives interweaved and shining, and I felt I already knew what was to come.

Yeshua turned to my husband.

'Judah,' he said. 'I need you to be the one who hands me over to my death.'

'No!' Judah threw himself back against the wall with his arms spread out. I knew he felt as though he had been struck with a sword.

'Sit down and listen,' said Yeshua, wearily. 'It is hard enough. Please, just listen.'

Judah sat down, shaking, and bowed his head.

'It has to be someone responsible and reliable,' said Yeshua. 'You are the only one I can fully trust. Cephas is too impulsive and emotional, John is too much in the higher worlds to listen to simple physical facts, and the others, I'm afraid, would simply not understand.'

'And you think I do?' Judah was shaking his head in perplexity and anguish.

'No, not yet, but hear me out.'

'I can't bear this.' Judah stood up again and began to pace around the room.

'Bear it, Judah, please, bear it for me.'

I could only listen, tears standing in my eyes. Despite his agony, Judah had the love and kindness to touch me on the shoulder, feeling for my pain as well as his.

'But, Lord, how can I? How could *I* betray *you?* Even if I could do it, how could I live after betraying you to the Romans? And if I did, the others would surely kill me.'

'They know the sixth commandment.'

'They know everything you've taught them. We all do, but reality is different!'

'No, Judah, that's exactly it. Reality is not different. Everything I have taught you is reality. It is the flesh that is the only weak world. It has to be transcended to prove the strength of the other worlds. My body is all I have to offer which can be seen and believed by all men who cannot see the other worlds. This has got to be lived in reality. And reality includes death.'

'It would mean my death too.' Suddenly Judah was speaking with a new authority. I sat still as a captive bird, hugging my knees with my arms, looking from face to face and seeing the light shine in both of them. All my senses were heightened, and though the coldness within me was deep, it was also thrilling. This was right. I knew that, for all my fear.

'Perhaps,' said Yeshua. 'Perhaps it does

mean your death. If they have not learnt the teaching, perhaps they will kill you. If they have learnt, they will see with their eyes open and understand why it was necessary and there will be no blame. And you will live. If they cannot see, what good was the teaching to them anyway? They did not hear it.'

'But, Lord, what about Deborah? What about the continuation of the teaching? If I am killed and they have not understood, the teaching dies too.'

'No. Not everyone is blind, even if you are killed. And Deborah has her own work to do. She will be spared.'

'I still can't do it.' Judah began to pace again.

For the first time I spoke.

'Must it be?'

My brother took my face in his hands and kissed my forehead. Then he looked into my eyes.

'It must be,' he said. And I knew again that if Judah failed him, then it would be my duty to take him to the death that was his destiny.

'God, give me strength,' I prayed in my very soul.

'It must be,' said Yeshua again, sitting back against the wall and watching Judah's pacing. 'Listen. If you give me up to the Romans, I shall die publicly and shall be remembered by all the followers, all the Jews in the city; by all the Romans and all those who are in

283

Jerusalem at the time. Jerusalem is the centre of our world. The holy place where Abraham was willing to sacrifice Isaac. This time the sacrifice must happen. It is not enough simply to be willing; it must be translated into the physical world. The knowledge and the teaching will be spread from person to person and many will see the resurrection of the body and know it is the truth.'

'Resurrection?' Suddenly Judah's face lit up.

'Of course. How else would this be of use to God?'

'You will come back?'

'Yes, on the third day, I shall rise again. That is my message to the children of Israel. That death has no dominion and the Kingdom of God can overcome all evil.'

'The evil I do in betraying you.' He spoke bitterly, but I could see that the thought of resurrection was swaying him.

'Judah, if you do not do this for me, then Deborah must. And if she will not, I shall be taken without warning and you, and Deborah too, and the others will be killed with me. Miriam and Magdalene and so many that I love. That is for certain. The teaching then will die. My death now is the only way forward for all of us. There is no future for me on this earth. I have done my work. That is my Father's wish and how could I deny him?'

I spoke again. 'Are you not frightened?'

'Of course. I am a human man. I do not look forward to the pain of death. But death itself is just the passing through to my Father and I am tired, Deborah. I want to go home.'

'You want to die?'

'Yes. I have done nearly all that I came to earth to do. This is the final task on earth.'

'But why me?' Judah cried in distress.

'Because you are the only one I can trust. The others will refuse or deny me. Each of those is a far greater betrayal. When you do it, Judah, I will kiss you for gratitude, for being the strongest of my friends and the beloved of God. Those who are awake will see that and understand.'

'And those who sleep will not. Why can't you tell them? Why me? Do you really think they would not listen?'

'They will see the resurrection,' he said. 'If they have understood at all, they will see.'

'And me?' I leant forward. 'What can I do for you?'

'Oh, Deborah, I have been so proud of your faith. Understand that death is nothing. Just moving between worlds. This is greater than all of us. It is the beginning of the taking of the Torah—the teaching—to the whole world. You have much more to do here. Judah may still be with you. And after a while we shall all be together again in the greater world.'

'It will be all right though, won't it?' I asked, a little child again. 'They will see, won't they?'

'God grant they do,' said Judah.

Yeshua stood and held out his arms and the two men embraced for a long time. When Yeshua pulled back, he had tears in his eyes.

'Judas,' he said, using the Greek form of his name. 'I thank you from the bottom of my heart.'

*   *   *

In the days that followed we thought of every reason why not. If he were sacrificed, what guarantee was there that everyone else would not be slaughtered too? What if the Romans killed Judah (and me) as well? What if Yeshua were deluded at last?

'But that means everything we have learnt comes to nothing,' said Judah despairingly. 'And to be honest, Deborah, life would not be worth living if this knowledge were taken away.'

I agreed, but we cried ourselves to sleep those nights with the horror of the knowledge that life as it had been was over, whatever happened now. The price was there to pay and the reward Eternal Life. Just how much did we really believe?

The third morning Judah was awake before I. He was standing, praying, swaying back and forth by the door of the house. I looked at his beloved form and tried to swallow the fear that rose again in my throat.

But when he turned to me his face was brighter than I had ever seen it, older and stronger, and lined with the terrible wisdom he had received.

'I was visited in the night,' he said. 'They told me this is what I have to do and why. I know now why it is right.'

'Can you tell me?' An old jealousy raised its head within me that he had been visited by angels when I had not.

'Some,' he said, coming to sit on our bed and taking my hand. 'It is a debt I have to pay to reach Eternal Life. I have refused it before, many times, and if I do not do it again, the price to pay will be even greater another time.'

'But how can betrayal be a good thing?'

'Look at the wider picture,' he said and laughed. I had not seen him laugh all those bitter days. 'You always tell me that! If this is done, I place my faith in the Highest. I keep my word to one I love more than myself. No greater love exists than to lay down my life for my brother. Yeshua lays down his life for mankind, so how can I refuse to sacrifice myself for him?'

So, he would die then. My heart wept and I covered my face with my hands.

'I can't bear it. Both of you. And left alone. Can I not at least come with you?'

'You see.' His face was brilliant now. 'You do understand! Death is the beautiful place. I have the easier path, Deborah. I will be leaving

287

soon after my Lord and what more could I ask? But you, you blessed woman, are strong enough to continue. Oh, price above rubies!' He took me in his arms.

And it was then, when I finally accepted God's will and understood that, for all my knowledge, I understood nothing, that the angel spoke to me too. It was a light without shape in the corner of the room. Intangible but real. 'Fear not,' it said. 'All is well. Speak of me to Miriam and she will comfort you. She knows what is to be and you will be each other's greatest strength.'

*   *   *

Once Judah had left to be with Yeshua and the other eleven, who were going ahead of the rest of us to Jerusalem for Pesach, I packed up and made my own journey to Kfar-Nahum, where Miriam would be. It was a full day's trek even on the little donkey and I wrapped my cloak around me closely, afraid that anyone who saw me would be able to look inside and learn the terrible secret I carried.

It was dusk when I arrived, the time for families to meet up for evening worship and the meal. My errand was not the kind that would mix well with the convivial mood of the evening, so I tethered the donkey and lay down to sleep in an olive grove just west of the town. I was fortunate; the night was fair, but I could hardly appreciate that as I tossed and turned, feeling lost and tiny under the midnight sky.

In the morning I waited until the time when the women went to collect the water. Miriam's face lit up when she saw me and, putting down her jug, she held out her arms. 'Look at you,' she said. 'I never tire to see you upright and strong. But what is it, child? Are you troubled?'

'No,' I told her, but looked into her eyes with a different answer, knowing she would stay behind after the other women, to hear me in private.

'Let us sit a little,' she said. 'We can catch up with the others.'

It took some time for the last stragglers to pass us; many of them knew me and stopped for a greeting. We spoke of tiny things, which would have seemed important had I not been so eager to be alone with my earthly mother. Miriam held my hand tightly in unspoken understanding.

'You have seen him,' she said quietly, as the last woman's figure went from our sight.

'Seen who?'

'Gabriel. I can see it in your face. You only recognise the look if you too have seen him.'

'Gabriel?'

'Yes, God's messenger. It will be concerning my son.' Suddenly she began to cry. 'Has the time come then?'

Such gratitude swept over me when I realised she already knew. And such compassion for the mother who must have lived in fear for . . . how long?

'Since he was born. No, before,' she said. 'No such blessing would bring an ordinary life with an ordinary end. And the priestly astrologers . . .' She was looking up now, into the heavens, her tears falling slowly, elegantly, delicately. 'They told me when they came after he was born. At the time I thought it unkind of them, but I have thanked them a thousand times since. It is better to be prepared. Then you treasure every day.' She turned to me. 'Is it soon?'

'Yes.' I took her face in my hands. 'And it is Judah who leads them to him. It is what he has asked. And, Imma, I don't know how to bear it.'

'We will go to Jerusalem together,' she said. 'There will be much to do.'

We sat, together, in each other's arms, rocking back and forth in our grief. Finding the love of woman, the Shekhinah, within and without. Nature growing, dying and being reborn around us as we wept.

*   *   *

And so he was crucified. My husband led them to him as he had been asked to, so Yeshua was at least arrested in a place and a time when he

290

could be prepared and where his execution would be made public.

We women were not there. Yeshua had chosen to be alone with his twelve apostles that night in the Garden of Gethsemane.

I heard later that he asked the men repeatedly to be awake and to watch, but they did not understand and their eyes were closed to any world but the one they wanted to see. No one noticed the love and mutual honour in the pain of the two men who met together with that sacred kiss. Two men who together made the holy bond that led to the resurrection, telling the whole world that death could be transcended. Instead, they blamed and cast off the one who had had the courage to make the miracle come about.

With the other women, I had cleared up from the Passover supper that we ate in Jerusalem and had gone to another place on The Mount of Olives to pray together. Miriam and I had half-hopeful and half-heavy hearts. We knew he could rise above death. We knew who he was, but not knowing just what was happening was the hardest part. We were glad to have Magdalene lead a service that we had developed for ourselves over the last few years and to immerse ourselves in worship. There were seven of us there; Miriam, Magdalene, my sister Salome—in Jerusalem with her family—Joanna, Susannah and Martha. At the end, Miriam began to pray aloud for Yeshua, and the others, knowing intuitively that something important was happening, joined in.

We heard the hullabaloo after the arrest; the shouting and the running through the streets as followers of the heretic Jesus of Nazara were hunted. That was something we had not anticipated. The others stayed, paralysed with fear, in the grove, but I went down into the streets of Jerusalem to find out the truth.

I was there when Cephas denied him. It was as though a light went out inside the big fisherman as he said the words and I turned dizzy with horror. What if it had all gone wrong? What if the only outcome of this were death and misery and pain? What if Yeshua simply died and all the talk of resurrection were just illusion? What had Judah done?

At that moment I too was grabbed by servants of the High Priest, my arms twisted behind me and questions thrust at me like daggers. 'You are one of the heretics!' they accused me. 'You are one of his people! Aren't you? Aren't you?'

Cephas's face, flooded with desperation and panic, was before me. He knew I could betray him to his death with one word.

'Yes, I am the sister of Jesus of Nazara,' I said. 'Let this man go. You have no business with him. It is me you want.'

It was not because I was a greater soul than those who ran away; God knows, I have my failings, but I was beyond caring what happened to my physical self. Either Yeshua was right and all this would end in glory or what point was there in going on?

I was glad to be taken; glad to be hauled before the Sanhedrin and the High Priest; glad to be thrown into the darkened hole of a prison; glad to share the shame of being spat upon and whipped—and worse—in that dreadful long dark night of the soul before I was handed over to Pontius Pilate for sentence. Some angel carried me through it all so that my faith was not dented and my soul untouched.

I looked him in the face, this man who had condemned my brother. He was small and slightly bent, as though he had bones that ached with the effort of controlling this unruly outpost. His hair was thin and his nose sharp, but there was a strange fear deep within his eyes, which I had not expected to see. Some part of me was amazed that I could not hate him, nor hate my captors, who had tried so hard to debase and humiliate me, but I did not. I was not there. I was standing above myself, detached from the dirty, dishevelled and aching body down below me. I had charge of how and where she looked and what she said, but that was all.

I had nothing more to fear. Pilate looked at me with astonishment and at the priests with distaste.

'And who is this?' he asked.

'The heretic's sister, Deborah Bat Miriam, also a heretic,' they said. 'The wife of the one who betrayed him. She has been teaching insurrection too. She will not answer us. She will not admit her crime. A woman! She is as warped and as dangerous as he.'

'I do not think so,' he said, looking at me with a strange, sideways stare. 'Sit down, woman.'

I sat. He walked around the room, deep in thought, then he turned sharply.

'Tell me, Deborah Bat Miriam, do you teach what your brother taught?'

'I do,' I said.

'Then you are a brave woman, even if you are a foolish one,' he said. 'Did you know of your husband's action in bringing him to the priests?'

'I was there when they agreed it between them.'

'Then I have no need to punish you, do I?' he said. 'You shall have a lifetime to consider what has been done. We have much in common, you and I.'

Then he turned to the priests and gestured wearily at them.

'Have done. You have had your way enough. I do not make war on women,' he said. 'Set her free and leave her be. I will not have her made a scapegoat too. And if I hear of any harm coming to her, I shall bring the wrath of Rome

294

down on your Temple. Believe me, for I will do it. I give you my word.'

One of the soldiers was kind and gave me a mug of hot ale to drink before I left. Now, just when I had so much to do and to find out, my strength seemed to have left me and I wanted to lie down in a tightly curled ball and fall asleep for ever.

I took the potion gratefully, hardly noticing the woollen cloak he wrapped around my shoulders as I drank.

I saw that he was one of those who had abused my body—was it that day or the day before? I could not remember. I did not care. He was young, perhaps fifteen, and he found it hard to meet my eyes.

'My name is Vintillius,' he said. 'If you need help, go to my father at Bethlehem. He is the centurion posted there. Say that you come from me and he will shelter you.'

I think I thanked him; I hope I did. All I remember is walking stiffly up the cobbled streets of Jerusalem towards Golgotha. It was a few hours before the Sabbath eve and people were bustling on the streets as they made their way home for the evening service. It seemed so strange and unreal that they did not know, or care, what was happening on that hill outside the city wall.

I saw the crosses as I went out through the gate. I knew his would be the one in the centre and I kept my eyes on him, praying as I stumbled along. I must have been still a hundred paces away and could see the people waiting at his feet, when I heard Magdalene calling to him.

'Look up, up to the Kingdom of God, not down to the world of men!' Her voice was so full of love and faith and it was that which finally broke my iron resolve. When he died, I was at the foot of the cross, sobbing uncontrollably and wishing only that I could die too.

Miriam was so very kind to me—God knows she had enough to bear but she at least knew everything. To the others, I was simply the wife of the traitor. One who knew he would be betrayed and who did nothing to stop it.

I think I spent that night in our lodging house, but a fever had taken me and I was barely conscious as the disciples and the women spoke and lamented and grieved. At one point Magdalene bathed my brow and the part of me that was still in this world understood that she knew everything and did not judge me. But it was hard to know where I was and what was happening. For hours I believed myself back in her sweet-smelling basement room, being cared for after the stoning at Emmaus.

I was still feverish when the news of the miracle came back to us. It was Magdalene who saw him first and that was such balm to our hearts. That he remembered his sisters' care and grieving and came to them first. The others too were ecstatic and dances of joy were performed in the secrecy of the little house.

They knew they were still in danger and it was decided that they should disperse back to Galilee to let their notoriety die down. They expected Yeshua to join them on the road and, from now on, they would have the world at their feet.

But first they had to deal with me.

No one had to tell me Judah was dead. I knew. I had heard some of the whisperings and rumours. Some said he had killed himself, but I did not believe that.

I hid that parcel of knowledge and grieving deep inside to be called on at a later date, when I was strong enough. Now, I had to fight for my own life; I who had not seen him; who had been excluded from his resurrection and to the others was simply the wife of the traitor.

They cursed me and told me I would be better following my husband to his death. I was no longer one of them and was not even welcome to the small place they were willing to allot to his women disciples in their life.

I did not even try to explain, for they would not have listened. Thomas was sad for me— but he did not yet believe in the resurrection. Cephas stepped back from the group and would not speak or meet my eyes, but he did not condemn me as some of the others did.

I was simply outcast, and any woman who

went with me would be outcast too.

'Stay,' I said to Magdalene, who was wondering if she should come with me. But her eyes were shining with her knowledge of his risen life and I thought her place was there with the others. She could at least fight for the place of the women. She had the strength.

Miriam he had given into the care of John and she would stay with him. She would have taken me gladly and could even have persuaded John too, for he was a good man, but I did not want to live that kind of life, being accepted on sufferance and having to keep in my place.

Instead, I took my woollen cloak and left while they were still arguing over me. My donkey was stabled outside and some kind person had bundled up all my possessions and put them beside her, together with a pouch of bread and fruit.

I mounted and turned the donkey's head to the Jaffa Gate. We followed the walls of the city before we took the south road and I wondered whether I would ever return. For a few moments a wave of anger and grief threatened to overcome me. Again, my life was in ruins.

'I've done it before, and I can do it again,' I said, gritting my teeth and nudging the donkey into a trot. 'If one word of what he taught me is true, I can do it, alone, if needs be.'

Perhaps they would take me in at Qumran

while I grieved and wondered what God's plan was for me now; perhaps I would find another group of worshippers in the desert. If I trusted and prayed, somehow all would be well.

The weather was fine and the donkey strong. We made good progress towards the arid lands. I stopped and ate, numbly, tasting nothing, too frightened of the depth of grief and betrayal that I had locked inside to dare to look within again. I did not know if I could live once it was released, but I knew it would kill me if it were not.

The afternoon sun was sinking over the hills but it must have caught some reflection in the rock, for suddenly the light was behind me. I heard the sound of footsteps and a voice called my name. Wearily, I turned—and the years and the pain fell away as I dropped from the donkey's back and ran into his arms.

'Did you think I would leave you?' said Yeshua, my brother, as I sobbed and sobbed and his strong arms held me tightly. 'I shall come and go, my beloved, but I will always be with you in the higher worlds. Keep looking. Keep searching. Go your way in peace.'

I think we sat together by the side of the road and shared the last of my bread and fruit. Then I know I slept, with my head in his lap, my hand curled tightly around his robe as if to hold on to him for ever.

I awoke, stiff and dry-mouthed, just after the dawn, alone on the dusty yellow grass.

Nearby the donkey was grazing and at my feet lay fresh figs and olives and a chunk of rye bread. Suddenly desolate, I jumped up and searched the horizon for him, but there was no one there.

I sat down and wept and wept and wept. The first layers of the grief began to wash away and the donkey pushed at me with her nose, as if to ask why I was making so much noise.

About noon I found a stream and drank to replace the ocean of tears I had shed for my brother, my husband and my lost life, and I did a thing forbidden to women. I said Kaddish for Judah. Then I turned the donkey loose and walked off the track into the desert.

I don't know how many days and nights I was there, or what I ate or drank. I watched the moon rise and set, wax and wane, and I wept and lamented and prayed and thought.

For some of the time I did feel him with me, but not in the physical world and I grieved for that as much as, if not more than, I grieved for my husband.

I relived every time Yeshua had taught me and every time I had learnt or failed at a lesson of life. I looked so deep into my soul that at times I wished only for death. At others I knew that, linked with God, I was invincible.

At last I felt it was enough and set my ragged feet back towards the west and the road I had come from. I had no idea what I would do then, apart from turning south to see if I could reach Qumran.

Something within me half expected the donkey still to be waiting, but she was not. Wrapping my cloak around me, I began to trudge southwards, head bent, along the dusty path.

By noon the sun was high. I stopped to drink and rest and found a pile of dates on a leaf by the water. At that moment I was, yet again, in need of proof that God lived in all the worlds and that miracles still happened, even if Yeshua were gone.

As I ate feebly, with my back to the road, it seemed that, as before, I heard the sound of footsteps behind me.

There was no one there. As I swallowed the disappointment, I noticed figures in the distance. There was a woman on a donkey; and, leading it, another woman and a man, all coming towards me. As I stood, watching and waiting, they seemed to grow so familiar. And surely the donkey was my donkey! I peered into the light, which seemed brighter by the minute, brushed down my dusty clothes and climbed up to the path towards them.

If my eyes did not deceive me, I saw dear, faithful Joseph Barsabbas and Magdalene, leading a younger woman on the back of my donkey.

'It's me,' I thought stupidly. 'I must be dying. I am seeing my own life again.'

Then 'Deborah!' they called as one person,

and the woman on the donkey slipped down and began to run towards me.

'Oh! I have found you! I have found you!' cried Rizpah as she ran into my arms and I held her so very tightly. 'The sign came: the one you told me to expect. Your brother came in a dream and told me to go to you. I went to Cana first and they sent me down to Jerusalem. Your mother was really worried because your donkey had come back. She told me you should be travelling south to set up a new group to study the Word. But Joseph and Magdalene said the beast had come back to fetch us and that they would come with me to find you. I must come with you, Deborah, I must! I have finished with the old life. Look, I have brought you this. He said you would want it.'

She laid the olive-wood box at my feet. The box my brother had carved for me. As I looked at it, the strength came back and I knew I could meet my dearest friends in this world with the welcome they deserved.

*   *   *

Later, as we all set off together towards Qumran, Rizpah tugged at my cloak.

'Look!' she said. 'Look! That light behind us! What is it?'

This time he was not in the flesh of this fragile country, but in the centre of the heavens where he belonged, smiling and showing us that his love was eternal. And by his side stood Judah, my husband, reunited with the friend and master he had loved to the bitter end. But this was not the end. This was, yet again, the beginning.

Hear, O Israel, the Lord our God is One.